PROMISED LAND

PROMISED LAND

Brandon Dean

Indigo River Publishing

Promised Land

© 2020 by Brandon Dean

Editors: Liesel Schmidt and Regina Cornell
Cover Design: Nikkita Kent
Interior Design: Nikkita Kent

Indigo River Publishing
3 West Garden Street, Ste. 718
Pensacola, FL 32502
www.indigoriverpublishing.com

Ordering Information:
Quantity sales: Special discounts are available on quantity
purchases by corporations, associations, and others. For details,
contact the publisher at the address above.

Orders by US trade bookstores and wholesalers: Please contact the publisher at the address above.

Printed in the United States of America

Library of Congress Control Number: 2019950477
ISBN: 978-1-950906-18-5 (paperback), 978-1-950906-93-2 (ebook)

First Edition

*With Indigo River Publishing, you can always expect great books,
strong voices, and meaningful messages.
Most importantly, you'll always find . . . words worth reading.*

Silhouettes of yesteryears
And scenes we never saw;
Foreign forces, domestic fears,
And the shortest straw we draw.

No more flowers are left to bloom
Above overflowing plots;
The darkness falls upon this tomb
And on the lives that time forgot.

I hear her call, dear lady Death,
As she sits upon God's throne.
But, no matter what, on my last breath,
I will not die alone.

PROLOGUE

It's so quiet, so serene. Pure nothingness, apart from the mechanical churning of the truck engine ahead of me. I'm on my way back home now. Or, at least, the closest thing to a home I have. A house of God transitioned into a temple of sin. The ones I align with are broken, no matter which side I choose or what angle I look at. One side of the coin is made up of men morphed into monsters, skewing the world to fit their own twisted agenda. The other is made up of men filled with pure helplessness, worker bees in a hive of catastrophe, unsure whether the breath they're taking right now will be their last. But fear not—I have a plan, and I have a prayer. They aren't going to get away with this.

The people I've met along the way, as well as the people I've lost—it does a lot to a guy, especially when that guy is just a teenager who's trying his hardest to grow up on his own. German bombs blanketing the ground don't do much to help matters. Go ahead and paint that picture in your head: foreign planes systematically gliding through the sunset as far as the eye can see, and in one flawless and precise brushstroke, everything you've ever known is gone.

Sometimes I wonder how I'm going to survive all this. Sometimes I want to give up. But what can you do when giving up isn't an option? You see, I'm past done. I don't fear death, but I fear a world where the ones I love have to fight this battle alone. And maybe that's what keeps me going.

I hope that one day this can all be over, that one day I can wake up to see Hazel by my side. I hope that one day I can prop my own grandkids on my lap and tell them silly stories. I hope that one day I can look myself in the mirror without guilt and regret staring back. I hope that one day we can all learn to move on and be happy. That's all I want now, just to be happy.

I hope that one day, we make it to Promised Land.

CHAPTER 1

My father, James, impatiently tapped his finger on the steering wheel of the family sedan. We had been sitting in the traffic of downtown Cleveland for nearly an hour, and he must've been craving a cigarette. He must've left his Marlboros on the kitchen counter again.

"I wonder if this damn light will ever turn green!" he shouted. My mother, Amelia, placed her hand upon his shoulder, telling him to calm down in the kind tone she always seemed to possess. Dad scoffed; he didn't want to start an argument—not today, at least. It was my seventeenth birthday, and as a celebration, we'd decided to go to the Indians and Athletics game.

I looked out the window at the pedestrians walking on the sidewalks. I saw a paperboy waving his goods in the air, hoping to make a sale to whatever passersby he could. "Do the Germans Have the Upper Hand?" the headline shouted. It was a dark time that seemed to jeopardize our very way of life. It hadn't affected me directly, however—not until the Japanese attacked and so many people in my own little world had to go overseas. It really is amazing how tragedy can bring people closer together. It's also disheartening to realize it takes those very same tragedies to form unity on the home front. And going on with our everyday lives was easier for some than others. My best friend, Riley, had said goodbye to his father that day, and there I was, sitting in the back seat, being driven to a baseball game by my own. There was a tinge of guilt that rested somewhere in my heart and soul. It didn't seem fair, but I wasn't about to complain.

"Clint," I heard my mother say, breaking into my thoughts to bring me back to the present. I was scared—most of us were. We just didn't know how to admit it, and a lot of us, myself included, didn't know what exactly it was we were scared of.

"Oh, sorry, Mom. What is it?" I replied.

"I was just asking you if you've thought of any baby names," she said.

Mom was about six months pregnant. I was excited; I'd always wanted a younger brother to take under my wing, but I supposed a little sister would be just as good.

"Boy or girl?" I asked.

"Boy, hopefully," Dad interjected.

"Oh, behave yourself, James," Mom said with an eye roll. "Just tell me what you have already," she said, directing her attention back to me.

To be honest, I hadn't given it too much thought. I was a teenage boy—I had other things on my mind besides baby names. I did, however, have two—one for a boy and one for a girl.

"I like Logan for a boy and Violet for a girl," I told Mom.

"Violet . . . Violet," she whispered to herself. I knew that, despite the fact that my dad was hoping for a boy, she desperately wanted a girl. "I think I like Violet," Mom said.

"Like hell I'm naming my son Violet!" Dad protested. I couldn't help but notice that he was trying to hide a smile.

Mom laughed. She always laughed at my dad's jokes, even when they weren't funny. She'd always said that was one of the reasons she'd fallen in love with him, and I believed it. She was either really easy to make laugh or she simply humored him because she adored him so much. I think it was a little of both.

I wondered what my future sibling would look like. I had inherited traits from both my parents—my mom's blue eyes and my father's dark hair. Life really is an amazing thing. To think that we all start off too tiny to see. One of God's many unfathomable miracles, I supposed.

We were approaching League Park. I had been excited for the game since my father had promised to take me the week before. It didn't even matter that the 1943 Indians were an average team up to that point. I just wanted to do something else besides school and chores. We found a space to park not far from the field. I brought my glove in hopes of snagging a foul ball.

"That glove isn't gonna do any good if you don't know how to use it," Dad taunted playfully.

"Yeah, yeah," I replied. "Just you wait until I get one hit to me—then you'll see."

Dad smiled at me and helped my mother out of the car. "Maybe our next boy will be a little slugger, maybe teach you a thing or two," he shot back.

"Maybe, or maybe he'll end up like me and have the coordination of a one-legged spider." I laughed. Dad did have a point, though. I was the first male in the Brodsky family who didn't excel athletically. My father had been the star quarterback at his high school, had been offered a free ride to play in college for the University of Tennessee, but he'd decided to take a different route and had joined his uncle Paul to work in one of the many steel mills the area was known for. I guessed the thought of leaving the only place he'd known was too much for him to swallow.

We headed toward the field. My parents walked together, their hands locked tightly, with me following behind them. We approached the counter and were able to get three tickets just a few rows up behind home plate for a little less than four dollars. It usually would have cost more than that, but prices had gone down quite a bit—along with attendance—due to the current state of affairs.

My father grabbed a pack of cigarettes from the machine once we entered the stadium, pulled one from the pack, and lit it quickly. "That's much better," he said, taking a long drag. "Now, let's go find our seats."

We sat behind home plate and had an absolutely perfect view of both teams as they passed balls and did short sprints back and forth on opposite ends of the outfield. My dad was staring ahead nervously; he must've thought I didn't notice.

"What's wrong?" I asked.

He looked at me, coming out of his trance. "Oh, nothing," he said.

I knew better, though. I knew what was bothering him, deep down. "Dad, you aren't going anywhere," I said, hoping my words would be truth. "You're staying here with Mom and me."

Dad turned back to the field and muttered, "We aren't talking about this, Clint."

"Dad, I—"

"Stop!" he interrupted. "Did we come here to be sad, or did we come here to have a good time?"

I could see what looked like tears welling up in the corners of his eyes. He didn't mean to snap the way he did; he just couldn't bear the thought of saying goodbye to his family, especially since his second child was about to arrive. I didn't reply; I didn't know what to say. On one hand, I didn't want to drop the topic. On the other, I knew he would shut down anything else I had to say about it.

I looked to the field again, trying my best to enjoy the game. The Philadelphia Athletics were lined up on the third-base side, while the Cleveland Indians were on the first-base side, along the chalk lines. The caps of both players and spectators were placed over chests as the national anthem played throughout the stadium.

The game began, and three innings passed without either team getting a single hit. At the top of the fourth, however, a large, burly man from Philadelphia swung at a fastball over the heart of the plate. The sound of his bat on the leather ball cracked and echoed through the stadium as it cleared the left-field fence with several feet to spare. Groans and sighs rippled through the air as the home team found themselves at a disadvantage.

"How 'bout them Indians?" Dad asked me.

"They still have five innings, Dad. They'll pull through."

"Twenty dollars says they won't," Dad replied.

"Dad, I don't even have twenty dollars," I said.

"I know—that's how sure I am," he said with a smug look.

Four more innings came and went, and neither team did much to help their cause. The Indians managed to get a couple of men on base only to leave them stranded, and the Athletics were able to score one more run. The score now sat at two to zero. My dad looked at me, rubbing his thumb and index finger together and grinning.

I rolled my eyes. "Smart-ass," I muttered.

The ninth inning was just as slow paced as the rest of the game. Philadelphia couldn't get a man on base, but neither could the Indians, having gone down on three straight strikeouts. The crowd was full of disappointed faces, their heads shaking as they streamed out of the stadium after the loss.

Thunder started to rumble through the sky as we got up from our seats. "Well, at least Mother Nature waited until the game was over,"

Mom said as Dad helped her up.

"Yeah, now we get to wait in all that traffic again," Dad replied.

"After the way Cleveland played today, I think you couldn't possibly be any more let down," I said to Dad.

He laughed. "'Bout time we agree on something."

We made our way back to the car, and less than a minute after we were settled in and had the car started, the sky opened up and poured down rain. Dad turned on the windshield wipers, but it did little to help his view of the road ahead of him. I watched as some pedestrians casually walked along the sidewalks under the cover of their umbrellas, while others scurried like mice as quickly as they could to get to some kind of shelter or to their vehicles.

"I can't see a damn thing," Dad said, leaning forward in his seat with his eyes squinted.

"Do you think we should wait it out somewhere?" asked Mom.

Dad paused for a moment before responding. "Hey, Clint?"

"Yes, Dad?" I replied.

"You hungry?" he asked.

"Always." I laughed.

Dad looked back to Mom. "Yeah, we can wait."

I could tell Dad wanted to wait it out just as much as she did; he had asked me so it would seem as though he was being respectful of what Mom and I wanted. Dad valued his pride and did everything he could to prevent his masculinity from taking even the smallest of hits.

We turned right at the end of Twelfth Avenue and into the parking lot of a small hole-in-the-wall burger joint called Vicky's. I had never been there before, but my dad swore by their burgers and milkshakes. We stepped inside and walked to a small booth in the back of the restaurant, near the kitchen and away from the other customers. I looked around to take in the atmosphere. There were about half a dozen tables but only three other booths in the dining area, one of which was twice as large as the rest. I looked over to the front door, where a calendar hung. *May 1943*. I needed that reminder, because the décor and furnishings looked as if they hadn't been updated in over twenty years. There were some visible cracks peeking through the beige-painted walls as well as a few rips in the vinyl on our booth. I quickly forgave the sad state of the dining room, though, as soon as the smells wafting from the kitchen hit my nose, making my mouth water.

A thin waitress stood over our table and carelessly laid silverware in front of us, her uninterested gaze focused on the small notepad she held in her hand. "What can I get you?" she asked, noisily snapping a piece of chewing gum.

"Just three burgers and fries," Dad said to her.

She kept focus on her notepad as she hastily scribbled down the order. "Anything else?" she asked disinterestedly.

"Three drinks, as well. That'll be it for now," Dad said, giving her a smile that went unreturned. The waitress walked away and into the kitchen, chomping on her gum with increasing intensity every step of the way.

"Hope she doesn't expect a tip," Dad said.

"Oh, James, she might just be having a rough day. Be nice," Mom urged.

"Yeah, yeah, you and your kind heart," he said while buffing a water spot of off his spoon with a napkin. "So, did you enjoy your birthday present?" Dad asked me.

"Yeah. I would've enjoyed it more if the Indians knew how to get on base," I said.

"I heard that. Well, there's always next time," he replied. Dad had never liked baseball much—he was more of a football man—but he knew how much I liked it, so he tried to put his own prejudices aside for me.

The waitress came back, looking as uninterested as ever, and placed three empty drinking glasses stacked inside one another on the table. She walked away even more quickly than she'd come.

"Thank you!" Mom called after her.

"Uh-huh, sure," the waitress replied, never looking back.

Dad placed his now-clean spoon on the table and turned his head slowly to Mom. "So, how much of a tip do you think we should leave?" he asked.

Mom rolled her eyes and faced ahead with her arms crossed, huffing in irritation.

I grabbed one of the drinking glasses from the stack and went up to the counter. "Root beer, please," I said to the young-looking soda jerk.

"You got it!" he replied.

I sat on a stool at the counter while I waited for my drink.

"Hey, kid," a harsh voice to the right of me said. "How old are you?" The voice came from a husky older man sitting at the counter.

"I'm seventeen."

He reached down to the ashtray next to him and extinguished his cigarette. "You just might luck out, then," he replied.

"What do you mean, 'luck out'?" I asked.

"You know exactly what I mean," he said through a raspy cough.

"And what about you?" he asked the soda jerk.

"I'm nineteen," he said, sliding my root beer in my direction.

The old man laid his bowler hat on the counter and reached into his shirt pocket to grab another cigarette. "Got a girlfriend?" he asked the soda jerk as he placed the butt between his lips and lit the end.

"Yeah. I do, actually."

The old man laughed. "Not for long, you don't."

The young soda jerk refrained from lashing out at him. "Would you like another sundae, *sir*?" he asked through gritted teeth.

"No, I'm fine," the man said, sliding his empty glass dish away.

The radio behind the counter was tuned to our local news station. "Turn it up, will ya?" the old man demanded.

The soda jerk sighed as he increased the volume. The radio was now loud enough for anybody within a few feet to hear.

"This is Wilmer Foster with a breaking news update. Reports from an undisclosed military source are indicating that German military personnel are conducting tests for a new type of explosive weapon. It is believed that this new type of weapon was developed using some form of atomic energy. The validity of these reports is not certain as of yet. We will be sure to update you as we gain more information. Thank you all, and have a blessed evening."

"You know what that means, don't you?" the old man said.

The soda jerk and I looked at each other, confused. We knew this news wasn't good, by any means, but we had no idea of its significance—not yet, at least.

"No, not really," I said to the old man.

He laughed at me in condescension. "Figures. You dumb kids think you know everything. But when it actually matters, you don't know jack-shit."

I gave him a sharp reply in response to his insult. "Well, since you're *obviously* a genius, why don't *you* tell us what it means?"

The old man glared at me. "Hey, how 'bout you show some respect, you little prick?" he said before taking a drag on his cigarette. "What it means is those Krauts are going to blow us to kingdom come. And there ain't nothin' a goddamned one of us can do to stop it."

"You don't know that!" the soda jerk insisted.

The old man diverted his attention behind the counter again. "Look, kid. I know this is hard to accept. But the world's going to hell in a hand basket. And it's going pretty damn fast."

I saw the young man behind the counter grow pale, with a few beads of sweat forming on his brow. Just a few minutes ago he'd been as cheery as someone at work could possibly be, and suddenly, he was anxiously waiting for the devil to call his number.

I walked away from the counter with my drink, taking an occasional sip as I pondered what the news update truly meant. Was the old man simply running his mouth, just a lunatic who had nothing better to do than scare people? Or was he more knowledgeable than he let on, I wondered as I reclaimed my seat at the table with my parents.

"Did you make some new friends?" Mom asked me, cocking her head to the side in interest.

"What do you mean?"

"Well, it took you ten minutes to get a drink. You seemed pretty invested in conversation over there."

"Oh, it's nothing," I replied, "just some old geezer trying to give a couple of kids a scare." I reached down and picked up my burger, the grease dripping onto the wax paper below, and took a bite. Dad was right: this sure was one hell of a sandwich.

"Tried to scare you how?" Dad asked through a full mouth. He'd been attacking his own burger like a starving lion would a wildebeest.

Mom looked over at Dad from the corner of her eye in disgust.

"Just the news," I said, trying to sound nonchalant.

"What about it?" Dad asked.

"Something about the Germans using atomic energy to develop weapons," I replied, taking another bite of my burger.

Dad started to chew more slowly, with his eyes locked onto me, not necessarily looking at me specifically—more as if he were looking through me, as if he were trying to focus on something in his own head. Dad slid the other two drinking glasses toward Mom. "Amelia, can you please get our drinks for us?" he asked.

"Sure, hon. What do you want?" Mom asked.

"I don't know, just . . . surprise me, okay?"

Mom nodded and walked toward the counter as Dad watched her for a moment.

He swallowed the food he had been chewing. "Tell me everything you know about this," he said in a low voice.

"I did. That's all I know," I replied.

"Well, what in the world took you so long to come back to the table?" he asked.

"Just that man at the counter—he was trying to blow this out of proportion."

Dad chuckled to himself for a moment. "Blowing it out of proportion, huh?" he mumbled.

"Yes, that's exactly what it was," I insisted.

"And how do you know that?" he asked.

"Well, I—"

"If I recall, you just told me you don't know anything about it. But now you know it's blown out of proportion?"

I looked silently at him, having no response.

"Who reported it?" Dad asked.

"Wilmer," I replied.

Dad leaned back in the booth, looking a bit relieved. Wilmer had a reputation around the community for being dead wrong on his reports half the time. His shotgun approach to journalism and desperation for a breaking story had even gotten him into some hot water over the last few years, since he never bothered to fact-check anything that left his mouth.

Dad reached down for his burger again and took one last, massive bite to finish it. "I guess you're probably right," he said around a mouthful, "but you can never be too safe, just in case."

I nodded.

Mom came back with the drinks, unaware that Dad's errand had merely been a ruse. She handed my father a glass of tea, settling down with a club soda for herself. "Did I miss anything exciting?" Mom asked as she reclaimed her seat next to Dad.

"No, just watching Dad here inhale his food," I replied, receiving a grin from Dad and a giggle from Mom.

We finished our dinner about fifteen minutes later, looking outside to see that the rain had cleared and the sun was peeking above the buildings around us. Dad pulled out a five-dollar bill and paid our two-dollar-and-twelve-cent tab. He left the remainder as a tip.

The car ride home was the same as always—casual discussions about my dad's work and my mom's chatter about a piece of jewelry in a catalog she absolutely had to have.

"Put it on your Christmas list," my dad would always say, to which my mom would point out how far away that was. "Oh, great, just enough time to save up for it," was his classic rebuttal. He never meant it, though. He was a softhearted man behind that rugged exterior. He always found a way to get her exactly what she wanted and, typically, when she least expected it. The most memorable of them all was the silver locket he had given her several years back. She'd been so excited, and now she always wore it around her neck. When sunlight hit the ornate charm at just the right angle, it almost seemed to glow. Inside the locket, she had a baby picture of me on the left and a picture of my father on the right.

We made the usual right turn into the driveway of 1919 Ashford Lane, our home, a small two-bedroom that was just under 1,200 square feet. The old brick exterior of the home was practically begging to be washed as a dark layer of dirt moved up the house, fading as if it were a gradient of mud. The flower bed to the side of the front door, usually vibrant with whatever blossoms were in season, now sat near barren apart from a few out-of-place weeds. Ever since Mom had gotten pregnant, she hadn't had the energy to tend to her plants, and Dad wasn't one to take on such a "feminine" task. I supposed even chivalry had its limits.

Dad stepped out of the car and went around to help my mom. When we walked up to the front door and opened it, we were greeted by the creaking of the glass outer door.

Mom spoke: "Are you ever going to—"

"Oil the hinges? Yeah, one of these days," Dad interrupted.

Mom sighed. It was like an act of Congress to get my dad to do any work on the house. He felt his weekly forty hours at work were enough of a burden as it was.

Even so, there wasn't a speck of dirt anywhere inside our home, courtesy of Mom. She was fastidious about everything being absolutely immaculate at all times. "You never know when someone will drop by," she always said. But I also believed she truly found some form of accomplishment in her day as she wielded her broom and dustpan to leave the house sparkling.

I walked to the kitchen, which was too small to accommodate a full dining table, so our breakfast table had to prove sufficient. It was an old table; my father had picked it up at a yard sale at a price that was practically free. It had surely been a beautiful piece at one point, but the white paint was chipped and scratched along its round surface. As I approached the table, I was greeted by the sight of my math homework from the Friday before. I had never been good at arithmetic, but tomorrow was Monday, and time to complete my work was running short.

I sat at the table, while Mom ran herself a bath just down the hall-way. I could hear the water heater hiss like a snake stuck in a lead pipe as it kicked on.

"Square root of two-fifty-six," I murmured to myself, counting on my fingers as I watched Dad enter the kitchen.

He stopped at the back door, next to me, to look out the window for a moment. He turned his head toward me. "I'm going to get that oil for the hinges," he said before opening the door to the backyard, where the entrance to the cellar was. The catch-all for all the things we had no place for in the house, the cellar was filled with all of my father's tools, holiday decorations, and miscellaneous items we didn't have the heart to throw away. I thought it was strange that he felt the need to explain himself to me, but he'd been seemingly more on edge in the last couple of days, so I dismissed his behavior.

I looked up at the clock that hung on the floral-paper-covered wall above the oven. The time read 8:30 p.m., and I still had home-work to do. I typically tried to be in bed at ten so I could be at least somewhat motivated to get ready for school. I'd never been a morning person, and it wasn't out of the ordinary to see me crawl out of bed at noon on the weekends. About ten minutes passed, and I finally found the answer my first question. *Sixteen*, I thought, feeling like an idiot for having taken so long to work out the problem.

My mother, now finished with her bath, walked into the kitchen sporting house clothes, her hair still wet. She waddled to the sink, grabbing an empty teakettle from the counter as she passed me. "Where'd that father of yours go off to?" she asked, filling the kettle with tap water and placing it on the burner to boil.

"He went to go get some oil from the cellar," I said.

"You mean he's actually going to fix those hinges?" she asked in sarcastic shock.

"Yeah, I guess so," I said, trying to focus on my homework. I was on question seven and had only four problems left. I took a quick glance at the clock—9:12 p.m. I pressed my dull pencil to the paper once again and then stopped, realizing that Dad had been gone too long simply to be getting oil for the hinges.

"Mom?" I said.

She turned toward me. "Yes, honey?"

"What's wrong with Dad lately?" I asked.

The corners of her mouth turned down, making her look grim. She pulled out the chair next to me and took a seat. "He's just scared he's going to have to leave us," she said.

"Why? He's still here, isn't he? It isn't like Dad to be acting like this."

"I know," she replied. She paused for a moment, her face indicating she had something she needed to say. "But he didn't have to serve in the last war. He was lucky and got to stay home, and that's why he's so scared of this war. He can't stomach the thought of leaving us—especially right now, with the baby coming soon."

Mom was obviously upset, so I stood up from my chair and gave her a hug. I heard the back door creaking open behind me, and Dad walked in with a small bottle of oil in his hand.

"Now, what's this all about?" he quipped, sounding overly chipper. I knew he was hiding it now; he didn't want us to be scared. But little did he know, sometimes it was okay to be scared. I ended my hug with Mom and immediately followed it up with one for Dad.

I placed my half-finished homework in my folder, settling on copying the answers from Riley in the morning. "Love you, Mom. Love you, Dad. Good night," I said before walking down the hall into my bedroom.

CHAPTER 2

T ime for school!" my mom shouted as she rapped on my door.

I grabbed whatever clothes were clean and threw them on. I groggily walked down the hallway into the bathroom and immediately noticed that the mirror reflected a worse version of myself than I'd imagined possible. I hadn't gotten much sleep the night before; I'd been worried about Dad. I couldn't wait for this war to be over so he could go back to being himself again.

I hastily brushed my hair and teeth before heading to the kitchen for breakfast. The radio was on. Thankfully, though, it was just playing a song. Not sure which song exactly, but my mom seemed to know it; she was humming along while she set the table. She'd made her usual Monday-morning breakfast of biscuits and gravy, a favorite of both my father's and mine. She felt that we needed to start the week with something to look forward to. It really was the little things that mattered most, regardless of how trivial they may have seemed. I wish I had realized that before it was all gone.

I looked down at the table as I sat and saw that there were only two plates and two glasses of orange juice. Mom walked over to me, placed a biscuit on my plate, and covered it in a thick, white layer of gravy.

"Where's Dad?" I asked as she sat down to make her own plate.

"Oh, he went into work early today," she replied.

"Is everything okay with him?"

She reached across the small breakfast table to take my hand gently in hers and looked me in the eyes. "You don't need to worry about your father, okay? This will pass; everything will be fine."

"What if he gets drafted? How will it be fine then?"

"You can't sit around thinking about what-ifs all the time; it'll take away from what's happening right now," she said.

"Yeah? And what's happening right now?"

Mom smiled at me. "You have both of your parents, you have your friends, you have your health, and you have your future. *That's* what's happening right now. And soon, you'll have a new brother or sister you can show the world to." I smiled back at her, and she pulled her hand away slowly. "Now, eat your breakfast before it gets cold."

I nodded. Mom always had a way to make me feel better. No matter what, she was someone I could always count on.

I finished my meal, grabbed my school supplies, and gave her a hug goodbye. I stepped outside and noticed that the creaking of the front door had become a faint sigh. I guessed Dad had gotten around to those hinges, after all. I began my mile walk to school and met up with Riley about halfway. We always walked together; it seemed to help time pass when I had someone to talk to.

"How ya doin', Brodsky?" he called as he walked toward me from his driveway. Riley wasn't someone who would typically have been seen hanging out with someone like me. I wasn't a dweeb, by any means, but I was a slim kid who usually kept to himself, valuing quality over quantity as far as friends were concerned. Riley, on the other hand, was about as popular as a high school guy could ever hope to be. He must have had dozens of girlfriends to my zero, and while he was an inch or two shorter than me, he made up for it with his athletic build. Before his father had gone off to war, the biggest worry on his mind had been whether he wanted to accept the offer of a scholarship for basketball or football.

"Pretty good, Riley. You?" I replied.

"Eh, not so bad, all things considered," he said.

"Have you heard from your old man at all?" I asked.

"No, not yet, but I'm not worried about it. He's gone face-to-face with these Krauts before, and he came back. I'm sure he will again. After all, he signed up for it on his own," Riley replied.

Riley's father was a patriotic man, from what I knew—always putting others ahead of himself, whether or not he knew them personally. He had already fought in the first war with the Germans. Needless to say, he knew his way around a battlefield and how to handle himself.

"That's good to hear. Hey, did you finish that homework Mrs. Cunningham gave us?" I asked

"Yeah, why? You slack on it again?" he asked with a smirk.

I rolled my eyes. "Will you quit busting my chops and just let me copy it?" I groaned.

"Yeah, yeah. On one condition."

"What condition is that?" I asked curiously.

"You set me up on a date with that Melissa girl who sits in front of you."

I laughed. "Typical Riley—she's only been here a week, and you already have her on lock?"

Riley chuckled. "Hey, buddy, I'm surprised I waited this long. Not often you see a dame as pretty as her just walk in like she owns the joint."

"So why can't you talk to her?" I asked.

"I would, but if I get caught passing notes again, Mrs. Cunningham already told me she would read it out loud. And let's face it: sometimes my notes aren't exactly kosher. Can't risk that embarrassment."

I gasped in mock surprise. "You mean to tell me Riley Jennings *isn't* a fearless womanizer? Wow, I'm in shock!"

"Yeah, yeah, wise ass. So you gonna help me, or what?"

I reached out a hand, and Riley gave me his homework to copy. "Here's what's going to happen, pal: you're going to let me copy this homework, and then you're on your own with Melissa."

Riley groaned. "You can't blame me for giving it a shot, can you?"

"No, but you missed your target by a mile."

"*Now* look who's the one busting chops," he said.

We walked together for a while longer, kicking rocks and exchanging small talk as we made our way toward school. At the end of our neighborhood, we spotted what looked like a government vehicle parked at the end of one of the driveways. A glossy white star was painted on the side of it, and a soldier in pristine dress uniform was climbing out.

"Oh, no," Riley muttered. "That's where Milo Varney lived. You remember him?"

Milo was destined to be a farmhand since the day he was born, a simple guy that valued his hunting, fishing, crops, and chewing tobacco over everything else. I'd never known him that well, personally, since he was a few years older than me, but it was my understanding that he desperately wanted to trade his city roots for the countryside and run his own farm—fields of crops instead of his small three-by-five plot of onions and tomatoes.

"Yeah, a little bit. What about him?" I asked Riley.

"You don't know?" he replied. Riley exhaled deeply through his nose. "That's what happens when a person, you know . . . dies at war."

I was in disbelief. I'd been fortunate enough never to have lost anyone very close to me. Death was a foreign reality that hadn't struck me up to that point, so this was something hard for me to process. Remembering someone so full of life, only to have that end abruptly. We continued to watch as Milo's mother answered her door to speak to the soldier. The man in uniform removed his hat from his head, and from a distance, I watched his mouth move. Milo's frail, elderly mother covered her face with her hands, her legs began to shake, and then we heard distraught weeping from where we were walking, which had to have been about two hundred feet away. I could tell this was harder for Riley to watch than it was for me; this was the worst possible outcome for many people across the country, himself included.

"Poor bastard," Riley muttered. "We better get going. Gonna be late if we don't put a little pep in our step," he added after a short pause.

We left our small, tucked-away cul-de-sac of Ashford Heights and walked into a more rural area. Homes were far too expensive for a steelworker in the heart of the city, so we were located in a small town just outside of Cleveland by the name of Mayfield. It had never made a difference to me, though. It was what I was used to, and it was nice not having to be burdened by the claustrophobia that came with crowded city streets.

We were just a few hundred feet away from our daily dose of imprisonment. "West Hills High School: Home of the Chiefs," declared the sign decorated in our school colors of blue and yellow.

Riley reached into his pocket and looked down at the gold-plated pocket watch his father had passed on to him. "Yeah, we made it. Barely, but we made it," he said, relieved.

"If you didn't have twelve tardies, you wouldn't have to sweat it so bad," I said.

"Thanks for the advice, Pop," he replied. Riley was a smart-ass, but that was probably what made us such good friends, because so was I.

We stopped at locker 112—Riley's. He reached inside to grab a pencil, which he used more to scribble notes to every bombshell he laid his eyes on than he did actually doing schoolwork.

"I'll meet you in class," I said before walking to room fourteen, Mrs. Cunningham's homeroom math.

Most of my peers were already seated, exchanging pleasantries with one another or sharing the traditional high school gossip. I took my usual spot in the second desk on the far left of the room, next to the window. Looking outside was peaceful, in a way, but at times, I found myself envious of the freedom possessed by the little squirrels and birds on the other side of that glass.

I pulled my unfinished work from my folder and took Riley's from my pocket. I began to copy the answers before Mrs. Cunningham came into class. Riley came in as the bell started to ring and took his seat directly behind me, and I passed his homework to him behind my back as stealthily as I could. Mrs. Cunningham wasn't in class yet, but there were a couple of brown-nosers in our midst. Especially Peter Gale, your typical poindexter, who weighed all of 120 pounds soaking wet. When a teacher called on the class to answer a question, you could rest assured that the little kiss-ass would have his hand up faster than anyone else in the room. Needless to say, he wouldn't have hesitated to rat me out.

"Good morning, class," Mrs. Cunningham said in her usual monotone as she entered the room with her customary mug of coffee in hand. She took a seat behind her desk, then sipped her piping-hot black coffee, her lips puckering at its bitter flavor. Mrs. Cunningham was probably as old as dirt; I never understood why she refused to retire. Maybe some people were just so obsessed with their work that it was all they could think about, and the very thought of not punching in and out seemed more of a punishment than a reward.

The loud speakers blared to life for our usual morning announcements. "This is Principal Bowen. Today is Monday, May third, 1943. All students in the senior class should be reminded that class photos will be taken after school on Thursday, the sixth. Now please stand for the Pledge of Allegiance."

My classmates and I all stood for the pledge, then followed it with a moment of silence.

As we reclaimed our seats, Mrs. Cunningham spoke up: "I'm sure you've all completed the work you were assigned on Friday, so now I would like for each of you to pass it to the front of your row."

"Yes, Mrs. Cunningham!" Peter yelped in response.

I snickered.

"Yes, Mrs. Cunningham," Riley mimicked. Somehow, I managed not to burst out laughing.

Mrs. Cunningham collected the papers from each row and placed them on her desk before taking another sip of her disgusting coffee. "Okay, class, since I'm sure you've all done so well on your homework, I've decided to test you on it today."

Every student in the room—except Peter, of course—groaned at the thought of taking a test with no time to prepare. Our groans, however, were interrupted by a faint, high-pitched screeching in the distance.

Sirens blared from outside. There was an overpass just in view of the window I sat next to, and I counted five police cars zooming down the road with a convoy of no fewer than twelve sage-green trucks following. Each truck had the same star painted on the side as the vehicle at Milo's house, and I could spot what appeared to be unmanned machine guns above the cabins of the trucks. Everyone in the classroom, including Mrs. Cunningham, rose to their feet and huddled around the window. When the sirens stopped and the vehicles were out of sight, everyone began to buzz with questions.

"Was that the army?" one of the girls asked.

"No shit, it was the army. Who else could it be?" one of the boys growled back in reply.

Mrs. Cunningham cleared her throat. "Take your seats, please," she said fruitlessly. The class was still huddled around the window, in awe of what they had just witnessed. "Take your seats! Now!" Mrs. Cunningham shouted, louder than the sirens themselves had been. The class fell silent; I could sense the impatience in Mrs. Cunningham's voice, intensified by the dead stare she gave us. A vein protruded above her brow, which, in most cases, would have been intimidating. But given that she was a frail, old woman whose stature barely hit five feet, it was mostly just hysterical.

Peter was the first to reclaim his seat, of course. Slowly, the rest of us followed suit.

Mrs. Cunningham passed out a quiz to each member of the class, and I immediately hated myself for cheating on the homework instead of learning the material.

"You have fifteen minutes, starting now," Mrs. Cunningham said before taking yet another slurp of coffee.

I glanced at the clock; minutes felt like seconds. I was on question four of fifteen, with six minutes remaining, so I opted to blindly guess on the remainder. Knowing I had just failed my test, I waited until everyone else had theirs turned in, as well.

Mrs. Cunningham valued silence, and we usually spent the second half of the period sitting quietly while she had her radio at a volume between ambient and audible. Loud enough for the room to hear if we were silent, but soft enough that even the faintest whisper would drown out the noise. On the radio played a classical melody— Mozart, if I was guessing right—a song one would typically listen to while trying to sleep or what an expectant mother would play for her child in utero.

The tune was interrupted. "This is Wilmer Foster, with a news update on the war in Europe. We have just received news from high-ranking US officials that the Soviet Union has surrendered. Some details have been withheld, but what we can confirm is that the cities of Moscow and Saint Petersburg have taken a devastating blow. The number of casualties as of now is unknown. The Department of Defense has advised all US citizens to proceed with their daily lives but to do so with a heightened sense of caution and preparation. More information will be revealed when available. Have a blessed morning."

The air in the classroom grew heavy; it was hard to breathe for a moment. I could see a few beads of sweat on Riley's forehead as he stared off, at no particular person or object, with concern, no doubt thinking about his father.

The entire class was nearly silent, apart from some nervous whispers.

"Does this mean we're next?"

"I thought the Soviets had this under control."

"How did they kill so many people?"

I didn't know what to think. Perhaps my father's paranoia had been justified all along. Maybe that old man at Vicky's knew what he was talking about, after all. All of us were just high school kids—we didn't know how the world worked; we didn't know the significance of atomic weapons. What we *did* know was that shit had just hit the fan. I looked around at the other students in the class. Nearly all of them were perplexed and confused, including Peter—even the brainiac who always had all the answers was at a loss for words at this one. The thing that kept repeating in my head was, *This is real. It's serious now.*

CHAPTER 3

No sense in worrying about it right now," Riley said, taking a deep breath. "What are you gonna do, you know? Can't change the world—not two kids from Mayfield, at least."

I nodded. "I suppose you're right."

"Yep, well, we best get on home. See you tomorrow, bud," Riley said before walking down his driveway and going into his house.

School had been different that day, for obvious reasons. The talk in the hallways between classes wasn't of how everyone had spent their weekend or about after-school activities, like it usually was. There was a spectrum of emotion I'd never seen before. Some students seemed to be on the verge of tears, while others looked unfazed. I couldn't really blame them, though, the more I thought about it. It was like Riley had said: What could we do about it now? The only option we had was to carry on and hope it didn't bite us in the ass.

I walked up the steps to my house after taking a quick look at the driveway. Dad was home. Admittedly, I had been so busy thinking of myself that I hadn't even considered how Dad might feel about the news. I sighed and opened the front door.

Mom was just inside, sitting with a sewing needle in hand on our old, worn-out couch. Years of use had started to turn the cushions into a color more gray than its original white.

"Hey, Mom," I said.

She immediately waved me off with a "Shh! Just a second!" She had a look of unbreakable focus; she loved to sew. The only problem was, as much as she loved it, she never seemed to get the hang of it.

"Almost done," Mom muttered to herself. "Voila! What do you think?" she asked, sounding pleased with herself. Mom was holding up a white blanket with frilly, sea-green trim. The accents were so uneven that even a blind man could have spotted the errors from a mile away.

The side of my mouth curled into a slight smile. "Looks great, Mom. Always does."

Mom's face lit up with pride.

I took a seat next to her and asked where Dad was.

"In that lousy cellar again," Mom said, sounding agitated.

"I take it you heard the news update?" I asked.

"Yes, I did. But I already told you: this will pass, and it will all be okay," she insisted.

I wanted to believe her, I really did, but I knew that she knew about as much about the situation as I did, which was almost nothing.

Dad came in through the back door, wiping sweat from his brow. Another fake smile; another fake, upbeat greeting. "Hey, champ, how was school today?" he asked.

"It was good. So I'm guessing you've heard?" I asked.

Dad barked out a phony laugh. "Oh, boy, that's Wilmer for you. Knowing him, he made the whole thing up just to get noticed."

I was growing tired of Dad's charade and the macho façade that really did nothing to hide his fear. "Stop, Dad," I said.

The smile slipped from Dad's face. "Stop what?" he asked, his voice taking on a more serious tone.

"I know you're not okay right now. I know there's a lot on your mind, and I know that this is hard for you," I said, trying to let him know he didn't have to put on a front for my mother and me.

Dad didn't respond right away. His face was shadowed with sorrow, but there was a tinge of relief, as well. He didn't have to hide it anymore. "I'm sorry. I didn't want you two to see me like this. *I'm* supposed to protect *you*, not the other way around."

I placed a hand on Dad's shoulder. "We're all supposed to protect the ones we love, Dad. But you don't have to be ashamed of being afraid. There's a lot going on in the world that's nuts, and we're all trying to figure out what to be afraid of and what not to be."

I gave him a hug with one arm, pulling Mom in with the other.

Dad gently rested a hand on Mom's belly, and said, "You know what? I think I like Violet, too." He let out, for the first time in days, a genuine smile. Despite the worry, despite the possibility of impending doom that lingered in the back of our minds, I was overcome with joy at seeing the peace in him at that moment, now that he wasn't keeping that secret.

"Who wants to watch a movie?" Dad asked, wiping away the last remaining tear from his eye.

Both Mom and I were ecstatic at the idea; Mom, because she loved getting out of the house—it didn't matter the reason. Slaving over a hot stove and cleaning the house like a typical Midwestern housewife were things she didn't mind doing, but she always appreciated a change of pace. I, however, was excited because I had heard talk about the new Mickey Rooney film, *A Human Comedy*. I was always one who could appreciate a good laugh, and the fact that Marsha Hunt was also in the film—well, let's just say I could appreciate that, too.

I also loved that we were going to the drive-in, instead of an actual theater. Watching a movie with my family, out in nature, was something I loved. For me, it was the epitome of relaxation. The fact that the drive-in was only an eight-minute drive made it more convenient than the theaters in the middle of the city, anyway.

I looked out the window as we drove. Mom and Dad were talking about the baby; they were both so happy. I tried my best not to feel like chopped liver, but I guessed it was inevitable; there were things bigger than me now, and that was okay. I couldn't wait any more than they could; I'd always wanted to be a big brother. And seeing my parents light up when the baby was mentioned gave me a warm feeling I couldn't describe.

The car came to a stop at a red light about a mile from home. On the left-hand side of the road was Mayfield Grocery, an older place where my parents were regulars. Nearly all of my mom's weekly grocery runs were to this small hole-in-the-wall that doubled as a Mayfield landmark. On the right side, attached to the town's pharmacy, was Charlie's Liquor Store, a newer place where my dad sometimes stopped. My dad wasn't a heavy drinker, but he had his days when, after a long day at work, he wanted nothing more than a couple of ice-cold beers. Just in front of the liquor store was something—or, more specifically, *someone*—I'd never seen before and didn't have much interest in seeing at that very moment. I wasn't in the mood for it, nor was anyone else in the car.

A gaunt old man stood atop an inverted milk crate. The look on his face was a mixture of disdain and insanity. A Bible was gripped in his hand as he preached his sermon of the end times. There was no clear path in his ramblings, no rhyme or reason in his method of speech—only a random spouting of verses. My father turned the radio on to its fullest volume, tuning him out. I looked to see some people pass him by, wanting no association with him, while others stood by him, clapping as he preached his gospel.

The light turned green, and my father peeled out like a bat out of hell. Seconds passed, and he turned the volume back down to where it had been before. He glanced around the car at my mom and me. "Sorry," he said, then redirected his focus to the road ahead.

A short while later, we arrived at Full Moon Drive-In.

"Three, please," my dad said to the attendant at the ticket booth. We drove inside and got a good spot—a perfect spot, actually; it always paid off to get there as early as possible to avoid the gargantuan lines to get inside and to keep from having to park a mile away. My father opened the trunk of the car, revealing our gloves and a baseball that had seen its fair share of fields as well as bat barrels. He lit a cigarette and signaled me to follow him as he headed toward a plot of grass a few feet in front of the movie screen. I grabbed my glove and ambled after him without a second thought.

Dad took one last drag of his cigarette and threw the butt to the ground as he slid his glove over his left hand. He made a weak throw in my direction. The trajectory the ball took was as if it had a mind of its own—three feet to my left and a foot above my head. The ball settled on the edge of some weeds several feet behind me. I laughed aloud, as did Dad.

"I guess I'm pretty rusty, huh?" he asked through his chuckles.

"Hey, look at it this way: I don't think Spud Chandler could throw like that even if he tried," I said to him through an ear-to-ear smile.

Dad waved me off. "Yeah, yeah, how about you put your money where your mouth is and show me what you got?"

I picked up the ball from the weeds, feeling dampness from a thin layer of dew from where it had settled. I threw as hard I could, with what I believed to be impressive speed. It landed in the middle of Dad's glove with a satisfying smack.

"Ain't nothin' but luck. You know, you should go to Puerto Rico and play that lottery thing I keep hearing about," Dad joked.

The sun eventually descended, and the sky grew dark. Cicadas began their nightly patrols along the branches of trees, emitting their indescribable sound, a song of nature. The projector screen lit up white, with a countdown from ten. Everyone, us included, tuned their ears to the loudspeakers set up around the grounds of the drive-in.

My parents sat in the front of the car, with me in the back. Mom gave Dad a kiss and wrapped her hand around his, resting her head on his shoulder. It made it a little hard to see the screen from where I was, but I adjusted my own position—I could hardly interrupt the two lovebirds, could I?

The movie began, and while it had its funny moments, it wasn't the comedic masterpiece I had been anticipating. I wasn't sure if it had something to do with my own mood, but overall, I was pretty disappointed in the movie. Maybe I'd had my hopes set too high. It eventually became more of a chore to watch than a pleasure, even to the point where seeing Marsha Hunt plastered on a thirty-foot screen couldn't reclaim my interest.

By the time the film had about ten minutes remaining, the predictability of the punch lines had actually gotten so repetitive that I had begun to cringe at the cheesy humor. Mickey Rooney opened his goofy little mouth one more time, and I waited to endure yet another half-witted joke.

Suddenly, static played through the speakers instead. My parents looked confused, but Dad also looked irritated at the possibility that he wouldn't be getting his money's worth. Everyone in the cars and the lawn chairs scattered around the grounds began to complain and groan in irritation and confusion.

Finally, the nervous voice of a young man came over the speakers. "I regretfully inform all of our patrons tonight that we will be closing before our scheduled time. As of now, we are unsure if refunds will be issued. However, please keep your ticket stubs to exchange for one free entry on a day of your choice. Th-thank you."

"What a crock of shit!" Dad yelled, angrily shifting the car out of park.

"*Temper*," Mom reminded him.

"How about some music? You know, to change the mood?" I suggested.

"Fine," Dad growled, adjusting the radio back to our local mainstream station, which was smack dab in the middle of "Tangerine" by Jimmy Dorsey. It wasn't a bad song, but I had heard it so many times that it had grown stale to me weeks ago. It didn't make a difference, though; I'd have listened to the sound of nails on a chalkboard if it would've helped settle Dad down.

From our position on the grounds, we were one of the last cars to exit the drive-in, and when we pulled out onto the main road, we were immediately caught in the bottleneck of traffic.

I had never seen so many cars backed up in one place in my entire life. Three to five minutes would pass, peppered by a few swears and snarls from Dad, and in that time, we would only move ahead a whopping ten feet. This went on for what seemed like ages, and I knew it would take all night at that rate. Several songs on the radio came and went, and it was in the middle of "Serenade in Blue" that it began.

A voice came in over the radio, interrupting the song and taking over the airwaves. It wasn't Wilmer's voice, though—this one lacked his signature goofy lisp. Instead, this voice sounded professional, completely calm. Almost robotic.

"This is the US Department of Defense, warning all US citizens receiving this broadcast to take shelter as soon as possible. Our mainland has been invaded aerially by a foreign power believed to be Germany. In coordination with previously undisclosed military information, it is believed that the cities of Los Angeles, Seattle, Boston, Indianapolis, New York City, Philadelphia, San Francisco, Cleveland, and Jacksonville are or may be in imminent danger. It is advised that all citizens of the aforementioned cities please cooperate in an orderly and civil fashion. Please gather the following supplies for your own personal health and safety: food, water, clothing, hygienic supplies and toiletries, a form of AM communication such as a radio, and a portable light source. We will update you all with information to come."

"Enough!" Dad screamed as he turned the radio off.

"What does that mean?" I asked.

My parents ignored my question.

"What does it *mean*?" I asked again, louder than before.

"It means nothing!" Dad barked back. "You hear me?"

"James . . . he's just scared. Don't be so hard on him," Mom soothed, gently rubbing her hand on his forearm. I could tell Dad was upset, too; he just didn't know how to express his emotions in a way that didn't make him look like an asshole to anybody who didn't know him.

"Look," he said in a deep exhale. "This guy's probably just like Wilmer. A total idiot. Everything's going to be—"

Dad was interrupted by an explosion of deafening noise that seemed to come from everywhere. It was the most terrifying sound I'd ever heard, sirens that pierced the air around me. Mom immediately covered her ears in a vain attempt to drown them out.

"What is that?" I yelled over the sound. The sirens were now accompanied by what sounded like a swarm of mechanical wasps in the distance.

Dad looked up to the sky past his windshield. "Get out of the car!" he yelled.

"What's happening?" I shouted fearfully.

"Get out of the damn car! Both of you!" Dad screamed urgently.

I opened my door to step outside; about a third of the people stuck in traffic had done the same, while others who had a farther distance to go helplessly hoped the traffic would move.

"Come here," Dad said to Mom as he opened her door and began to carry her.

That's when I made the mistake of looking up into the sky.

There were so many of them that I couldn't have counted them all even if I'd wanted to.

Metal birds of death wearing red crosses on the side. I had always been told that airplanes were angels up in the sky—how I'd been misled. I knew what the plan was without being told; I knew what had to happen if we wanted to live to see another day.

We had to run.

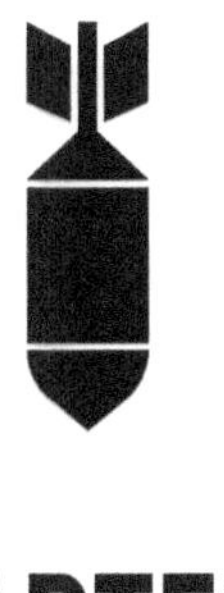

CHAPTER 4

We have to go!" Dad shouted.

I was worried that Mom would slow Dad down, but she didn't. She was in no position to make a two-mile walk on her own, let alone run that distance. Dad ran through the never-ending rows of cars that were sitting at a standstill. I'd never known how much adrenaline the human body could produce once it was kicked into fight-or-flight mode, but I was finding that out.

I ran after Dad. He would occasionally look back to see where I was before refocusing ahead to keep up his pace. I heard what sounded like a whistle as I looked to my right to see the flock of Nazi aircraft. The bombs were beginning to drop, and even with as many planes as there were, the artillery being released by them outnumbered them ten to one. I could hear the sirens of emergency vehicles practically being drowned out by the sounds of war.

Nearly everyone had left their cars behind at this point, and a mass of people was running to grasp what little chance of survival they had. Dad kept hauling ass as I followed closely behind.

Explosion after explosion rang loud and clear as I watched the city of Cleveland being reduced to nothing more than an ashy pile of ruin. The bombs seemed as if they were never going to stop. The screams, the frantic prayers, the self-spoken eulogies were never-ending. *This is it, the end of all of us*, kept repeating in my head.

Dad was gaining distance from me; he looked back. "Keep up, Clint! Keep up!" he urged.

I sprinted as fast as my legs could take me, closing the gap between my parents and me. I could see Charlie's Liquor Store in the distance. We were getting close to shelter, close to home—or, at least, what might be left of it.

Amid everything, for some reason, my mind chose to focus on my mother's cries, one of the most unnerving sounds I'd ever heard. Even so, despite the chaos, despite our seemingly guaranteed death, it reassured me that we were all still breathing. She couldn't cry out if she were dead.

I was then only about ten feet away from my parents. My body had started to give out, and surely, my father's had, as well. My chest began to clench, and my legs felt as if they would buckle under me at any second.

"Stay close!" Dad forced out the words in an exhausted breath.

The whistling sound was so loud I couldn't hear myself think. I looked behind me to see where it was coming from as more bombs fell on the line of parked cars we had just run through. I was a football field's distance away from complete annihilation.

"Almost there! Keep pushing! Don't stop!" Dad screamed, his voice practically gone.

I could now read the flyers on the inside of the windows of Mayfield Grocery and Charlie's Liquor; I was about sixty feet away. My sprint slowed to a quick jog as my body began to shut down. Dad was gaining distance again.

The aircraft blitzed my hometown as bombs fell atop both Mayfield Grocery and Charlie's. I was pushed back by the force of the blast a few feet, and then I blacked out. I'm not sure how long I was out, but I felt someone slapping my face, bringing me back to consciousness. Despite my blurred vision, I knew it was Dad. He had settled Mom on the ground for a moment to wake me. I didn't know what he was saying; all I could hear was a high-pitched ringing in my ears.

I looked around. The places I'd once passed without thought on a regular basis were now piles of concrete, brick, and glass. I saw a little girl, no older than five, on her knees, speaking to her dead father. I didn't need to hear what she was saying; I read her lips as well as the look of horror on her face.

"Wake up, Daddy! Wake up, Daddy!" she chanted in a panic.

The man's body was mangled and torn to shreds, limbs several feet away from the rest of him. The child's hands became coated in blood as she repeatedly banged on his chest in a feeble attempt to rouse him. I saw a few corpses scattered along the road—some scorched, some intact, some ripped apart beyond recognition. Images I'd never be able to forget, no matter how desperately I wanted to.

My sense of sound came back to me, and my father grabbed me by the shirt and lifted me from the ground. "We've got to move, Clint!" Dad shouted before grabbing Mom in a frenzy and taking off again.

I collected myself, dusting off small pieces of rubble and bits of dust from my clothes, then followed Dad again. He looked back at me to assure himself I was still behind him.

We ran and ran and ran, and it looked as if—against all odds—we were going to make it out of this alive.

My body was sore from the impact of the blast and from so much running, but it was better to be sore than dead. I could see it—Ashford

Lane. My God, I'd never been so happy to see so many cookie-cutter houses. The fact that they were all still standing comforted me. I found consolation in knowing that if it were to end tonight, I'd at least be at home and not on the side of the street somewhere.

Three hundred feet—only three hundred more feet, give or take. We were almost there. My dad's legs were shaking; my mom covered her eyes as tears flowed freely between the cracks of her fingers. We had pushed ourselves to the limit. We had nothing left in our bodies, so our minds needed to carry us.

We had not come this far just to die in our front yard.

We reached our mailbox at the end of the driveway, and a million pounds of pressure released from my shoulders. But not for long. I heard something, a new sound—loud, clanking mechanical gears in a synchronized rhythm.

Dad looked back to me, making sure I was there, and then took a glance at the sky. A wide-eyed expression of sheer terror stretched across his face. "Backyard! Now!" he screamed. I looked behind me. In the sky was a single aircraft whose size far outmatched the other plane I'd seen.

We ran into the backyard.

"Cellar!" Dad instructed.

I looked to the sky once more over my shoulder as I descended the steps behind my parents. One bomb, one the size of a small house, released from the underbelly of the aircraft. That telltale whistle filled the air.

I rushed inside the cellar and slammed the door shut behind me, making sure to lock it from the inside.

The whistling grew louder and louder, to the point I was sure my eardrums would burst from the pressure.

I felt a wave of motion under my feet and above my head; the world around me shook as if the very earth were having a convulsion. The explosion was so loud that I heard it for less than half a second. It was as if my ears couldn't process the decibels given off by the impact of the behemoth bomb that had been released. The only sound audible to me after the explosion was like being in the center of a tornado, with the rushing and whooshing of the wind all around us outside. The cellar doors started to shake and rattle, as though the hands of God himself were trying to pry them open.

"Help! Get the doors!" Dad yelled to me. He grabbed the door on the left by the handle, while I took the right. The vibrations of the door hinges rattled against the wooden frames as we pulled the handles toward our bodies to prevent them from flying open and exposing us to whatever was outside.

A small, one-inch-wide chunk of wood burst from the center of the door, exposing a foggy orange light coming through the gap. The ray focused on Dad's right shoulder as his flesh started to burn and sizzle like bacon in a cast-iron pan. He winced in pain and repositioned himself out of the beam's path. Just as I was sure I couldn't hold on for another second, the force of the explosion subsided. Other than my mother's cries, the entire world was suddenly silent. The overwhelming stillness we were suddenly plunged into was nerve-racking—eerie, even. It was the sound of a nothingness that could only mean doom.

Dad shakily pulled his cigarette lighter from his pants pocket and lit a small oil lamp on the floor. Suddenly, I had a clear view of everything around me. Mom was curled in a fetal position in the corner of the room, shaken by what had just happened.

I looked around the cellar. Three gas masks hung on the wall, a hunting rifle propped up on its butt end in the corner next to it. Boxes and shelves full of food and dozens of Mason jars full of water were against the wall behind me, and three sleeping bags were pushed together at the far-most wall of the cellar, with blankets under them for additional support. All of my dad's tools, all of our stored items had been pushed to the other corners and crannies of the room.

This was what Dad had been doing in here all this time.

This was what he had seen coming. And despite the anger and frustration I'd felt toward him earlier that week, I had never been so thankful for his urgency.

I sat against the cellar wall, drenched in my own sweat. The three of us inhaled deeply, trying to catch our breath.

"That was close, huh?" Dad tried to joke.

Neither my mom nor I found humor in this.

Dad's forced smile faded to a look of sadness. "I'm sorry you had to see that, both of you," he said.

"How did you know?" I asked.

Dad sighed. "I didn't—I just had a feeling. I guess it paid off, huh?"

"For how long, though?" I asked.

"My work in here wasn't done, Clint. We'll just have to make do with what I stored in here. Don't worry, though. We'll cross that bridge when we come to it. We should be safe for a while."

I gestured at the shelves of food and water next to me. "A week, two if we're lucky. Then what?"

Dad looked irritated. "Then we leave and start over somewhere else."

I let out a derisive laugh. "Start over *where*, Dad? Where can we go? Did you not see what happened out there?

"And why did they pick Cleveland? It doesn't make sense. What makes you think we can even leave here to go somewhere else without getting killed out there?"

"I don't think you realize that I saved our lives," Dad said, raising his voice with each syllable.

"Maybe for the time being," I said sharply. "It looks to me like we're living on borrowed time now. We both know we should have died out there." I paused to take a breath, easing my tone. "Thank you—thank you for giving us a chance. But if you had a feeling this was going to happen, if you had a feeling we would be living in a hole in the ground, then you must have some sort of plan in mind for what happens now. I love you, and I love Mom, and none of us deserve to starve to death in a hole."

Dad nodded, his attention now fixed on the hole in the door. "I know. I'll think of something, but we aren't going to be able to do it right now. None of us are thinking straight. Talking straight. And it's chaos out there still. Get some sleep. I'm gonna try to fix that door— can't risk letting whatever it is out there in here."

Dad grabbed a small piece of scrap wood he had lying around, a few nails, and his hammer. He ignored everything around him as he worked, trying to mask his fear.

I curled up in a sleeping bag near Mom. She was still weeping, but significantly less than before. I gave her a peck on the cheek in an effort to comfort her. She was scared senseless—not that anyone could blame her.

"Good night, Mom. Good night, Dad. I love you both."

"Night, Clint," Mom whispered in an unsteady tremble.

"You, too," Dad said, his voice muffled by the nail he had clamped between his lips.

I rolled over, turning my back to my parents and closing my eyes to try to get some semblance of sleep. I didn't want to have a dream that night. I was hoping that maybe I was just in the middle of a nightmare.

CHAPTER 5

When I opened my eyes the next morning, I could see that sunlight had found its way in through the cracks of the doors, making the glow of the still-lit oil lamp unnecessary. I rose to a seated position and felt the ache of torn muscles that must have settled in overnight, making me grimace involuntarily in pain.

"Oh! Look who's awake!" Dad quipped as he handed me a tin can half full of black-eyed peas. "Sorry, I forgot to pack silverware," he said with a shrug.

"It's fine," I muttered.

I looked over to Mom; she looked a little flushed. I thought it could've been the lighting or stress or perhaps even exhaustion from the night before. She was chewing her so-called breakfast slowly. Her mascara was streaked and dried on her cheeks from the path her tears had taken.

"This has nothing on your biscuits and gravy, Mom," I said, hoping to make her smile.

She laughed feebly, then coughed.

"Are you okay?" I asked.

"As okay as I can be. Don't worry, sweetie."

I nodded, unconvinced.

"I'll make them for you again someday, I promise," she said with a forced smile.

"Hey, Clint! Look what I found!" Dad exclaimed, holding out an old paddleball game I'd played when I was younger.

"Where'd you find that?" I asked in surprise.

"It was just in a box full of your old stuff. Say, you never did beat my score, did you?"

I laughed. "Oh, you mean that wild claim of yours that you got three hundred in a row? Gee, I don't know, Dad, you tell me. Did I beat it?"

"Hey, now, call it what you want, but the truth's the truth," he replied with a smirk. Dad handed me the paddleball, then went back to his treasure hunt.

Mom chimed in. "I remember the first time you ever tried to play with that as a little one. We were in the grocery store, and they had that at the counter. I didn't understand why a one-year-old wanted a paddleball so bad, but I couldn't say no to that little face," she said with a wink. "Watching you run around the house in your diaper, flailing that little arm around like a wet spaghetti noodle . . . it was truly something else," she said through a snorting laugh.

I smiled at the thought.

All those times I'd cursed my parents under my breath when I was angry, all those things that irritated me over the course of a day—spilling a glass of water, the lawn mower getting clogged, having to clean my room—were now suddenly so meaningless in that reality. There we were, scraping flavorless black-eyed peas from a tin can, living in a hole in the ground, hoping just to see another day and thankful for every moment we had now.

Day two was much like the first.

Dad rummaged through boxes we had scattered in the cellar, digging up old mementos. The pain of seeing my old baby clothes, four old photo albums full of past memories, die-cast trucks—it was close to unbearable. It seemed to help Dad, though.

Those same four photo albums had their pages flipped through an infinite number of times as my parents sat next to the oil lamp and examined them. They both smiled every time they saw the pictures. For Mom, I think it was a reminder of happiness. But for Dad, I think it symbolized hope. We had lived through the attack; we were out of sight and out of mind. But we would have to resurface before long. I tried reminding him of that, but he either refused to accept it or he chose to avoid it.

Day three, we dined on canned beets for breakfast and dinner. Dad noticed how low on food we'd gotten, so we no longer had lunch. Dessert did make its way into the mix, though: butterscotch-flavored powdered pudding poured into a wiped-down tin can with just a splash of water. It wasn't like any pudding I'd ever tasted. The mixture was more like wet sand than anything, with a subtle sweetness that left behind a chalky residue on my tongue. I hated the taste of it, and I knew that if I never had to eat that again, it would still be too soon. But I didn't have a choice—it was either eat shitty pudding or starve. The bright side was, I wouldn't have to suffer through it long. There were only three boxes of pudding mix to start with, minus the one we had just choked down.

Mom was starting to get purple crescents ringing the underside of her eyes, and her hand shook a little as she placed beets in her mouth. Her favorite blue sundress, something she'd always loved to go out on the town in, was soaked by the sweat pouring from her chest, back, and underarms. I was also beginning to notice her health start to decline. But she had always been a strong woman, so I told myself she would be okay. She *had* to be okay; we couldn't afford for her not to be. She kept insisting it was a cold, and Dad believed it. He couldn't bear to believe anything else.

I think that was the day everything finally sank in, though, the gravity of what the world had become.

I didn't know what time of day it was. I couldn't see the faintest hint of sunlight peeking through the cracks anymore. What a world we were living in; even the sun had given up trying.

That was the first night—the first of many—that I finally broke down. This was no nightmare, no matter how desperately I wanted to believe it was. I cried myself to sleep on day three. And I cried many, many times afterward.

Day four, it was beets again, for both breakfast and dinner.

Mom didn't look any better. But on the plus side, it didn't look like she had gotten any worse, either. There was a gag-inducing stench coming from the far-most corner of the cellar, where we had a bucket for relieving ourselves. Dad had placed an old tarp over it in an effort to contain some of the smell, but as far as I was concerned, it wasn't working. It was funny, though, in a way. Once upon a time, had someone told me that their family used a bucket as their shared bathroom, I would have retched at the thought. And now here I was, facing that as my new normal.

After all, I was in a hole, with no light other than an allotted few hours a day via oil lamp, eating cold canned food with my fingers, sleeping on the ground in a cellar with my parents—what was pissing in a bucket? No big deal, at that point.

When the bucket reached its capacity, we had no choice but to empty it, and the duty fell to Dad. To get through it, he wore his gas mask as he lifted the bucket by the handle. It was more than unsettling to hear the fluids slosh around inside the bucket; it may have been worse than the smell itself. He opened the cellar doors, and that was the first time I caught a glimpse of outside—albeit, just the sky, really. What I saw was pitch black, like an endless void, absent of all stars.

Dad poured the contents of the bucket onto the ground as he tilted it on its side with a grunt. The sound, once again, was almost indescribably unsettling.

Dad came back inside and closed the doors behind him. "My goodness! That thing was filled to the brim!" he said, his speech muffled through his gas mask.

"That's just lovely, Dad. Thanks for that," I said.

Dad removed the mask and hung it back on the wall, then wiped his hands on an old grease rag.

Mom began to cough again, and I was once again reminded of my frustration at my father for not making a move in getting us out of there.

"So what's the plan?" I asked Dad.

"Haven't really thought of it much yet. Just gimme a few days and—"

"We don't *have* a few days, Dad," I said, cutting him off.

"Being negative isn't going to get us anywhere," he replied.

"You're right. Being negative won't, but being realistic just might."

"And what do you know about life, Clint? You're just a kid."

I scoffed at the remark. "*A kid?* No, I can't afford to be a *kid* anymore, Dad! You know just as well as I do that we aren't going to last on two boxes of pudding, three cans of carrots, two cans of beets, and six jars of water. Not to mention that Mom's sick."

Dad looked agitated by my backlash. "She's just got a cold. She'll be fine," he insisted.

"*Colds* don't make you shake to the point that you can barely feed yourself! *Colds* don't make you too weak to speak! Wake up, Dad!"

Dad took a seat on the floor next to Mom, reaching his arm around her frail, trembling frame, and took a long pause. He began to cry. "I don't know what I'm doing, Clint." He stopped to take a breath. "All I ever wanted was to take care of you, your mom, the baby . . . I can't even do that."

I sat down next to him. "You can. You will—you always have. But please, let me help. We have to do something. This hole is not a house, and we can't stay here."

Dad's glossy eyes looked up at me. "I'm sorry, I'm so sorry."

I reached my arms around my parents and hugged them both. "I know, Dad. This isn't your fault," I said, releasing my grip and leaning back to look at him. "None of this is your fault. This is going to take all of us if we want to get through, though."

Dad wiped his face with his sleeve and nodded.

"I'm going to try to get some sleep, Dad. We've had enough for one day."

Dad agreed. "I love you, Clint," he said.

"I know, Dad. I love you, too."

Day five, I was awakened early by the sound of screams.

"Amelia, listen to me! Breathe!" Dad yelled, waking me from my slumber.

"What's going on?" I shouted.

"Something isn't right with your mother, Clint! Hurry! Turn the light on!"

I scurried across the cellar floor, making my way through the darkness. "Dad, where's the lighter?" I yelled.

"On the bottom step!" he shouted back. "Amelia, please, slow breaths. Come on, sweetheart, you can do it. Please, listen to me," he said as my mom wheezed and gagged. "Clint! Today, please!"

Dad yelled.

I felt around on the cold stone step, and the tips of my fingers finally closed around a small, rectangular piece of metal. I made my way to the other end of the cellar, where my parents were, bending down to feel my way along. I flicked the flint of the lighter to help me see what I was doing and lit the lamp.

My blood went cold at what I was watching. Dad shook Mom in a panic, trying to talk her to wakefulness. Blood and saliva trickled out of the corner of her mouth as she lay helplessly on her side.

"Oh, God. Oh, God, please, no!" Dad screamed as he watched the life begin to fade from Mom's eyes. The color was draining from her skin.

I couldn't just sit there and watch, but I had no idea what to do.

Suddenly, Dad sat Mom upright, draping her upper body over one forearm while thumping her back with the open palm of the other. Blood began to mist from Mom's mouth in a harsh wheeze as she desperately tried to catch air.

"Come on! Come on, Amelia!" Dad shouted. He followed the urgent words with another blow to her back, and another, and then another. Finally, green phlegm flew from Mom's throat and onto the dirt floor.

"That's it, Dad! I think it's working!"

Dad reared his hand back once more and channeled his remaining energy into the last strike. The sound of Dad's hand hitting Mom's back resonated like the beating of a drum.

A solidified chunk of dark red goop the size of a golf ball escaped Mom's chest as she wheezed to reclaim her breath.

"Oh, thank God! Oh, thank God!" Dad gasped as he held Mom close to him, rocking her back and forth. Mom was panting, still breathing heavily, but she was breathing.

"I'm so sorry I had to do that. I didn't know what else to do," Dad whimpered through his tears, Mom's head buried in his chest.

I noticed something that didn't look quite right with Mom's side—a spot on her dress was covered in blood. "Dad, what is that?" I asked, pointing at her side.

"What is what?" he answered, looking confused.

"That, around her rib cage," I replied.

Dad felt around in the dark through Mom's dress. There was a small tear in the fabric. "What in the hell?" Dad said as he took out his pocketknife and cut a small area of the fabric away, revealing what it was.

It was a chunk of something buried into Mom's side; must have been shrapnel from the explosions days ago. The area around the cut was badly infected, the skin pigmented yellow with puss seeping from the edges.

"Oh, no! Oh, no!" Dad moaned. "I have to go get help," he said to me.

"Help from who?" I asked.

"It doesn't matter who—we need to do something! She's going to die if this is left untreated."

My father was right. She had already flirted with death, and for her to have any chance at all, we would have to get help.

"Well, I'm going with you," I insisted.

"No . . . *no*, you need to stay here with your mother in case she gets worse," Dad said.

"*Worse?* If she gets worse, how is my being here going to help? Face it, Dad, you don't know what's out there. You really want to walk through a wasteland alone?" I asked.

"*Want to?* No—but you have to stay!" Dad spat back, clearly losing patience in his frenzy to do something.

"No . . . ," I murmured.

"Excuse me?" Dad boomed.

"*No*. I'm going with you. I'm no doctor; I don't know how I'd help if something happened to Mom. And what if *you* need help? You can't go out there alone," I answered.

Dad looked me in the eyes for a moment, coming to the realization that what I was saying made more sense than he wanted to admit.

"Fine," he said at last. "But do exactly what I say. Nothing more, nothing less. Understand?"

"I understand," I said, nodding.

Despite my fear of what was waiting outside, a fear I'm sure was shared by my father, I knew it was the only option. We would have to face the world and whatever it had become.

CHAPTER 6

It was still the fifth day, the worst of all of those days in that hole. I didn't know it yet, but that was the day that, for the first time, I would have to say goodbye forever to someone I loved. Someone who had held me immediately after I'd taken my first breath on this planet. Someone who had always had an open ear for me to confide in and a warm embrace that sheltered me from all that was evil. Someone who had always believed in me, pushed me to become something bigger.

I sat in the cellar, anticipating what waited on the other side.

"Ten total," Dad said. His words brought me out from my reverie.

"Ten what?" I asked.

"Ten cartridges," he replied, strapping his hunting rifle to his back. "And we'll return with all of them. Got it?"

"What if we—"

"All ten!" he interrupted. "Do as I say, and it'll all work out."

"Okay . . . So what's the plan?" I asked.

Dad picked up an old black duffel bag that hadn't been used in years. Spotted layers of white mold covered its exterior. "Here," he said as he handed the bag to me. "Put some water in there in case we need it. The plan is to stop at the pharmacy in town. We don't want to go into the city unless we have to. Penicillin and any disinfectants—that's what we need the most."

I nodded and placed two of our last five jars of water into the duffel bag.

Dad leaned down to Mom, who looked as if she could slip away from us at any moment, and gave her a kiss as well as a gentle rub on her enlarged belly. "You're gonna be just fine. Just try to relax, and keep taking care of that baby. Okay?" he said, obviously holding back tears.

I followed Dad's example and gave Mom a light peck on the cheek.

"Put this on," Dad instructed as he handed me a gas mask from the wall.

"This really necessary?" I asked, hesitating as I took the mask from his hand.

"It is unless you want to die of radiation poisoning. Now put it on," he barked.

I groaned as I placed the mask over my head and watched Dad do the same.

"Remember," he said as he turned around to face the cellar door. "All . . . ten . . . rounds."

"Got it," I replied. "All ten."

Dad flung open the cellar door, and we were immediately overtaken by a blast of freezing air.

"What in the world . . . ?" Dad muttered, his voice muffled by the gas mask. Neither of us knew why it felt like the inside of an icebox—it was May, after all—but it didn't matter at that point. "Let's go," he said.

We climbed the steps of the cellar and stepped onto the frigid ground. I heard a crunch; I looked down at my feet to see layers of frozen dew on the discolored earth. "This doesn't make any sense," I said.

"None of this makes any sense. Now let's quit stalling and get on with it," Dad responded.

I took in my surroundings, my attention immediately caught by the sky. The shade was a dark orange, not like a normal sunset—more a strange shade between tangerine and dark gray. There weren't any clouds, either. Not like any clouds I'd ever seen, anyway. It was as if a dense sheet of fog had been stretched across the entire world.

"Beautiful, huh?" Dad asked in a sarcastic tone.

But *any* kind of sky without planes flying through it was beautiful to me at that point.

We walked around the house and into the front yard as our feet crunched with every step. The entire street seemed dead, with shingles ripped off the roofs of houses as well as broken windows. The place was empty, like a ghost town. If there were any survivors left, I knew they'd gone somewhere else. Ashford Lane was ours alone. The cookie-cutter houses still remained standing, but now each had its own unique degree of damage.

Dad removed his gas mask to wipe the foggy lenses before placing it back atop his head. "You know," he said, "this isn't exactly what I had in mind when the real estate agent said it was a quiet neighborhood."

I managed to smile at his cheesy joke.

"Let's go," he said. "Mom's counting on us."

We walked side by side in the orange, frigid silence until we could see the pharmacy in the distance, several blocks away from us.

"How are you feeling?" Dad asked as we made our way toward the pharmacy.

"Hungry as hell . . . but I'll be all right," I replied.

"I hear that. We'll try to come back out and get some food after we help Mom," Dad said.

"You think Mom's going to be okay?" I asked anxiously.

"Yes," Dad insisted.

"The baby, too?" I asked.

"The baby, too." He sounded resolute, as though he couldn't give room to a thought otherwise. "We can't let anything happen to either one of them. I don't know what I'd do. You'll know what I mean when you meet someone special."

"How will I know?" I asked curiously.

"You just will. And the thing is, you won't be expecting it. So every little feeling you get when you see her, it's real. Hits you like a ton of bricks," Dad said.

Even though I couldn't see his facial expression through his mask, I knew he was smiling and thinking about when he'd met Mom.

Dad chuckled to himself softly. "Yep, might happen anywhere. You really never know until it happens. And when it does, you'll get this burning feeling in the pit of your gut. Like a million little firecrackers blasting away in there. And then one day, you'll be looking at her, wearing a long white dress, and sometime after that, she'll be holding your little baby. The way she looks when she does . . . There's nothing else like it in the world."

"I think I get it," I replied.

"Trust me," Dad said, giving me a light, playful shove. "You don't."

I saw a new side of Dad in that moment. He'd always tried his damnedest to make sure everyone knew how strong he was, but he was also incredibly gentle and thoughtful—much more so than he'd ever admit. His love was endless, and he was a hell of a man. The best that humanity had to offer.

As we were inching our way closer to the pharmacy, I felt a frigid, wet chill ripple down my spine. "You feel that?" I asked, shivering against the cold.

"Feel wha—" he started to ask as the same chill hit him. It was starting to snow—in May, of all months. "What . . . in the hell . . . ?" Dad chattered. We both looked up to the sky to see a light flurry of snowflakes glide through the wind. "I've seen it all now," Dad said as he shook his head in awe. We watched intently as the flakes touched down to the ground and then dissolved immediately. "At least it isn't sticking," Dad said.

We could see the city of Cleveland in the far-off distance, a shell of its former self. Even from so far away, it looked like a ghost town. Our small suburb was no better, either. We saw the state the Mayfield Pharmacy was in as we approached the storefront. Debris and rubble littered the entire crossroads, and bodies were scattered across the ground like common pieces of garbage, some intact, some torn to shreds and mangled beyond all belief. Every single one of them, though, was blackened and scorched, like the charred remnants of a piece of charcoal that had been on the grill. There was one particular scene that stuck with me the most and, to this very day, haunts me at almost every waking second.

Two bodies intertwined, their cracked, carbonized flesh fused together as if they had been deliberately welded into one piece. The larger of the two bodies had its arms wrapped protectively around the entire frame of the smaller body. That smaller body was what tore my heart to pieces.

It was clearly that of a small child, its head buried into the chest of the larger form. And held within the curled fingers of the child were the frayed, ashy remains of a teddy bear, missing an eye, with a leather patch sewn onto the top of its head. I could imagine that kid, crying, begging frantically . . . pleading. So scared, so confused. And the one holding the child was doing his damnedest to deliver comfort. They'd never stood a chance, though, and in the end, all they'd had was each other and that one last embrace.

My chest clenched tightly, and my breathing grew unsteady. My stomach began to churn as my mind desperately tried to piece together everything I was seeing. Tears streamed from my eyes; I pulled my gas mask from my face and vomited on the ground below me. "Dad . . . Dad, I can't do this!" I cried out, wiping the traces of bile from my mouth with the collar of my shirt.

Dad rushed to me and pulled my mask back over my face. "Keep it on, Clint. Keep it on," he said.

"Why, Dad? *Why?* Why did this happen?" I asked, my words slurred and barely intelligible.

"Clint, listen to me!" Dad shouted as he grabbed me by the sides of my head and stared directly into my eyes.

"Dad, I can't—" I repeated.

"Listen!" he said even louder, finally getting my attention. "There isn't anything we can do to change this. What happened here, it's horrible. But we have to keep it together for your mother, okay?"

"This is terrible . . . Nobody deserves this," I replied.

"I won't argue with you on that point. But we can't think about that right now. We need to go inside," Dad said as he gave me a pat on the back. "Can't let this keep us from taking care of Mom."

I nodded and followed Dad to the front of the pharmacy. The door was locked, but thankfully, the glass door pane had been shattered enough to reach an arm inside and unlock it. Dad reached in and quickly pulled his hand back out to reveal a small piece of broken glass lodged inside. As he yanked it from his flesh, a small amount of blood dripped to the ground.

"You okay?" I asked.

"Yeah—it's nothing," he replied, pushing through the door.

The door slowly creaked open, and we walked inside, the broken glass snapping and crunching beneath our feet. The entire place looked as though it had been ransacked, with shelves and cabinets overturned and left barren, documents and papers scattered about the dirty tile floor.

"Start looking. You know what we need," Dad said as I removed the duffel's strap from my shoulder and unzipped its main compartment.

Dad ran to the back of the pharmacy and into the storage room. I could hear loud rummaging as he slung drawers and boxes about the small, confined space. I walked over to the front counter and started opening all of the cabinets and drawers, finding two adhesive bandages still in their wrapper as well as a sealed bottle of rubbing alcohol and an unused syringe. I threw all of it in the bag and called out for Dad. "Find anything?"

"Sure did!" Dad yelled back, holding up a half-empty bottle of penicillin. Even through his gas mask, I could imagine the smile I was sure he was wearing.

"Good job! Is that gonna work?" I asked hopefully.

"Only one way to find out," Dad replied. "Let's get outta here." He handed me the penicillin; I threw it in the bag and zipped it shut. I rose to my feet and began following Dad back to the front entrance.

"Help me! Anybody, please!" I heard a man's voice scream from outside the pharmacy.

"Who is that?" I asked.

"How the hell should I know? Quick, get behind the counter!" Dad instructed.

We scurried over to the counter and crouched down, trying our best to remain hidden. The man's voice kept pleading for help; it grew louder and louder.

"We have to help him!" I insisted.

"You know we can't risk anything. Just stay down."

A gunshot rippled through the air, and the voice was silenced.

"Oh, shit," Dad whispered as he peeked his head around the counter.

"What is it?" I asked frantically.

"Shh!" he hissed.

"Is there someone out there? Did they kill him?" I asked in a whisper.

"What do you think? Shut up and stay hidden," he commanded.

"We can't just stay hidden! We have to help!" I said, rising to my feet.

Dad pulled me back down. "Don't you *dare* move," he said. "Do you have any idea what would it would do to your mother and me if something happened to you?"

"But, Dad—"

"I said *be quiet*!" Dad snapped.

"Hey, he have anything?" I heard a man's voice say from outside.

"Jesus Christ," Dad whispered. "They're speaking *English*. They aren't even German."

That was the first time I really saw the world as I do now, became aware of how cruel and dark a place could become in a matter of days. How desperate people could become when the odds were stacked against them and everything was stripped away. It scares you, makes you wonder if you'll ever go down that road yourself. Makes you wonder what happened to make these lost souls fall from grace.

I came back to my senses when I heard a second man respond to the first. "Nope. Nothing. Typical."

"Shit, old man ain't gonna be happy 'bout this," the first replied.

"We gotta go back with *something*!" the second man insisted.

"How 'bout that pharmacy? See if there's anything in there!"

"Oh, shit," Dad whispered under his breath. "Don't make a peep," he instructed quietly.

Our backs were still pressed against the counter as we heard the door creak open slightly. Footsteps atop broken glass and filthy tile echoed through the room.

"Just a waste of time! This place looks like a tornado went through it," I heard one of the men say.

"I suppose so. Let's go on, then. Gotta find something," the second replied.

Dad exhaled in relief, and my heartbeat began to slow down. We heard footsteps make their way back out the door when, all of a sudden, they stopped.

"What's that on the floor?" I heard one of the men say. Dad and I looked at each other in confusion and fear.

"Looks like blood to me. And it's fresh," the other man replied.

Dad looked down to the cut on his hand and began shaking his head.

"Anyone in here?" one of the men shouted.

Dad and I stayed silent until the second man chimed in: "We will burn this place down! Show your faces!"

Dad looked at me and gave me a single nod. "Don't shoot!" he said as we rose to our feet with our arms in the air. The men inched their way toward Dad and me with smirks painted across their faces. It wasn't long before Dad and I were backed into the wall, with nowhere to go.

The men were tall, about the same size as my dad, and about ten years younger. One was much thinner, while the other was slightly older and stockier. Both of their faces were covered in layers of filth and grime, like they had just gotten off from a shift at a coal mine. The larger man's face was deformed on one side, as if he had been badly burned by chemicals. Perhaps he hadn't been in a safe zone when the bombs fell. Their clothes were little more than torn rags, their pants and shirts full of holes. The larger man wore a thick, black leather jacket that would have swallowed me.

"We never saw you, you never saw us. How about we just go on about our days?" Dad asked the men.

"How about this: I do all the talking, and you only open yours if I ask you a question. Ya hear?" the smaller man said.

Dad nodded.

"What's in the bag, boy?" the larger one asked, directing the question at me.

"Nothing," I replied.

"You got that thing glued to your chest—seems awfully important for it to be nothing," he replied.

"Please . . . you don't have to do this!" Dad spoke up.

"What the hell did I just tell you?" the smaller man screamed, raising his shirt slightly to reveal a handgun in his waistband.

"Now about that bag, boy," the older man said again.

"Medicine for my mom. She's dying," I answered.

Both of the men took a look at each other before letting out a harsh bark of laughter.

"Poor baby," the smaller one said. "What makes you think we give a damn about your mom?"

"Please don't—" I pleaded.

"What's yours is ours now. Best make this as easy as you can on yourselves," the older one said, cutting me off.

I slid a look at Dad, and we nodded to each other.

I could see Dad's eyes scan the men through the lenses of his mask as I did the same. Only the smaller one had a gun visible.

The larger one had a large hunting knife shoved in his waistband. I didn't know what the plan was, but I knew Dad had no intention of letting Mom die.

"Hand over the masks," the larger man demanded.

Dad and I both knew it was already too late for them—they'd been exposed to far too much radiation, so the masks would likely be useless by that point. But considering we didn't want to get gunned down, Dad and I slowly reached to the backs of our masks to unzip them and slide them off our heads. Dad and I handed the men the masks, and they promptly put them over their own faces.

"Now the gun!" the larger man said.

Dad didn't immediately hand it over; instead, he asked the man a question. "You're going to kill us, aren't you?"

The man went chest to chest with Dad before giving a condescending snicker. "Maybe you ain't half as stupid as you look. A man's gotta do what a man's gotta do. Surely you can understand that this town don't have enough for all of us to share. Quick and painless, or suffer—choice is yours. You best cooperate."

"I understand," Dad said before looking at me. "I love you, Clint," he said, taking the rifle off his back and slowly handing it over.

The man reached for the gun with both hands, and that was when I found out we didn't have a plan at all. This was a showdown, and we were about to fight for our lives.

Before I knew what was happening, Dad reached down into the man's exposed and vulnerable waistband and grabbed the hunting knife, quickly plunging it into his heart and then shoving it in farther with a quick twist. The man groaned and gagged as the life left his body, falling to the floor like a sack of potatoes.

"You son of a bitch!" the smaller man screamed, pulling his gun from his own waistband and firing two shots into Dad's chest. Dad immediately fell against the wall and slid down to the floor, grunting in pain as he left a streak of blood behind him. I saw red and, without thinking, charged the man who had shot my dad. The pistol flew from his hand and slid across the floor, out of reach.

I had the man on his back; I swung my fists at his face from every direction.

"Get off me!" he shouted, wriggling out from under me and breaking free when he gave me a quick kick to the ribs.

I was facedown on the ground; he grabbed my hair and kept slamming my face against the floor. My head throbbed and my vision faded as I watched a pool of my own blood form on the floor's surface. He flipped me over and buried his knee in my chest, choking the life out of me. My eyes drifted over to Dad, and I could see him barely hanging on. He was crawling to something, but it wouldn't be until a little later that I knew exactly what it was.

"I'm sorry, Mom . . . I'm sorry," I groaned weakly as I began to gag on my own blood.

"Go to hell, you pig! Just die already!" the man screamed at me.

It was at that moment that I accepted it: I was about to die. I reached out and gave one last feeble swing at his face, but he slapped my hands away like those of an annoying infant. My right hand landed on something; it was a shard of glass. I gripped it tightly, knowing it would be the only chance I had to make it out of there alive—I just had to wait for the right time to strike. With my eyes starting to close and my limbs growing numb from lack of oxygen, though, I knew I didn't have much time to wait.

Just in the nick of time, another gunshot echoed through the pharmacy, and the man on top of me had his chest blown apart. He screamed in pain, and his grip loosened. As air filled my lungs again, I saw a small window of opportunity to strike back. With all the strength

I had in my beaten body, I drew the broken shard of glass deep across the man's throat.

The look on his face was pure shock as his blood rushed from the wound like a geyser. I think the pain of getting shot paled in comparison to what was happening at that very moment. He knew he was done; he knew he was dying. It hit me hard, the fact that I had just ended another human being. It made me question who I really was.

His eyes closed as his limp body fell from on top of me. I stood to my feet, my muscles aching, and hobbled over to Dad. He was lying on his back in a pool of his own blood.

"So much for all ten, huh?" Dad tried to joke. He was wheezing, and his skin was sickly pale.

"Let's get out of here," I replied, trying my best to drag him.

"Stop," Dad said with a harsh cough. "Go home . . ."

"I'm not leaving you! Let's go!" I insisted.

"It's too late for me, son. I need you to take care of her. I need you to look after her. You're the man of the house now."

"Dad! Stop!" I shouted.

"It hurts so bad, Clint. My God, it hurts so bad," Dad said as he started to choke.

I turned him over on his side, and blood drained out of his mouth. He took in a deep, wheezing breath. "I need you to do it," he said.

"That's not an option!" I replied.

"Don't leave me like this . . . please . . . ," he begged.

"There's another way! There has to be another way!"

"I want you to know something," Dad said before letting out yet another bloodied cough. "You always were a special kid. Light of my life." Dad stopped to take in another ragged breath. "I remember when I first held you, the deep talks we always had. I guess all good things come to an end, right? Teaching you to play ball, teaching you to be the man you are now. And I couldn't be more proud."

"Don't talk like that!" I said, my eyes burning with tears.

I gripped Dad as tightly as I could and gave him the longest hug I'd ever given him. Just like the two bodies in front of the store, we were having one last embrace. I could feel his thready pulse bouncing to no particular rhythm. He kept trying to speak, but soon it was nothing more than exhausted noises and groans.

I looked Dad in the face one more time, memorizing the face of the man I'd always admired, the man I'd always thought of as a superhero. The look Dad gave me, that stare—he knew it was time, but I didn't want to accept it. I had never seen someone feel so much pain at once. And despite my strongest wish, I knew he was right. I couldn't leave him like that, just barely clinging on and in so much agony. I picked up the rifle as I watched Dad mouth the words "Goodbye. I love you." And then he closed his eyes, waiting.

"I love you, too, Dad. I love you so much," I whimpered back.

I aimed the gun as best I could through my tears, my trembling, unsteady hands clutching the very thing we had tried so hard not to use. Now, it had only nine rounds left. I moved my finger to the trigger.

And in an instant, the nine became eight.

CHAPTER 7

I gathered all the supplies that could possibly be of use to me, along with my mask, the handgun our attackers had brought, their knife, and the thick leather jacket, which had a small glass jar of some type of food tucked into the side pocket. I looked outside and saw that the rate of snowfall had dramatically increased.

I glanced at the young man staring back at me in the reflection of the shattered remains of the pharmacy's front window. A black eye, bruised jaw, and bloody mouth. I was taken aback by the fact that if it hadn't been for my dad and a piece of glass, I wouldn't be walking back through that front door. I pulled my gas mask over my face with sigh of disbelief.

I don't think I could've beat a snail in a race, moving at the rate I did as I made my way back home. I dragged my feet as I watched stray drops of my own blood spoil the clean surface of the now ankle-high snow. My feet had grown numb, but who knew if it was from the cold? Everything was numb by then.

The sun had started to set, but the typical orange hues of the sunlight bouncing off the horizon were replaced by blackness in this strange sky. Had it not been for the tiniest bit of moonlight, I would've been lost and left to freeze. A week ago, having my ass kicked with no way to navigate myself home would've been a scary enough situation, but the pain I was feeling now reminded me that I was alive. Besides, I had much bigger issues to worry about. My mom, for one. I had no idea if she was even alive, and if she was, I was going to have to tell her that Dad was dead.

All those thoughts kept rushing through my head. What if Mom hated me for what I had done? I debated whether I should even tell her. Would she understand? She needed to know the truth—and it wasn't like I was Superman: unless I were to miraculously heal my injuries before I walked down those cellar steps, she would know that things had gone terribly wrong without me even opening my mouth.

We were in a dog-eat-dog world now, and I either had to get used to it or die. There wasn't any room left on the table for choices anymore. The choices I'd had to make since the bombs fell had been getting more and more difficult. There wasn't a way out of it; this was a nightmare we couldn't wake from, a world that made me question everything I'd ever been taught. If God loved his children, why let them suffer? Why allow evil to win? I didn't even care that I was having blasphemous thoughts. Why fear the hell below when you're living through hell on earth?

I eventually dragged myself down the streets of Mayfield and then down Ashford Lane until I arrived at the remnants of my home. The cellar was blanketed by a thick layer of snow—it must have been at least six inches deep by that point. Ohio was no stranger to heavy snowfall, and had it been a few months earlier, the sheets of white would have been an expected sight. But it *wasn't*. It was May. I wiped the snow away from the cellar door with my arm and placed my hand on the handle, taking a deep breath.

"Come on, Mom, pull through for me," I uttered prayerfully as I opened the door and closed it behind me. I placed my duffel bag against the wall before removing the medical supplies. Mom was motionless where I had left her, but I could see she was breathing.

I removed my gas mask, dropped it on the floor, and began looking for one of Mom's old sewing kits. A single needle and a bit of thread was all I needed; I hadn't had any luck at the pharmacy in finding some proper stitching supplies. After scrounging through a few boxes, I found what I needed. The needle was slightly rusted, but beggars couldn't be choosers. I'd just have to sterilize it with alcohol and buff it out the best I could. I lit the oil lamp again and began reading the back of the penicillin bottle to find out how much I should use.

I lifted Mom's dress just enough to expose the back of her thigh, then slowly and carefully injected the penicillin into it. She flinched, but other than that, she hardly moved. I poured some rubbing alcohol into my hands and rubbed them together before grabbing the chunk of shrapnel that had wedged itself into her side with my thumb and index finger. She opened her eyes slightly as I began to wiggle it back and forth, trying to break it free from its burrow. Once I could move it just enough, I knew what my next step would be.

"Sorry, Mom, this isn't going to feel good," I said before quickly pulling it out. Her eyes were wide open now; she thrashed and screamed in pain. "Mom, calm down!" I urged, trying to soothe her. "I know it hurts, but you need to save your energy. And I need you to stay still."

She wept in pain for another couple of minutes before focusing her eyes on me. That was when she saw my beaten face and torn clothes. Her eyes grew wide as she looked around the cellar. I dreaded the question she was going to ask, and I couldn't think of an easy way to answer her.

"Where is your father?" she whispered weakly.

"Dad . . ." My throat choked on the words. "Dad didn't make it."

Mom looked at me, more confused than upset. "But he's on his way, right?" she mouthed with little volume.

"No, Mom . . . He's gone," I said, my shoulders sinking in shame and grief.

Tears streamed from her eyes like a flowing river, and her lips trembled.

"Mom, please . . . don't cry," I said, my own voice cracking.

She just looked at me. "How do I not?"

"I don't know, Mom," I said, breaking down. I was tired of crying; I was tired of suffering. I gave Mom a tight embrace. "I miss him, Mom. When does it end?" I cried.

She ran her fingers through my hair like she'd done when I was a little boy; it was the most comforting thing I had felt since all this had begun. We sat in that cellar for hours, trying to cope with our new reality. We were all we had.

Mom went back to sleep after I finished treating her wound. I poured a small amount of alcohol inside, then stitched it the best I could. It wasn't neatly sewn, but it was closed, and that was all that really mattered. I pulled an old wool blanket over her and gave her a light kiss on the cheek. "Good night," I said before sitting against the wall. I was in no condition to sleep; there was too much on my mind. I saw the cellar door start to leak, and while I knew it couldn't hold the weight of the snow forever, I also knew it *had* to—we couldn't leave yet. Neither of us would get very far in the shape we were in. We needed time, something I knew we didn't have much of.

I thought about Dad's last words; I felt like I'd done right by him. *"I need you to take care of her."* It kept playing in my head. I heard him, and who was I to deny him of his final wish? I wondered how he was doing, wherever he was. Funny, all my life I had been told about heaven and hell. I'd always looked forward to those pearly gates and being surrounded by everyone I loved. It had always given me peace of mind, too, knowing that the end wasn't the end. Streets of gold with no crime, no pain, no goodbyes. It was a nice thought, and if there really was a heaven and hell, I was sure Dad was in heaven. He deserved nothing less.

Still, the longer I was awake, the more I thought. I was beginning to wonder if it even existed at all. Was it a lie to trick us into being better people? Or was it perhaps a lie to unite us as a society into conformity? I didn't know—still don't, and I don't think anyone ever will—but part of me couldn't bear the thought of Dad being gone completely. I didn't want him to hurt anymore, I didn't want him to be scared. I wanted him to be happy, but I wanted him here, with us. Still, I tried to think of him having the time of his life up there, and realized that maybe, just maybe, that was why so many still believed: because we could never truly let go of the ones we loved.

But on the other hand, the more pessimistic side of me insisted that it was all a sham, a construct of deceit. *"Jesus loves me, this I know . . ."* Well, I was beginning to think I needed some kind of evidence of that. What all-loving father, what divine creator without sin, would idly sit back and watch his children be slaughtered like cattle?

I spent the next four days watching Mom heal. The first day, she ate green beans. She needed all the energy she could get; and though I felt as if I were going to die, whether it be from my physical or emotional pain, I knew I could likely spare a couple of days without food. My stomach disagreed, though, growling at me every time I watched Mom take a bite. She stayed awake a little longer than usual—to me, that was a good sign.

Just before I went to sleep, I rammed the cellar door open with my shoulder; that had become a daily task for me during our time underground. The door had grown heavy from all the snowfall, and I knew it wasn't a good idea to let it accumulate. On one hand, it could have collapsed on top of us. On the other, it could have gotten too heavy to budge when the time came to make our escape, and then what? Still, I was determined: I would not die in a hole.

The second day, I went without food again, sustaining myself on only water. I usually let Mom have the clean stuff we had jarred, and grabbed some snow from outside and waited for it to melt for myself.

My stomach was beginning to resent the abuse I was giving it. The jar of food I found in the coat pocket turned out not to even really be food but sorghum—poor man's honey. In what I can only call desperation, I scraped a big finger-ful of the sweet, gelatinous goo and stuffed it into my mouth. My lips puckered tightly as I tried my best to swallow. It wasn't exactly food, but I figured anything was better than nothing, so I decided to use most of it to mix into Mom's meals to help stretch them. I didn't know what I was doing—I was no doctor—but she began to pull through. She was still much too weak to walk around for long, but she could now walk distances of about ten feet or so, and she could feed herself without me guiding the food to her mouth. She still needed my help using the bathroom, but I didn't mind. I wasn't about to give up on her.

Day three rolled around, and I had my first bite of actual food since coming back into the cellar. Brussels sprouts. I'd always hated brussels sprouts.

It was at about that time that I noticed the state we were in, as far as hygiene went. The body odor I kept trying to mask with rubbing alcohol was plain as day now. If we didn't blow our cover somehow, I was sure it'd be just a matter of days before some wild coyote sniffed us out. I would wipe whatever plaque I could off my teeth with an old grease rag I found, and then insisted Mom do the same. I'd fill an empty tin can with snow and allow it to melt, dipping the same rag into the water and wiping dirt and grime off the both of us. It was a far cry from any proper bath, but it would have to suffice.

Mom got back most of the clarity in her voice then; she was still hoarse in comparison to her usual soft tone, but she was healing. I needed any glimmer of hope I could get, and I only wished Dad could have seen her pull through. We often talked about him. Memories mainly, the goofy, childish things he'd always do. What he would say to us right now if he saw us upset, how he was a man of values before all else. It was comforting. It was almost like he wasn't "gone" gone, like he had just "gone to the store to pick up a pack of smokes" gone.

There was something tearing away at me, though, something I couldn't quite understand.

"Mom?" I said.

"Yes, honey?" she asked.

"Why didn't you let us know you were hurt?"

She stared off in the distance for what seemed like minutes, though I was sure it was just a few seconds. "I didn't want you to go out there. Lord knows what's waiting for us," she said.

"What were you thinking? That you'd just be able to wait it out and get better on your own?" I asked.

Mom shook her head in regret and forced a smile. "Yeah, that's exactly what I was thinking. And look what I caused," she said with a blank look.

"Mom, trust me, it isn't you who deserves the blame."

"If not me, then who?" she asked.

"Mom," I said, my voice cracking, "I killed Dad."

She looked at me, confused.

"Two guys approached us. They were going to kill us; we didn't have a choice but to fight back. I had to do it out of mercy. He was shot and in pain, and he knew he wasn't going to make it. He asked me to do it, and I felt like it was the only way to honor him." I felt the hot sting of tears in my eyes.

"Clint, honey," she said softly.

"Mom! What if I'd done things differently? What if I'd acted faster? All I needed was just a second, and Dad would still be here. I froze, I was scared, and now Dad is gone because I was a coward!"

"Clint! Stop!" Mom urged. "Your father would hate hearing you say that!"

"Yeah, well, he *can't* hear me say it. And it's all my fault!"

"No! It isn't!" she insisted. "Things happen for a reason! He's with God now—"

I interrupted, letting out a frustrated laugh. *"God?* God let this happen! If there even is a God, I'd love to have five minutes alone with him to make him answer for what he's done to us!" I screamed.

Mom caught me off guard with a smack to the mouth. She pointed her index finder sharply at me. For a weakened woman, she sure could deliver a sting. "Don't you *ever* say something like that again! You were raised better than that."

"You don't understand," I muttered back.

"I don't?" she replied. "Do you know what it's like to see your child beaten black and blue, or to have the person you love more than your own life taken away from you forever?"

"No, no, I don't," I replied. "But do you know what it's like to see the town you love full of dead bodies or to see both of your parents slipping away?" I asked softly.

"No. I don't," she murmured back.

"Face it, Mom, neither of us are cut out for this. Maybe that Darwin guy knew what he was talking about, with natural selection and all."

Mom chuckled. "I don't think a guy who thought we came from monkeys had any clue about how the world works."

I laughed; Mom had always known how to make me laugh. She'd always had a way to make me feel better, one way or another.

"It's gonna take a miracle for us to make it out of all of this alive," I said.

"Life's full of miracles, Clint. After all, I have you, don't I?"

I smiled. "Yeah, and you always will."

That was about it for day three. I really needed day three. A million pounds of pressure lifted from my shoulders. I had desperately needed to talk about the guilt and horror that were chipping away at me. And, of course, Mom was there for that. She always was.

By day four, Mom's voice was almost back to normal. We *both* ate that day—not much, but just enough. By then, we were down to our last two cans of food and half the jar of sorghum.

Mom could also use the bathroom with less help now, and her hand wasn't as shaky when she fed herself. That was when I felt it, for the first time in a short forever: happiness, pride. I had done something right. I thought of what Riley had asked me a few days before, or maybe it was a couple of weeks or months by then—it was hard to keep track of time. "What are a couple of kids from Mayfield gonna do?" Well, I didn't know what my old friend was doing, or even if he was still alive, but I knew I had made a difference. A small change in the vast scope of things, maybe, but a colossal one to me.

I knew we had to leave soon. But in that moment, I had to focus on cherishing every breath we took. Laughs, smiles—for once, they were genuine. I rummaged through miscellaneous boxes in the cellar.

In a box buried underneath an old roll of duct tape and a box of nails, I found an old set of checkers. "What do you say?" I asked Mom with a smile, holding the game in front of the lamp's light.

She grinned back. "Sure. Beats sitting here, doing nothing."

I removed the box's contents and laid them out on the cold floor.

"I call red," Mom said before I could even set up the game.

"Maybe *I* wanted to be red," I said playfully.

"No, no. I want it more," she insisted.

"Why are you so bent on being red?" I asked curiously.

"Well, there's a reason we put this old game in the cellar in the first place," she said.

"Yeah, and why is that?" I asked.

"Because it's missing one of the black pieces!" she laughed with a snort. I let her have it her way; it didn't matter to me. Not even when she won eight games in a row.

We ended our night looking through old photo albums again, both of us tearing up whenever we saw Dad's smile. Sure, it was sad, but it was nice being able to cry over something worthy of our tears. Something special.

"Where do we go from here?" I asked.

"Does it matter?"

"Yeah, it matters. It has to. At least, I think it has to," I said.

"And why is that? Who knows what's out there?" She had a point; I didn't see the difference in going north, south, east, or west. As long as it was better.

"I guess we just pick a direction Dean keep going," I said.

"As good a plan as any, I suppose," she said. She was easy to convince that we had to leave. She'd always been a rational woman.

My one and only goal was to avoid the city. I felt that would be the safest course of action, with the least risk of running into anyone dangerous. Our landscape was filled with hills and trails, the type of outdoor scene you would see on a postcard. At least, it had been. As I ran my idea by my mom, I told her that, despite the fact that it would take longer to get wherever we were going, at least we'd be more likely get there. She didn't object.

"So, when are we leaving?" she asked.

"First thing in the morning. We'll get what rest we can and use the little light we have to our advantage before it gets pitch black out there when the sun goes down. Sound good to you?"

Mom shrugged. "Sounds as good as it can, I guess."

"Good. I'm going to get some things together, then I'll get to sleep. You should go ahead and get your rest. You aren't a hundred percent yet."

Mom agreed hesitantly. "Good night, Clint," she said.

"Good night, Mom."

I filled all of our jars with snow to let them melt overnight, wrapping some loose cloth around them to prevent them from freezing once we got out there in the cold. In my duffel bag, I packed the lighter as well as the remaining rubbing alcohol to use as a fuel source for fire. I held the jar of sorghum in my hand, sighing as I placed the disgusting goo into the bag. We had one chance, and we needed all the help we could get. I checked the ammunition in the rifle's magazine to confirm that there were eight cartridges left, as well as the handgun I had picked up in the pharmacy. Six in there—fourteen shots total. I sharpened the blade of the hunting knife I'd picked up against the concrete walls. It didn't have to look pretty—it just had to be sharp. And with some time and focus, it was.

Finally feeling prepared for what might be ahead, I closed my eyes. I woke up a few short hours later to see my mom waiting on me to rise.

"How long have you been awake?" I asked.

"Not long," she said, sliding me half a tin can of food.

I ate what could have been my last meal before Mom asked me if we were ready to leave. I nodded. "For the most part. We need to do something about your outfit, though," I said.

She must've been freezing the entire time we'd been down there; the thick blanket she'd used to cover herself almost never left her body. I picked the hunting knife up from the floor and cut a long strip off of the blanket.

"What are you doing?" Mom asked curiously.

"Making you a scarf. You'll be the talk of the town with this thing on."

She rolled her eyes with a slight smile.

I began cutting two more strips, smaller in length than the first had been.

"Now what?" she asked.

"You can't have a brand-new scarf without a pair of boots!" I said by way of explanation.

"Aren't you just the genius?" she said, surprised.

"Wrap these over your shoes," I instructed, handing her the fabric along with a roll of duct tape I had found the night before. "Make sure they're snug," I said.

As Mom was busy outfitting herself, I did the same, putting on the leather jacket I had picked up and zipping it up to the collar. I placed a gas mask over my head and then handed Mom one, as well.

"You've got to be kidding me!" she objected.

"You'll put it on unless you want the baby to be born with a third eye," I said.

"Fine," she said with a groan.

I took a good look at Mom. Strips of blanket were tied around her feet and draped over her neck, with the remainder over her shoulders as a cape. With the gas mask over her face to top it off, it was a hilarious sight.

"You look beautiful, Mom."

"Quit being smart and open that door, will you?" she insisted.

I threw the bag over my left shoulder, with the rifle over my right, and gave a hard kick at the door to dislodge any buildup of snow. "Gonna be a blizzard out there," I said. I grabbed the door by the handle and pushed it open.

What I was greeted with caught me off guard. Sunlight. The snow had stopped falling, and the sky looked normal. A wave of relief washed over me, and I found myself laughing almost maniacally.

"What on earth is so funny?" Mom asked, clearly confused.

"It stopped! I see the light!" I said.

"Honey, I think you're going mad," Mom said in a joking tone, though I could tell she was concerned.

We headed out in a direction opposite the city. The trails and woods had to lead somewhere eventually. Many of the trees closest to home had charred splits and cracks, their outer surfaces burned by the bombs. Mom trudged behind me, shivering the entire way with her arms crossed. The snow was up to our shins.

"Pretty damn cold, huh?" I asked.

"Watch your language, young man," she scolded through chattering teeth.

I couldn't tell you how long we walked that day, nor could I tell you how far. Every so often, we would stop to let Mom rest. The baby had been using most of her energy for everyday tasks, and now a sub-zero hike was added to the mix. I cleared a spot for Mom to sit. We used each break to have a drink, wring the frigid water from our drenched clothes, and try to warm ourselves with a small fire we made using twigs splashed with alcohol. We weren't in the mood for much small talk at these little resting spots; it was much too cold to be bothered with chitchat.

We continued like that for hours. My limbs were going numb, and I'm sure Mom's were, as well. The only time we really ever spoke was to repeat the declaration of how hungry we were.

Night fell eventually, and we had to find a spot to sleep. We decided to stop underneath an old oak tree, something to help protect us in case it started to snow again. I broke off several twigs, drying them with my coat sleeve, and began hacking at a small part of the ground with the knife. I placed all the twigs into the hole and lit a small fire. These fires were a pain in the ass, especially since we had only rubbing alcohol and damp twigs to work with. We sat with our hands stretched toward the fire, warming ourselves the best we could, the twigs snapping and crackling under the heat, with the flames casting a shadow on the surrounding wilderness.

Mom and I sat against the tree, staring at the stars above through the foliage.

"Beautiful, isn't it?" I asked.

"Sure is," she replied with a yawn.

"I've taken these stars for granted all my life. I assumed they'd always be there. Bothers you a lot more than you'd think when they go away one day."

"What are you going on about?" Mom asked.

I chuckled. "That's right; you didn't see it."

"See what?" she asked.

"The sky. On the day Dad . . . you know." I took a breath. "Days were like a grayish orange, and the nights were black. Not like normal night black, but pitch black. Not a star in the sky. Only light you had was what you thought was the moon. Crazy how you don't realize how much lightness there is to night until all the switches up there are flipped off. It's hard to explain, like the sky was one big cloud, but it wasn't a cloud. There isn't a way to describe it, actually. You'd have to see it for yourself, but I hope you never do. I never want to see it again."

Mom put her arm around me, both of us still looking to the sky. "He's proud of you, Clint," she said.

"I sure hope so," I replied. "It's all I ever wanted. He was a good man—the best I'll ever meet. Always took care of you and me. I guess I'm just trying to follow in his footsteps and make him proud. And it's an honor. If I end up as good a man as he was, then I can go to the grave knowing I've lived a life worth living," I said.

Mom pulled me in closer. "You already are, honey."

Minutes went by, and Mom was fast asleep. I took my coat off to cover her exposed skin and stayed awake to keep watch over her. I heard a rustling in the bushes far off in the distance. I dismissed it, however, assuming some snow had fallen off a branch. Then, almost immediately, I heard it again, closer than before. I gripped the hunting rifle in my hands firmly, and then I heard it: a menacing howl. I looked over to Mom, but she didn't stir.

I took one hand off the rifle and tried to shake Mom awake, trying my best not to make any sound. "Mom . . . Mom, wake up," I whispered. I heard a deep growling noise inching toward me, presumably attracted by the fire. "Mom, wake up!" I said, this time more adamantly.

She turned her head and groaned. "What is it?"

"We have to go!" I said with fear in my voice as I removed my mask to get a better view of my surroundings.

"Why? What's going on?" she asked nervously, rising to an up-right position. Before I could answer her question, I saw a glint out of the corner of my eye. Just beyond the campfire was a set of glowing eyes, increasing in size as the creature they belonged to stepped closer toward me. I was expecting a coyote, but I was wrong. A large brute of a dog came from the bushes, baring its teeth. It looked to be a mix of a Rottweiler and a mastiff.

Mom noticed it, too. "Is it rabid?" she asked.

Judging by the lack of foam coming from its mouth, the dog wasn't rabid but had gone feral and reverted back to its natural animalistic instincts. This wasn't like what had gone down at the pharmacy, though; I didn't have anyone to help me this time. Instead, I had a gun I'd never fired before, I had a sickly, pregnant woman by my side, and I had the knowledge of a dog's pack mentality. There was no telling how many others might be closing in on us or even if there really were any others. All I knew was that there was no way I was going to win a hand-to-muzzle fight with an animal bred for killing. And the sound of gunfire—the only high card I had to play at this point—might actually have been dangerous under the current circumstances. After all, it would have alerted other people of our presence.

"Good dog . . . *good* dog," I said, trying to talk it down from its bloodthirsty hunt. It kept inching slowly toward me, waiting for the right moment to pounce on me and tear me to shreds. I noticed a flash of metal coming from the dog's neck as the glow of the campfire illuminated the dog's massive frame. It was a tag buckled to a collar—this menacing creature had once been somebody's pet. I had to think of something to do. Mom was of no help to me; she was frozen with fear, and she'd covered her face—whether in an attempt to shield herself from an attack or because she didn't want to be a witness to a massacre, I wasn't sure.

The beast was standing mere feet ahead of me now. I slowly raised the rifle to my eye, making sure not to make any sudden movement that might provoke the dog. I readied a cartridge in the chamber and gripped the rifle tightly as I slowly began to push the bolt forward. The faint grinding noise of the small parts interacting made my heart sink into my stomach.

The bolt was mere millimeters from the back of the barrel now as the dog planted its hind feet firmly. It had made its mind up; it was going to strike. The only decision it had left to make was *when*. As the bolt came flush against the end of the barrel, it emitted a metallic ting. The dog's ears flattened back behind its head as its gums became visible and an aggressive snarl erupted from its throat. Too suddenly for me to react, it leaped through the air; and before I could move my hand back to the trigger and fire, the dog was on top of me.

Mom screamed in panic as the dog sank its sharp teeth into my right forearm. I desperately punched its rib cage with my left fist, but it wasn't budging. No amount of physical pain could deter the dog from its desire to attack. I felt around on the ground for the hunting knife before noticing out of the corner of my eye that I had left it near the fire. Even if I could reach it, it would be too hot to grip. I could feel my muscles tear as the dog twisted its head around, trying to free any loose meat it could. The dog raised its head, licking my blood from its lips; and as it eyed my throat and bared its teeth to take another bite, two gunshots rippled through the air. One entered the dog's side and exited the other with a mist of bone fragments; the other, taking a path through the side of its head, sprayed my eyes and mouth with blood.

I used my free arm to push the dog's warm corpse off of me and turned my head toward Mom. She was holding the handgun that had been inside the duffel bag, smoke still rising from the hot barrel.

I stood up, holding my arm. "Way to go, Mom," I said inan exhausted gasp.

She threw the gun down and rushed over to look at my wound; two small craters filled with rushing blood shimmered in the firelight. "Are you okay?" Mom asked.

"Yeah, I'll live," I said.

Another howl came from the distance, then another shortly after. There were at least two more of them stalking us in the woods. I didn't care what breed they were—I didn't want to know; I didn't want to ever see them.

"Let's go!" I urged Mom, and she more than willingly agreed. We took off running as fast as we could, leaving all of our supplies behind and stomping our way through the thick snow. It was like the day the bombs had fallen all over again, but this time, we were targets and not just consolation prizes.

I heard Mom yelp behind me and turned to find that she had stumbled over a tree root concealed in the snow. I ran back to her and looked up to see two sets of glowing eyes coming toward us. I picked Mom up, the same way Dad had several days ago, and pain shot through my right arm as my wounds opened from the strain. I cringed, but I couldn't let my own physical limits hold me back. I sprinted as fast as I could through the trees and plants, weaving back and forth to avoid obstacles.

I could hear heavy breathing creeping closer to me; it wasn't my own, and it wasn't Mom's. It wasn't even human. I heard one of the dogs lunge at me with a growl as it narrowly missed my calf, and felt its teeth brush against me, followed by its cold, wet snout. Goosebumps covered my skin, and the hairs on my body stood on end. I took a quick glance back to see the dog collect itself and shake the debris off its body.

My legs and arms were about to give out, and I had only run a half mile or so at that point. Dad had made this look so easy when he'd done it, but, of course, he'd had about thirty pounds of muscle on me. The fact that I had barely slept or eaten in days was taking its toll, and light-headedness started to overtake me.

"What is that? Up ahead!" Mom shouted.

It was a field with massive, round bales of hay scattered about it. And in the distance was a large eggshell-white farmhouse, seemingly unaffected by nuclear devastation. There was a light coming from a window of the bottom floor, casting the shadow of what seemed to be a person in a rocking chair on the front porch.

"Please! Help us!" Mom screamed in desperation.

"What are you doing?" I asked, panicked.

"The only thing we *can* do!" she replied.

The figure stood, alert now as we approached. I looked back to see how close the dogs were to us, and, to my dismay, I could see their glowing eyes still on our trail.

"Clint! Watch out!" Mom screamed.

I looked ahead, and at my eye level was a thick branch sticking out from where the woods ended and the field began. I heard a loud thud from inside my head and felt a surge of pain as I hit the ground and blacked out. That was my last memory of the night.

CHAPTER 8

I felt my eyes adjust to the light as they twitched slightly and crept open. I was in a bed, with a thick white comforter and sheets pulled over my body as my head rested on a fluffed pillow. I had no idea where I was or how long I'd been out, but I did know I hadn't felt this rested in days—apart from my body feeling like it had been hit by a bus.

I grabbed the blanket with my right arm and noticed a white bandage tightly wrapped around my forearm, a small, reddish-brown spot in the area I'd been bit. I tossed the bedspread off and swung my legs over the side of the bed, looking around at my surroundings. The walls were painted in a color that couldn't decide whether it wanted to be pink or white, resulting in a shade that rested somewhere between the two. The posts of the bed, along with the dresser near the door and the chest at the foot of the bed, were a dark-brown oak with intricate designs carved into them. This wasn't the cheap stuff you would find sitting on a sales floor. I dipped my bare feet down to the carpeted floor, wiggling my toes into its softness. It felt good; I'd never realized how good carpet could feel until then. I stood, and the soreness from my legs made an unwelcome visit. I got caught off guard by the pulse of pain running up my body and fell flat on my face.

I groaned as I grabbed the side of the bed and pulled myself up. I noticed a glare of light on the satin walls and turned to face a mirror standing in the far corner of the room, the frame matching the rest of the furniture. I stumbled over to it to get a better look at myself. I looked like hell. Forget Cleveland; it looked like they had dropped the atom bomb directly on top of me. Much like my arm, my head was wrapped in bandages, and a large knot protruded under the wrap. My left eye was black and slightly swollen, as was my bottom lip. I had bruises all over my arms and face. That's when I noticed the clothes I was wearing. I had never seen them before—dark-blue pajamas. I lifted the shirt to examine the rest of my body, seeing various cuts and scrapes, with one side of my rib cage almost black from bruising. I was clean, too, as though someone had bathed me. And I certainly smelled better than I had the last time I'd checked.

"Are you okay?" A soft voice startled me as the bedroom door creaked open.

I turned around to see a small, elderly woman in an apron covered by white dust. "Yeah," I said, confused. "Where am I?"

"Oh, young man, how rude of me—I forgot to introduce myself. My name is Beverly Maxwell," she said. "My granddaughter saw you and your mother out in that field, and it looked like you needed some help. So, here you are."

"Thanks for saving our skin. My name is—"

"Clint, Clint Brodsky. Your mother has told me so much about you," she said, curling her wrinkled lips into a warm smile. "Now, where are my manners? You must be starving! I mean, you were conked out for two days, after all."

I knew my face must have shown shock. "*Two days?*"

"Yes, two days. Well—give or take a few hours."

I couldn't believe it. I'd known I was tired, but *two days*? What had Mom been up to while I was playing Rip Van Winkle?

"Where is my mom?" I asked.

"She's right in the kitchen having breakfast. There's some waiting for you, too, if you're hungry."

I smiled at the thought. *Breakfast.* "Thank you."

"It's my pleasure. We'll be waiting on you downstairs. You best get going before it gets cold," she said before heading out of the room.

I was beginning to think maybe I had died in those woods and gone to heaven—it all seemed too good to be true. I stepped out of the bedroom and into the main hall. The floors were a beautiful shade of brown, so well polished and spic-and-span that I could see my own reflection. Paintings hung upon the walls between the doors of other rooms in the hallway, and at the end was a winding staircase. The white wooden railing was perfectly crafted, and not a single board on the tread of the stairs made a noise under the weight of my feet. Not one creak or groan. I was starting to think it was some kind of setup; everything was too neat and perfect—or maybe it had just been so long since I'd seen a real home that I'd forgotten what it felt like to be inside of one.

I descended the staircase to find that I was in the main sitting room; a record player sat in one corner, with a brown sofa next to it. The elegant area rug below the antique piano looked to be an heirloom and handmade. Potted plants, chairs, chaises, a bust of a horse, and baroque wall décor made up the graceful Southern feel of the room.

I heard light conversation and silverware scraping on dishes coming from the kitchen. I walked through the archway and was greeted by the sight of three women sitting at a breakfast table, engaging in pleasantries. My mom with her back to me, Beverly at her side, and a younger girl—about my age—facing me. I was unable to see the bottom half of the girl's face because of the book she held in front of it.

"Good morning," I said to make my arrival known.

Mom turned around with an ear-to-ear smile. "Well, hello there, sleepyhead. I was beginning to think you'd never wake up!" She stood and walked over to me to give me a tight hug; it was good to feel she was getting her strength back, and she looked fresh and rested.

"Why don't you sit down and join us, young man?" Beverly said, gesturing to the empty chair between my mom and the younger girl.

I sat between them and looked at my breakfast. Two fried eggs, lightly peppered, with the yolks busted, running into a piece of crisp toast that was on the edge of burnt. Mom must've told Beverly how I liked it, because this was right on the money.

"Clint, this is Hazel," Beverly said, nodding at the girl who still hadn't acknowledged me. "Hazel, why don't you say hi?" she prompted.

Hazel placed her book spine-down on the breakfast table and turned her head toward me disinterestedly. I had a good look at her now: her long golden-blonde hair draped past her shoulders; her eyes were such a light shade of brown that they almost matched. Her skin was fair, almost a sun-kissed peach, with just a few lone freckles on each side of her button nose. She was pretty—*really* pretty. So pretty that it was hard to find my voice and introduce myself.

"Hi," I said, a shy smile stretched across my face.

Hazel took a good look at me, scanning me with her eyes squinted in sharp assessment. "Geez, how are you alive?" she said with a scoff and then an eye roll, redirecting her attention to her book.

Beverly sat in shock, eyes and mouth wide open. "I'm sorry. You'll have to forgive her," she said before whispering something in Hazel's ear.

"It's okay," I muttered, digging my fork into my breakfast.

"Beverly says we can stay here until the snow clears and we can make our way to Cincinnati," Mom said eagerly.

I chewed my food and swallowed, confused. "What's in Cincinnati?" I asked.

"Safety!" Beverly exclaimed.

"Safety? What do you mean, 'safety'?"

"Cincinnati is under military control, *our* military. Not everywhere is a wasteland, you know."

I was in disbelief. "What else do you know?" I asked, dropping my fork onto my plate and leaning forward in my chair.

"Clint, where are your manners?" Mom said.

"I'm sorry. But, Beverly, if you saw what's out there—what those monsters have done—you'd understand. My mom and I, we really need some good news right now, at least some information."

Beverly shook her head, and Hazel stood from the table, storming out of the kitchen. "You'll have to excuse her. Her little brother and grandfather had gone into Mayfield for some fishing bait when this happened, and they haven't returned yet. She's fearing the worst."

"I understand," I said. "I know how that feels."

"She's taking it really hard. Her grandpa taught her everything. She was Papaw's little girl . . . And her little brother? Oh, he's as cute as a button, such a good, well-mannered young man. He has this little teddy bear he carries with him everywhere he goes. Old, weathered thing Hazel used to play with when she was little. Had to patch up the head with a piece of leather from an old saddle."

My heart skipped a beat as my mind flashed back to the two bodies outside of the pharmacy. My troubled look must've been obvious.

"Is something wrong?" Beverly asked.

"No, no, I'm sure they'll show up," I said, trying to cover with a fake smile. I felt horrible about lying, but there was nothing I, or anyone, could do for her, and I needed information and cooperation. There would be a time to tell her everything, but until then I would have to keep the information to myself.

"Anyway, you wanted to know what I know?" Beverly asked.

I nodded.

"To be truthful, it's been about like any other day out in these parts. You know, besides Art and Gabe being gone. And, of course, all this snow. We heard the radio broadcasts coming in for a couple of days after the bombs fell."

"What did they say?" I asked anxiously.

"We haven't surrendered yet—at least, not to my knowledge. Apparently, the Germans weren't the only ones with those big bombs. Next couple of days were spent focusing on dropping what we had on Germany, so I'd imagine it looks a lot like what it does here, over there. One side has gotta surrender one of these days. Everyone's hanging on by a thread, no matter where they are."

"But there really is a place for us to go?" I asked.

"That's the impression I'm getting. After the president was moved to a safe place, Lord knows where, the Department of Defense kept going on for a couple of days with the broadcasts. Apparently, quality checking wasn't as important to the Germans as mass production. Only half the atom bombs that fell actually detonated; the others were taken in for research and examination. The government thinks we can use those against the Nazis. Our bombs, fortunately, weren't duds."

I leaned back in my chair as I felt a surge of hope wash over me. I looked over to Mom, and she reached her hand out to rest on mine.

"We're going to make it, Clint."

"Yeah, I guess we are. I just wish Dad could've made it, too," I said before looking back toward Beverly. "Is there anything we can do to help you? It's going to take a while for all of this snow to melt."

"Well, yes, there is."

"Sure, I'll do it," I said eagerly. I'd do anything to stay there until we could safely move on to Cincinnati.

Beverly laughed. "Aren't you just the eager beaver! Nothing major, just chores, really. You know, help gather water and maybe go out to the garden for food on occasion. Help clean up around the house. That kind of stuff."

"That's it?" I asked, shocked that the things she'd requested were such basic, everyday tasks.

"Yes, sir, that's it," she said.

This had to be a dream, but even so, I sure as hell didn't want to wake up. I looked around at the faces of the two women next to me. Beverly was sipping a mug of warm tea, having resumed her small talk with Mom. And then my eyes crawled down to Mom's stomach, which looked as if it might burst at any second. *We're gonna make it. Hang in there, little one*, I thought with a smile.

I dismissed myself to the front porch as tears began to well up at the corners of my eyes. It was freezing, of course, but I didn't care. The thin wool pajamas I wore would be sufficient. My bare feet touched down onto the lightly frosted wooden planks of the deck as I made my way to the rocking chair I had seen swaying when I'd first noticed the house. I took a seat and really, truly enjoyed and appreciated what was around me for the first time.

I was surrounded by life. *Life*. I heard a few birds chirping, likely snuggled in their nests in distant branches. I watched greenery sway in the wind as snow was knocked loose and fell to the ground with a light thud. I heard rustling in the bushes around me; it sounded like some small critter moving around—a rabbit, probably.

Life. Every day, we take it for granted. Every breath, every blink, wink, laugh, and cry. All of it comes and goes. And all of it is ignored. My dad had had a life, and my mom still had hers, and two lives and two loves had made *my* life. It made me think of the man I'd had to kill in the pharmacy.

I hadn't wanted to think of what I'd had to do and, more specifically, who he'd been. What had he done for a living? Had he had a family? Wife and kids, maybe a pet? What had he been doing two weeks ago? Laughing with his loved ones? Grinding away in a world occupied by time clocks? Or maybe he was a big shot, with everyone else doing the grinding for him. What had been his favorite things?

The more I thought about it, the more questions I had—questions neither I nor anyone else could answer. The guilt had really started to settle in. He hadn't been a pesky rodent I'd had to kill; he'd been a *person*. A human being, with human emotions. I knew I'd only done what I'd had to do, but I hoped I'd never have to do it again.

I was between a rock and a hard place, both satisfied over having done what needed doing but also terribly overcome with shame. How, and why, did I feel so guilty about killing the man who had ended my father's life? Because he'd been a human, and so was I. And no matter what happened, no matter the lengths we would go to, we'd always have a little humanity deep inside.

I kept my eyes on the sky, looking past the clouds, focusing on anything beyond. "If you're up there," I whispered, "I'm sorry for what I said, what I thought, what I've done. I was afraid and angry. Please forgive me. There's a reason we found this place. There's a reason we know about Cincinnati. We can make it. Please, help us make it. Please prove that you care."

I slowed my rocking to a halt and stood from my chair. It was time to go back inside and join everyone.

I had a weird feeling, though. As beautiful and eye-opening as my little front-porch nature retreat had been, I couldn't help but think that there was something I had seen that morning that was even more beautiful. Something that was actually *someone*. And I couldn't shake the feeling that there was something special there.

And she sure was pretty.

CHAPTER 9

Tweets and chirps piercing the closed bedroom window served as my alarm clock the next morning, and I opened my eyes to see a new set of clothes folded neatly at the end of the bed. They must've belonged to Art, who must've been a pretty substantial man, judging by the size of the clothes. A gray, long-sleeved, button-up shirt and a pair of faded blue jeans swallowed my body, draping loosely over my frame. Near the footboard of the bed was an old pair of work boots, next to a black leather belt; the first hole was frayed and torn, presumably from a long period of use. The leather around it had softened from repeated flexing.

I walked over to the mirror to examine myself. I looked ridiculous. The shirt was tucked into the pants so far that its bottom hem was gently tickling the top of my kneecaps, and I had to stuff the pant legs inside the boots to avoid tripping over their extra length. I chuckled silently at my reflection. I was the perfect example of what would've happened if Goliath had eaten David.

A smile followed my laughter, which froze on my face when I noticed some slack in my head bandage. The lump on my head was shrinking. I gently touched the area and then quickly pulled away. It might have been smaller, but it was still unbearably tender to the touch.

I leaned toward the mirror and examined the swelling around my eye, which also seemed to be improving. I could open it a little wider now—still only about halfway—but even the color was less intense. Instead of a plum shade of purple, it had morphed into a wine-like red. I looked at myself for another few seconds, a half-smile on my face. I was making progress, and I'd be healed soon. Which was good, because I needed to be if I wanted to make it to Cincinnati.

I walked out into the hallway, anxious for breakfast, and was greeted by the faint sound of someone brushing her teeth. Across the hallway from my room was a small half-bathroom, with nothing more than a sink and a toilet. As I peeked in, I could see Hazel, standing in her pajamas—a vibrant blue nightgown—with her face an inch away from the mirror, brushing her teeth briskly. I don't know how long I stood looking at her, but no length of time would've been long enough. I was in a trance, one as deep as any hypnotist could have put me into.

That strange feeling I'd had before came back, but it was a feeling I didn't mind having. Something was flopping around in the pit of my stomach. I knew I was hungry, but that wasn't it. This was something else, something new. I broke myself from my reverie; I didn't want her to notice me staring. I didn't want her to think I was some kind of goon or something.

For some reason, I was captivated by her.

I turned and began to head downstairs.

As soon as my booted foot made contact with the hardwood on the bottom floor, Beverly shouted, "Hazel, Hazel, honey, is that you?" She poked her head through the kitchen doorway. "Oh, it's you! Well, good morning to you, Clint!" Beverly said happily.

"Good morning," I replied cheerfully. "Hazel's upstairs getting ready. I'm sure she'll be down in just a minute."

"That's good to hear, because I have a little task for both of you," she said.

"Oh, well, sure. What is it?" I asked curiously.

"I need you to go to the garden out back and pick all of the crops you can. In this cold, all that'll be left is probably onions and asparagus, but get whatever you can find."

I nodded. "Sounds fine. Yeah, no problem. I'll go ahead and do that," I said.

"It's probably buried under a foot of snow at this point. It's right in the backyard, but I don't think you'll find it unless you know where to look. Feel free to poke around, but I was thinking Hazel could help you—"

"Yes! Yes, that's a great idea!" I said with a smile so wide it felt as if the corners of my mouth were going to crack.

Beverly raised an eyebrow, obviously trying not to break out into a grin. "Uh-huh, well, just give her some time. I'm sure she'll be down in a jiffy." She walked over to a large metal pot on the stove. "Why don't you take a seat, young man," Beverly instructed, taking a wooden spoon in hand and stirring the pot.

I pulled out a chair at the breakfast table and sat down.

"Eat up," Beverly said, placing a bowl of oatmeal in front of me. "You'll need your energy if you want to be of any use to me," she said with a playful wink.

I smiled back at her. "Yes, ma'am," I said. I took a few bites and looked up to see Hazel dragging her feet into the kitchen. She was wearing a snowcap, a pair of thick gloves, and brown coveralls that covered every inch of her besides her head and fingers. It was cold, sure, but she looked as though she planned on spending the night out there.

"Oh, Hazel, finally!" Beverly chirped. "You know, it isn't polite to keep people waiting."

Hazel smiled at her. "Sorry, Mamaw. Won't happen again."

"I was just telling Clint here that maybe you could show him the garden, and you two could go collecting this morning," Beverly said.

"Yeah, sure," Hazel said with a shrug.

"You need to eat something if you're going to be out there all day," Beverly said.

"I'm okay. I just want to get this over with, as soon as what's-his-face here finishes his feast," Hazel said, gesturing toward me.

My cheeks went hot and red from embarrassment. "My name is Clint," I said.

Hazel looked over at me with a smirk. "I know."

"Hazel, be nice," Beverly said, her voice disapproving.

"Yes, ma'am," Hazel mumbled, looking back at me. "If you're finished, we can go now."

I followed Hazel outside through the back door just past the stairwell. She stopped on the back patio, handing me a small wicker basket while she took another.

"So where's the garden?" I asked, trying to make conversation.

Hazel pointed off to a horse field several hundred feet away; a snow-covered gazebo stood mere feet in front of it. "Over there," she said.

"I thought Beverly said it was in the backyard."

Hazel sighed. "Well, I guess this means we have a big backyard, then, doesn't it?" she snapped, turning to walk off.

I sighed to myself. "Off to a great start, you big idiot," I mumbled under my breath, but apparently louder than I had intended.

Hazel turned around to face me, looking absolutely disgusted.

"What did you just call me?"

"Uh, what?" I asked, flustered.

"Uh, what? *Uh, what?*" she mimicked, her jaw slack in mock cluelessness. To be honest, if I hadn't been the target of her disdain, I would've probably laughed. It was funny—kinda cute, even. "You called me an idiot!" she insisted.

"Oh, no! No!" I answered.

"Oh, yeah? So who else is here?" she questioned.

"*Me!* I called *myself* an idiot!" I said.

Hazel looked at me with blankly. "You called *yourself* an idiot? Are you crazy or something? You got a screw loose, buddy?"

"No! I'm just nervous. I think you're really pretty, and I want to get to know you!" I blurted.

Hazel crossed her arms. "So let me get this straight: you called me an idiot because you think I'm pretty?"

"Yes!" I replied.

She uncrossed her arms and made a fist with her right hand. "*Excuse me?*"

"Wait, no! That's not what I meant! I saw you brushing your teeth, and I—"

"What?" Hazel yelled. "You were watching me brush my teeth? *What are you?* Some kind of creep or something?"

"Damn it!" I yelled, covering my face with my hands.

Hazel pointed her index finger at me sharply. "Listen here, *pal.* I've been waiting on that front porch for my brother and my papaw ever since this mess happened. And when I finally see something coming from them woods, it isn't what I want to see. It's a pregnant lady with a pencil-necked dork of a son who looks like he just went twelve rounds with a school bus. Now I don't see why I saved you from all those puppy dogs that gave you such a scare, because apparently all that interests you is calling me names and watching me in the bathroom. So, got any more to say, wise guy?" she growled, looking as though she had every intention of burying my body in the garden.

I cleared my throat. "No, that's all," I said.

"Good. Now, unless *I* speak, *you* don't speak. We clear?" she asked.

I nodded.

The rest of that walk was probably the most awkward two minutes of my life. My eyes never left the ground as I watched my feet drag across the snow. I couldn't help but feel like I had completely messed up. And for some reason, even though I'd just had a girl who was about six inches shorter than me and several pounds lighter practically scare me out of my boots, *I'd liked it*. Sure, I would've liked her aggressiveness a hell of a lot more if it hadn't been directed at me, but it definitely helped me see the type of girl she was. A better introduction would've been nice, but now at least I knew she could stand her ground. She wasn't a pushover. She was confident, and until that day, I'd had no idea how attractive that could be. I only hoped all the stars would align just right and give me another shot. But right then, I wasn't winning any points with her.

"Okay, this is it," Hazel said, breaking into my thoughts. We stood before a small plot of land that hardly looked different than anything else around us.

"Are you sure?" I asked.

Hazel turned around with a huff. "You hard of hearing or something? I thought I told you to keep that big trap of yours shut! Now, I may be an idiot, but I think I know where my own garden is!"

I raised my hand like a student in class.

"What?" she barked.

I didn't say a word; instead, I pointed my finger about thirty feet to the right. Leaves, twigs, and weeds were just peeking out from the fallen snow, indicating the presence of something underneath.

Hazel's cheeks grew rosy in anger and embarrassment. "Okay. So maybe I was off by a little bit. You happy? That what you wanted to hear?" she huffed.

I shook my head.

"Wait here, don't move. I'll be back," Hazel instructed. I watched her walk over to the gazebo and pick up two small metal objects from the wooden bench inside; then she made her way back over to me. "Here," Hazel said, shoving a spade at me. "We dig, and when we find something, we put it in the basket. Simple enough?"

I nodded.

"Good. If an *idiot* like me can do it, then surely a sophisticated man like yourself should have no problem with it."

"Look, I already tried to tell you, I didn't call *you* an idiot. I was calling *myself* an idiot. I don't know how to keep saying this without sounding like a broken record," I said, feeling suddenly fed up.

"I don't believe you." Hazel turned around and got on her knees to begin digging.

Women sure are crazy, I thought. But I wasn't about to say *that* out loud.

It wasn't easy, but I was able to get a full basket—mainly of onions, with a few bunches of asparagus. I'd never even held a spade before, much less used one to dig for my food, but I was persistent enough to make sure the job I had to do was done. I was so focused on my own harvest that I hadn't noticed that Hazel had left me behind; I didn't even know when she'd gone. My fingers went numb toward the end, making using them nearly impossible. I found myself having to blow warm air onto them to get the blood flowing again, even standing at some points to shove them into my pockets for a few minutes.

Eventually, I returned to the house with my basket of harvested food. The back door creaked open, and I heard Hazel say, "About time he came back." I assumed that it was directed to Beverly, but she'd purposefully said it loud enough for me to hear, as well. Unfortunately for her, I was both too tired and too cold to care.

"Hey there, Clint. I guess you aren't much of a gardener, huh?" Beverly asked jokingly as I placed the basket on the kitchen table.

"You can say that again," I replied unsteadily as my lungs adapted to the warmer air. I spotted a pot of boiling water on the stove. With breakneck speed, I rushed over to thaw my hands over the steam. I let out a groan of satisfaction as my fingers regained their feeling.

"My goodness, Clint. Surely you didn't go out there and dig through that barehanded?" Beverly asked with concern.

"I did," I replied, not turning around to face her, keeping my focus on the hot steam in front of me.

"That was just silly, young man. There was a nice warm pair of gardening gloves sitting right next to those spades in the gazebo. You were more than welcome to use those," she said.

I slowly turned to face Hazel. "Silly me . . . I must not have noticed them," I said to Beverly, keeping my eyes steadily trained on Hazel.

Beverly looked quizzically over at her granddaughter. "And *you*, young lady! How many times do I have to tell you that—"

"Shh!" Hazel interrupted, slamming down the book she'd been reading and raising her index finger to her lips.

I didn't know what was going on, but what I did know was this could be an opportunity to get some sweet revenge. All I had to do was play it up a little bit. "Now, Hazel, that was very rude of you. After everything your grandma has done for my mom and me? Oh, goodness," I said, tsking softly.

Hazel looked at me with pure, concentrated anger in her eyes, a vein pulsing in her forehead, as she mouthed, "Shut up."

I gave her a sly, sarcastic smile and directed my attention to Beverly. "Please, finish what you were trying to say."

Beverly took a couple of seconds to look at Hazel and then me, completely flustered. "All I was trying to do was tell Hazel that she needed to wear her spectacles if she wants to keep her eyes from getting any worse." Beverly stopped to look at me. "She got picked on a lot as a little girl because of it—but she's sixteen now! She's practically a woman!" She reverted her attention back to Hazel. "You need to do what's best for you, my dear. Don't worry about the mean things people have said to you about it."

Of course! She wore glasses! Suddenly it made much more sense to me now—the way she'd had her face pressed against the bathroom mirror, the way she'd squinted to read, the way she'd looked at me the first time she saw me . . . Even why she'd been so wrong on the location of her own garden.

Hazel stood from the table and stormed out of the kitchen.

"Hazel, wait!" I called after her. I felt like scum; she was obviously insecure about having to wear glasses, and I understood. People could be cruel, and nobody liked to be belittled for something beyond their control. All I'd wanted to do was get a little payback. I didn't actually want to hurt her.

God, I really *was* an idiot.

She hadn't wanted anything to do with me before that; she was sure to hate me even more now. "Is she okay?" I asked. It was the only thing I could think of to say. But it was also the only thing I cared about right then.

"Yes, she's tough. She'll come around." Beverly paused for a moment. "Oh, I almost forgot to tell you. Your mother came downstairs to get a bite while you were outside. She said she wasn't feeling well. She looked a bit pale—clammy, even. She went to go lie down."

I had known Mom to be sick those last few days, and my heart began to pound as I asked, "Where is she now? Is she okay?"

Beverly laid a gentle hand on my shoulder. "She's fine, Clint. She told me everything that happened. I know it's hard for you to hear she's feeling ill, but she was walking and talking just fine. Who knows, could be just the baby being a little ornery in there."

I slowed my breathing, exhaling and inhaling deeply as I sat at the table. Her words comforted me; something about an elderly lady telling you it's all going to be all right has a way of doing that. She went from Beverly to Mamaw Maxwell really quickly, and it worked. "Thank you for all you've done for us. I should probably go check on Mom, though."

"I would leave her alone. She probably just needs her rest, is all."

I nodded, realizing she was probably right.

"You're welcome, by the way," she added.

I excused myself and headed out to the front porch again, remembering the peaceful mood it had put me in the day before. This time, though, I had shoes on. I walked outside to see the chair rocking back and forth slowly. It was Hazel. She gave me a quick glance before staring back out into the distance.

"Oh, sorry, I didn't know you were out here," I said as I turned to walk back inside the house.

"Wait," Hazel said.

I stopped dead in my tracks and turned to face her.

"It's okay. You can stay out here."

No way, I thought with a smile. I tried to keep a straight face—I didn't want to look desperate or too pleased—but I couldn't help myself.

"I get the chair, though, got it?"

I sat on the frosty ground next to Hazel.

"Pretty, isn't it?" she asked.

I watched as the snow glistened in the sunlight. "Sure is," I answered.

"Hey, Clint," Hazel said quietly.

It was the first time I'd heard her call me by my name. I didn't know what she was about to say—hell, I didn't care. She'd said my name. She *knew* my name.

"What is it?" I asked.

Hazel curled her mouth to one side in a sheepish smile. "I'm sorry for giving you such a hard time. None of this is your fault. And the way you look after your mom, if I'm being honest, I think it's kinda sweet."

I let out a chuckle under my breath. "Thank you. But I have to ask, why *were* you being so hard on me?" I asked.

Hazel laughed for the first time since we'd come. It was the most beautiful thing I had ever heard—and still is. "Papaw raised me to be tough, I guess. Always told me that no man is good enough for me. And I had the feeling you had eyes on the prize, you know? Just trying to do right by him, since I have no clue where he is," she said.

"Wherever he is, I'm sure he's thinking about you," I replied, hesitating before I went on. "But truth be told, I do kinda like you."

"No!" Hazel replied sarcastically, her eyes and mouth wide in feigned shock.

I laughed to myself, looking out at the landscape. "How could you tell?" I asked.

Hazel sighed. "Might've had something to do with the fact that you almost threw up the first time you ever said hi to me."

"That obvious, huh?" I asked.

"If you'd had the words painted on your busted-up face, it still wouldn't have made it any more obvious."

"Okay, okay," I said playfully. "But why were you scared to wear your glasses around me?"

"Well, if it weren't for all your bumps and bruises, I bet . . ."

"You bet *what*?" I asked.

"I bet you'd be handsome," she said nervously.

"Oh? Is that so?" I asked.

"Yeah," she replied, blushing.

Suddenly, we were interrupted by the sound of screaming.

"What was that?" I shot to my feet in alarm.

"I don't know," Hazel replied, following suit.

More screams rang out. It was Mom.

"Is that . . . ?" Hazel said.

"Yeah, it's my mom," I replied. "I have to see what's wrong!"

I rushed in through the front door. The kitchen and living room were both empty as I called out for Mom, darting up the steps and navigating through the hallway to the room she'd been using. I twisted the knob; it was locked from the inside.

I pounded on the door, yelling, "What's going on? Mom, are you okay?"

Hazel could see how upset I was, so she tried offering words of comfort.

The doorknob slowly turned as the door creaked open, and Beverly's head peeked out.

"What's going on? Is my mom okay?" I asked, my voice trembling with fear.

Beverly smiled. "Shh . . . Everything's okay. The baby's coming!"

By then the room had started to spin around me as both excitement and fear washed over me. I had always wanted a sibling—it didn't matter if it was a boy or girl. But what kind of world was this baby being brought into?

It seemed to go on forever, and the hours stretched endlessly as my eyes stayed glued to the ornate grandfather clock on the first floor of the house. Hazel and I sat on a perfectly fluffed sofa, awaiting news.

Why did she care? I wondered. Why did she feel the obligation to sit with me? It made me think that maybe the hard-ass attitude was just a ploy and she really *was* that gentle-natured girl I'd met on the front porch.

We talked as we waited. It almost made me wish the labor would last longer than it already had, just so I could keep living in that moment with her.

"So . . . Wonderful weather we're having," Hazel quipped. I'd realized by then that was her style of sparking conversation.

"Yeah. If you say so," I replied, my focus still on the grandfather clock.

"You *do* know that thing's not set correctly don't you? Hasn't been right in months!"

I laughed. "No, I didn't know that. So what time *is* it, really?"

"Does it really matter?" she asked reasonably.

I took a deep breath, then turned to face Hazel. "I really want to get to know you . . . if that's okay," I said.

A smile tugged at Hazel's lips. "Yeah. That's okay."

"I ask you some things, then you ask me. Sound good?"

"I'm familiar with how conversation works, but thank you for giving me a refresher," she replied.

"Okay, then. So . . . Beverly is your grandmother. What happened to your parents?" I asked.

Hazel sighed, obviously bothered by the question. "The Depression. Goods got too expensive, jobs didn't pay as much—that is, if you were able to even find one in the first place. Shortly after Gabe was born, the load became too heavy for Mama and Papa, and they just couldn't take care of us. They dropped us off here one day and headed west for Arizona. That was so long ago, though. So where they are now, what they're doing . . . Your guess is as good as mine," she said, staring down at her hands.

"What about you? What happened to your dad?" she asked.

"He, uh . . . he died, a few days back now," I said.

Hazel's eyes shone with genuine sympathy. "I'm sorry. I understand if you don't want to talk about—"

"It's fine," I said, cutting her off. "We had to find some medicine for my mom, out in the city. Met a couple guys at a pharmacy whose heads weren't right. Some bad things happened, and he got hurt. Really hurt." I paused, closing my eyes to muster up the strength to talk about what had happened. "I . . . I had to . . . you know. Out of mercy."

Hazel looked at me with clear compassion. "Oh, Clint . . ."

"It's fine," I said quickly, shaking my head and trying to clear my eyes of tears. "I did what I had to do, what he wanted me to do."

"Can I have another question?" Hazel asked.

"Sure. Shoot," I replied.

"Did you do what you had to do, with those other guys?" she asked.

"What do you mean?" I asked, confused.

"The guys at the pharmacy. What happened to them?" she asked.

"We . . . we . . . ," I stammered, trying to find the words. "I'm not a killer, Hazel. But I *am* a guy who's killed someone. If that makes sense."

"It does . . . I think," she replied slowly.

"It was either them or us. Guess there just aren't enough supplies to go around, especially when everyone needs all they can get."

"I understand," Hazel said.

"Please, don't think I'm some kind of monster. Don't be afraid; that really isn't who I am."

Hazel looked at me with a smile. "Trust me, wise guy, you don't scare me," she said.

I glanced over to the clock again. Another forty-five minutes had passed since I'd last looked at it. Talking to her helped pass the time, gave me something to do. And it helped for other reasons that hadn't yet occurred to me.

"My turn?" I asked.

"I guess so. Wise guy," Hazel replied.

"Well, I'd like to ask why you keep calling me that, but I don't want to waste my question on something so pointless. So here goes . . . Do you believe in God?" I asked.

"That question is dumber than the other one!" she replied. "What kind of buffoon *wouldn't*?"

I rolled my eyes. "The kind of buffoon that doesn't have a reason to," I answered.

"Okay, wise guy."

"Again with the wise-guy stuff," I muttered.

"Shh! Listen to what I have to say!" Hazel demanded. "Who made it?"

"It?" I replied, confused.

"*It!* Everything! All of it! If not God, then who?"

"Well I don't know—"

"Aha! *Exactly!* But I know who made it. *God* made it," Hazel said, confident in her answer.

"Oh, please. That's just what you believe," I insisted, rolling my eyes.

Hazel leaned toward me and gave me a sly smile. "You're right. And what's it hurt to believe in something good right now?"

That caught me off guard. I hadn't really expected that answer. She had a point, though, as much as I hated to admit it. Before I could think of a response, Hazel said, "Gonna take a while for that snow to clear up. Should be plenty of time to teach you some things. It'd be a real shame if you did all this just to burn in a lake of fire when you push up daisies."

I nodded. "Sounds fine to me," I replied, excited by the idea of spending more time with her.

The rest of our time on that couch was spent talking about basic things, things you would typically know before you had a deep conversation like we'd had. Guess the whole world was backward.

Hazel had been born October 14, 1926. Same year I was born. She was still sixteen, though; I had a few months on her. Her favorite color was yellow. I had never met anyone whose favorite color was yellow before, but I also hadn't met anyone *like her* before. Her favorite food was scrambled eggs, but with tomato catsup mixed in. She'd once tried to have a boyfriend, but her grandpa had run him off when he'd found out, using a twelve-gauge to intimidate him. *Thanks, Art,* I thought as I listened. The more I heard, the more I knew she was far from perfect. But luckily for me, I didn't want perfect. I wanted *her*.

Time passed, and night fell. According to the broken clock, though, it was only 3:00 p.m. Hazel's eyelids drooped heavily, and she slipped into sleep on the opposite end of the sofa from me. I grabbed a blanket from the backrest and tucked it around her, then spent another hour or so watching the clock, hearing the sounds of my mother groaning and a rustle coming from upstairs. I hoped all was going well.

And then I heard it.

Crying.

A tiny, fragile, and innocent cry. It was the baby.

I shook Hazel awake.

"Geez, Louise, wise guy! What is it?" Hazel asked in irritation.

I didn't have to say anything, though, because as soon as she heard the cries, her eyes grew wide in excitement.

Both of us hurried up the steps and opened Mom's door.

"Boy or girl?" I demanded to know as soon as I barged in.

Mom was propped against the headboard of the bed, obviously exhausted, crying tears of joy, with a little bundle swaddled in her arms. "It's a girl, Clint," she whispered. "It's your baby sister, Violet."

I walked over to get a better look. She was adorable. "She's so precious," I said.

Mom smiled back and gently held the baby out to me. "Why don't you get to know her?" she said.

I reached out to take the baby. "Shhh, shhh . . . Good girl," I said to Violet, gently rocking her back and forth in my arms.

Hazel peeked around me, trying to get a good look for herself.

"Would you like to hold her?" I asked.

"Really? You mean it?" Hazel asked.

"Of course I do." I handed Violet to Hazel, and, in an instant, she stopped crying. "I think she likes you!" I teased.

"Well, who could blame her?" Hazel replied smartly.

Hazel was squinting as she tried to make out the details of Violet's face. I walked over to Beverly to whisper in her ear.

"In the bathroom cabinet beneath the sink," she said to me.

I headed down the hall and into the bathroom, opening the doors beneath the sink. There they were, in a pristine black leather case. Hazel's glasses. I returned to Mom's room to give them to Hazel. "Put these on. You'll be able to see her better," I instructed.

Hazel groaned and traded Violet for the glasses, donning a pair of thick black frames that looked almost too big for her head. She looked down at Violet one more time. "Oh, my goodness!" she squealed. "She's beautiful! Isn't she beautiful?" Hazel said, looking me directly in the eyes with a wide, sincere smile.

"You have no idea," I said back.

CHAPTER 10

About a month went by. My injuries had almost entirely healed. It was a good feeling, getting my physical health back.

Mom stayed in bed for a few days after Violet was born, recovering. But she was tough, and she seemed to bounce back fast.

Violet's rosy-red newborn shade faded before long, and I could finally get a good look at her features. She looked just like Dad, and it wasn't until I saw how much she looked like him that I truly noticed how much I didn't. Sure, he and I shared a feature here and there, but Violet? She may as well have been Dad with wisps of hair and baby fat.

She had to be fed every two or three hours, waking us with her incessant crying, making my eyes pop wide in the wee hours. Not a single time, though, was I upset to hear her cry. That child was a monument to all of my persistence, Mom's fortitude, and Dad's selflessness. That child—along with Mom, Hazel, and Beverly—was a reason to fight another day.

Mom liked to rock back and forth with Violet swaddled like a caterpillar in a cocoon, singing seemingly every song she knew.

"You Are My Sunshine"—she loved to sing that one, and Violet loved hearing it, twisting her wobbly little head to look around with an adorably gummy grin. Before then, I'd never known how good a singer Mom was, but I imagined hers was a voice that could command rooms.

She loved Violet fiercely, and for the first time in what seemed like forever, she was happy.

Beverly taught me a few things, and I could've sworn that she saw me as her own grandson, at times. For times when food was scarce out in the wild, Beverly had stocked a lot of supplies. It hadn't been because she'd anticipated the bombs—she was just the type to make sure she didn't have to go to the grocer more often than she had to. The outdoors and her family were all she needed most days, and I took a lesson from that.

Beverly showed me how to cook properly, and I was thankful for it. We had plenty of food to last us for a while. Between Beverly's supplies and the garden, we could afford to spare some for cooking lessons, even if they went awry. And in a home surrounded by women, cooking wasn't such a bad skill to have. I could hardly have lived it down if I'd been the only one in the house who struggled to boil a pot of water while everyone else could make pastries and filling dinners in a snap. I guessed she was showing me how to pull my own weight, but in a different kind of way than I might have expected. And I could tell she had just as much fun teaching as I had learning.

Beverly kept mementos, photographs, trinkets, and everything of the like. I would spend hours late at night sitting at the breakfast table in the kitchen with her, sipping on a mug of hot tea and skimming through the pages of old photo albums. I would never have pegged her as having once been a professional model, but she had. Not a fashion model, though—a model for women's cosmetics. Beverly's picture had once been plastered in every magazine and newspaper across all forty-eight states. According to her, she'd had to wear a thick white powder with accents of red on her eyes, lips, and cheeks. I got a kick out of imagining that, but she said it had been the style back then. The photographs and newspaper snippets she showed me were all in black and white, so I'd had to imagine it. Even so, I could plainly see she'd been a looker back in the day. I could see where Hazel got it.

Among all the photos of herself and Hazel, Beverly showed me others. There were pictures of Hazel's father, Beverly's one and only child. The photos they posed for together as father and daughter indicated there was genuine love there, but it made me wonder how a person could leave his own children behind. Art and Gabe were also among the photos. Art was a larger-framed, husky sort of man, as the massive clothing I had to wear indicated. I got a look at the life he and Beverly had built together, from youngsters madly in love in their twenties to buying their first home—this home—in their early thirties. Hazel's little brother, Gabe, was obviously your typical little kid. There were plenty of photos of him playing outside or with his die-cast toys, opening gifts on Christmas morning. Blowing out the candles of his birthday cake—a cake Beverly must've made herself. I swear, I could've tasted it through the picture. A picture is worth a thousand words, and every single one of them spoke loudly of love and happiness.

When it came to Hazel, she was an ever-flowing river of surprises. She was something else. It wasn't long before I could describe the way she made me feel. Especially when she said my name, or laughed with me, or *at* me—didn't matter. I'd have walked a million miles to hear it. That feeling was exactly like Dad had said, like a million little firecrackers going off in the pit of my stomach. *I was in love.* And I prayed that she felt the same way about me. Hell, I'd even have taken a strong liking, truth be told. I'd have taken anything I could get.

Hazel taught me how to fire a gun. Art kept a rifle similar to the one Dad had owned, the one rusting in the woods where I'd left it. Hazel had made some snarky comments before about how she'd saved me from those "puppy dogs," and I saw firsthand how she knew her way around a stock and barrel as well as most people knew their way around their own house. She was patient with me, though, in teaching me about using the gun. I must've wasted twenty bullets before I could hit a stationary target, but—in my defense—they weren't very easy to hit: old sarsaparilla bottles at the end of a long driveway. We spent an hour or two every day outside, fine-tuning my marksmanship. I knew if it came to it, it would be a significant skill to possess.

Hazel was rough and tough out there in nature, but in the house, she was much more lady-like. There was a little bit of Beverly and a little bit of Art in her, and although I'd never met Art, I could tell which was which based on what she was doing or what she said.

The girl could also draw—well. *Really* well. Had I not watched as she moved her pencils across blank paper, I would've thought the finished product was by da Vinci himself. I suppose it was possible, though, that I was a little biased. She'd told me she wanted to be a cartoonist; that was her dream. She said there was too much bad in the world, that it was too serious and too dark. All she ever wanted to do was brighten up people's day. She sure brightened mine. She might as well have been the sun itself.

She taught me more about God, put it into a perspective that no preacher or pastor had ever been able to do. We would read near a lit candle in the kitchen every night before bed, getting up to Ecclesiastes. I kept asking myself, if God was real, why had the whole world turned upside down? It seemed I was the only person who even questioned it; Mom, Beverly, Hazel, and even Dad had all kept their faith. But after all those nights talking with Hazel and reading, I also reclaimed mine. I'd come to realize that maybe He really does have a plan. After all, if it weren't for everything that had happened, would I have met Hazel? Didn't there have to be some reason for all of it?

We had grown closer and closer with each day. And then came that one special night. The snow had begun to melt as it had started to get warmer, and drips from suspended icicles painted the front porch with chilled water. An old wool blanket was spread across a patch of thinning snow several feet from the porch, and we lay there together on our backs with our eyes on the night sky, another thick blanket draped over us.

Hazel raised her arm and pointed to a pattern of stars. "That one's Orion," she said matter-of-factly.

"What's that mean?" I asked.

"Beats me!" she said with a giggle. She raised her hand again. "Ooh! That one's the Little Dipper! See the handle?"

I squinted and desperately looked for anything that even remotely resembled a handle; I couldn't find it. "Sure! Yeah, I see it now!" I said, not wanting to sound like an idiot.

Hazel pulled her arms back under the blanket to warm them before poking one out again. "And that one . . . that one little star up there! The brightest of the bunch—see it?"

A star, so white it shone light blue, was separated from the all the others. "Yeah, yeah, I see it," I said.

Hazel propped herself on her side to look me directly in the eyes, the moonlight reflecting off the lenses of her glasses. "That one, that special little star, that's your daddy looking down on you."

I smiled at her. "You think so?" I asked.

"I *know* so," Hazel replied. " I wish I could've met him. Think he would've liked me?"

"Not a doubt in my mind," I said.

Hazel placed her thumb on my jawline and began to trace the shape of my face. She leaned in toward me slowly. "Can I tell you something?"

"You can tell me anything, anytime," I said.

"I think I love you, wise guy," she said, obviously nervous.

At her words, my heart started beating as if I were walking a tightrope between two skyscrapers. "Can I tell you something back?" I asked with a wide smile.

Hazel nodded.

"I think I love you, too," I said.

Hazel leaned in closer, and our lips met. That was the first time we'd kissed. Never had I felt so alive, and never was I so sure that I would do anything to keep that feeling.

We spent the rest of that night under those stars, our hands locked together, staring more into each other's eyes, each other's souls, than we did the night sky. Hazel looked happy.

I was happy.

Finally.

CHAPTER 11

You sure you know where you're going?" Hazel asked impatiently.

"Yeah, I think," I replied.

"Since when does 'I think' mean you're sure?" said Hazel.

We had decided to take a trip out to the woods to look for the stuff I had left behind. I guessed it was just boredom setting in.

"I'm freezing, wise guy. Let's call it quits on this, okay?" Hazel said, fed up with our little treasure hunt.

"Give me a minute," I insisted. "I know it's close."

We continued walking for another few minutes; Hazel groaned in annoyance the whole time.

"There it is!" I exclaimed, pointing to a small black pile off in the distance. "That's where the fire was!"

"Great. Now let's get your junk and head home."

"Why's it gotta be junk?" I asked, making my way toward the old campfire.

"Because it's a leather jacket and two nearly empty guns that have been sitting out in the snow for a month. *That's* why," she joked.

"Yeah, yeah, well, what else did we have to do today?" I asked.

"Something that doesn't require getting frostbite up our knees, for one."

"Oh, hush," I said, locking eyes with her and grinning.

We arrived at the campsite, and I got on my knees to stuff everything I could find into the cold, weathered duffel. I dug through the little remaining snow surrounding the fire site and grabbed the hunting knife I'd left. The blade had weathered from its rust-spotted shine to a fully rusted brown shank. It had seen better days, but it was still useful enough to keep. The leather jacket was now drenched, and as heavy as it had been before, it felt at least double its original weight. With some persistence, though, I was able to stuff it inside the bag with just enough room to spare for the pistol. I grabbed the familiar hunting rifle and handed it to Hazel. "Can you carry this for me?" I asked.

"Why? Expecting more puppy dogs?" she said with a wink, reaching for the gun.

"Ha ha, very funny."

"Thought you'd like it," she said with a smile, throwing the rifle over her back by the strap.

We began our walk back home.

"Think we'll get back by the time breakfast is ready?" Hazel asked.

"Hope so. Already got cold toes; last thing I want is a cold meal," I replied.

"Where'd ya get that joke? A Cracker Jack box?" Hazel asked playfully.

"Yeah, it was right at the bottom," I countered.

We heard a loud rustling noise in the woods behind us.

"What was that?" Hazel asked, stopping sharply.

Keeping my attention on the woods ahead of me, I shrugged and said, "Probably a rabbit or something."

Hazel cocked her head to the side. "A rabbit? What kind of rabbit is *that* loud, wise guy?" she said, looking behind us.

"It's nothing, Hazel. Let's get back home."

"You can say it's nothing all you want, but—"

"Excuse me?" growled a man's voice.

We turned around to see a man coming from behind a tree, his frame gaunt, the filth of his unkempt, long gray hair matching a beard. He looked like what I'd always imagined a bootlegger would have before the end of Prohibition.

"What do you need?" I asked, trying to be intimidating, straightening to stand as tall as I could.

"*I'm* the one with the gun, wise guy. You standing up straighter isn't going to scare him," Hazel whispered through the side of her mouth before looking down at my locked knees.

"Well, we can't just shoot him," I said.

"I'm looking for my sons. Have you seen them?" the man asked.

Hazel glanced over at me, giving me a nervous, suspicious look.

"No. We don't know your sons, and we don't wanna know 'em. So why don't you just go back where you came from! Go on! *Scram!*" Hazel boomed, gripping the rifle tightly as a show of threat.

"Calm down," I whispered through my teeth.

"Shh!" Hazel replied.

"Please, I'm so hungry and lost. Can you please help me?" the man pleaded, his arms in the air in surrender.

Hazel opened her mouth to say something back to him, but I intervened. "Fine," I said to the man.

"What are you doing? Do you not see what I see? This guy looks like he eats cats or something!" Hazel grunted.

"I guess I picked a good day to be human, then," I said.

"We have a baby and two women who couldn't fight their way out of a paper bag back home. This isn't something to crack wise about."

"What if he isn't some criminal? What if he's telling the truth? You really want leaving him to die out here on your conscience?" I asked.

"No, I guess you're right," Hazel said reluctantly.

"I'm gonna go check him out. Keep that rifle ready in case he tries something."

Hazel exhaled nervously and nodded.

"Hey, buddy. Keep your hands up," I instructed.

"Okay, sure thing," the man replied.

I walked up to him cautiously. I stood directly in front of him, scanning him up and down. His shoes were so muddy that it looked as if he had taken a detour through a sewer, and he smelled foul enough for it to be true. He had almost no teeth, and those that he did have looked more like coffee beans than actual teeth.

"You got a name?" I asked.

"Willard. My name is Willard," he said.

"Okay, Willard, we're going to get you taken care of. And then you hit the road. That's it. End of story. Got it?" I asked.

"Yes. Yes, that's all I need," he replied eagerly.

"Good. Get to walking," I said, pointing the way to home, walking backward to maintain eye contact with him.

After a few minutes, I stopped to let Hazel catch up to me, falling behind Willard but still close enough to keep an eye on him, and we began talking quietly so he couldn't hear us.

"Think this guy can be trusted?" I asked her.

"I sure hope so. But you're right: we can't just leave him out here," Hazel replied reluctantly.

Willard must have heard us talking. He turned to look back at us.

"Hey! Were we talking to you?" Hazel shouted. "We don't want to waste a bullet, so don't give us a reason!"

"That's twice you've threatened him," I said quietly.

"Gotta play it tough, wise guy."

"He looks pretty tired. What if he needs a place to sleep for the night?" I asked.

"Oh, Clint, that's a *great* idea!" she replied, her voice thick with sarcasm. "Sure! We can invite Jack the Ripper here into our home and show him everything, especially where we all sleep! That's not dangerous at all!"

I laughed aloud. "Reminds me of my folks, us going back and forth like cats and dogs," I said.

"Well, *I'm* the dog," she replied.

"Why's that?" I asked, knowing I'd get some kind of smart-aleck response.

"Because you're obviously no match for a dog."

"I guess I walked into that one, huh?" I asked.

"You walk into a lot of things—like, you know, tree branches."

"Ha ha," I said with a grin, remembering the run-in I'd had with a tree that had knocked me out cold.

Hazel smirked back.

"I don't know what we're going to tell my mom and Beverly."

"We tell them we were looking for your stuff," she replied.

"Okay, so we left the house to find my stuff, and we came back with a strange man we found lurking in the woods. Got it," I replied.

By now I could just see a glimpse of the house through the foliage and vegetation as we walked out from the woods.

"Stop here, Willard," I instructed him.

Willard stood still as I approached him.

"If it's not given to you, don't touch it. If it's not offered to you, don't ask for it."

Willard nodded. "That's fair," he said.

"Good."

"So, is it just you two here?" he asked.

Something about the question unsettled me. Why did he care if we were alone? "What's it to you?" I asked.

"Oh, no reason. Just making conversation, is all," he replied.

"Well, we're not here to get chatty. You're going to get warm and eat a meal, and then you're outta here. Now, go to the house," I ordered, staying where I was to speak with Hazel as Willard began to walk toward the house.

"Did you hear what he said?" I asked her.

"Yeah. I don't like it," she replied, staring pointedly at Willard's back as he walked farther away from us.

"Me, neither. Keep your eye on him; I'll do the same."

We ascended the steps and joined Willard at the front door; then I opened it and led our trio inside.

"Make a left at the door. Sit down at the table," I instructed Willard, my voice firm. "Mom! Beverly! We're home!" I shouted.

"Oh, well, it's about time," I heard Mom say as she walked through the kitchen doorway. Her jaw nearly hit the floor when she saw Willard with us. "And . . . who do we have here?" she asked, confused.

"This is Willard. We left to go search for the campsite, and we found him there," I said.

"Yeah, crazy how things happen, isn't it?" Hazel said in a tight voice.

"It is," Mom replied, still clearly flustered. "Please sit down, Willard. It's nice to meet you."

When Beverly came in, she set the table with a basket full of biscuits and a pot of hot tea. Hazel, Mom, Beverly, and I exchanged nervous glances as Willard scarfed down biscuit after biscuit, shoving them into his mouth with his filthy, grit-covered hands as though he hadn't eaten in weeks.

"I'm sorry . . . Where are my manners?" he said, belching quietly as he observed the disgusted faces around him. The only one of us that didn't look offended was Violet, who slept soundly in Mom's arms. "Were you all wanting any more?"

"No. But thank you for asking," I said in distaste.

Mom looked at me sternly, obviously displeased that I hadn't been more polite.

Willard licked his fingers clean after finishing the last biscuit, smacking his lips like a caveman. "So, is it just you who live here?" Willard asked, his eyes focused on Beverly.

I opened my mouth to answer, but Beverly said, "My husband and grandson live here, too. We're just waiting on them to come back home before we head to Cincinnati."

Willard rumbled with laughter. "When's the last time you saw 'em?" he asked, his voice almost amused. "Let me guess—before the bombs, right?"

Beverly looked disturbed. "Yes," she said quietly.

"Might as well forget about them coming back," Willard said.

"*Excuse* me?" Hazel demanded. "You've got a lot of nerve coming here and saying things like that!"

Willard leaned back in his chair. "You'll have to forgive me. Got carried away. I may have a lot of nerve, but I do know one thing for certain."

"And what is that?" I asked angrily.

"The world is screwed," he said. "Everyone and everything you once knew is dead." Willard leaned toward me, his foul, warm breath assaulting my nose. "Only two choices, boy: go too far right, where nothing's left, or go too far left, where nothing's right.

One leads to seeing another day, and one leads to rotting in a gutter. Choice is yours."

"And what choice is the correct one, Willard?" I asked, my patience running thin.

"I'll let you decide. I know what I'm going with," he said, following his words with a horrendous smile. Willard and I locked eyes, each trying to intimidate the other into backing down. His eyes were empty, though, like those of someone overtaken by insanity.

"Okay, settle down now," Mom said firmly, trying to defuse the situation.

Hazel grabbed me by the shoulder and gently pulled me away from Willard. "Take it easy," she whispered.

I stood from the table. "Come with me, Willard," I said.

"Whatever you say. You're the boss," Willard replied sarcastically.

"Where are you going?" Mom asked nervously.

Hazel rose from the table to follow us.

"No, Hazel. It's fine," I said. "I'll be back soon. I'm just going to show Willard something out back."

We walked through the back door, neither of us speaking. I kept my focus on the speed of Willard's footsteps the whole way. We walked to the gazebo, and I turned around to face him. "Who the hell do you think you are?" I asked.

"What? It's okay for you to threaten me with a gun, but I can't say what's the truth?" he asked.

"We did you a favor, dumbass. We didn't have to bring you here or give you anything to eat," I said.

"So why do it?" he asked. "Why help me at all?"

"I did it for myself. For a little bit of peace, knowing I didn't leave a man out there to die," I said.

"Leaving a man to die isn't so bad. You get used to it, the killing, especially when it means you're alive. Too far left, that's the only way," he said confidently. Crazily.

"No, you *don't* get used to it," I argued.

"You don't? Tell me what *you* know about killing, boy," Willard said.

"I've killed someone before. It isn't something I want to do again, something I can forgive myself for. So take your 'too far left' bullshit somewhere else. It isn't going to justify a thing."

"Why'd you do it, then, if it's so unacceptable?" Willard asked.

"Two guys in a pharmacy. That's all I'm saying about it. They had it coming," I said.

"So you kill 'em, and then you become a goody-goody, is that it?" Willard sneered.

"Go find your kids, like you were trying to do when we found you. Leave us be," I said, getting in Willard's face.

"*Kids?*" Willard scoffed. "They ain't no kids. Hell, they got about ten years on you." Willard paused to give me a condescending look. "And that stupid Cincinnati plan? If that ain't the cutest thing. Those Germans turned half our country into dust overnight; what the hell makes you think Cincinnati's going to stick?"

"The war isn't over. Now *leave*," I growled, pointing in the direction of the driveway.

"Ain't over?" Willard asked. "How so? They already won. Fightin' a losing battle is all that's happening now. Only matter of time before they find you, too."

"Are you deaf or something, old man?" I asked. Out of the corner of my eye, I saw the curtains in one of the windows move; someone in there must have felt nosy.

"Who are those women in there to you?" Willard asked. "The old one—she your grandma? How about the other? Your mom? And I'd bet that young little thing is your girlfriend. Am I right?"

"Choose your next words carefully!" I warned.

"That's who they may be to you, but to the Germans, they're targets. And don't think for a second they won't have their way with that pretty little piece of ass you got in there."

I grabbed Willard by the shirtfront and pushed him against the side of the gazebo, keeping a firm grip. "She's got a name! And you *will not* talk about her again—or so help me, I'll rip you apart!"

Willard laughed. "That's it! That's what you gotta do! Feels good, huh? Just go a little further left, and you know what? I'm done, that's it, ain't gotta put up with me anymore!"

"*No,*" I replied through gritted teeth.

"No? I knew it. You and all the others in there. Just a bunch of pussies!"

Beverly stepped outside to hear what was going on, using the guise of hanging the leather jacket on the clothesline to let it dry— not that it mattered; it had likely been ruined from the weather. She was just looking for an excuse to be outside where she could overhear.

I let go of Willard's shirt. "Leave this place, and never come back," I said.

Willard ignored me, his focus on the clothesline.

"Didn't you hear me? I said *go!*" I boomed.

Willard began walking over to where the jacket hung as Beverly scurried back inside.

"Look, old man! I'm not going to tell you again!"

Willard turned to fix me in a cold stare. "Shut the hell up, boy. I leave when *I* say I leave." He picked up his pace, almost to a run, as he made his way to the clothesline.

"Where do you think you're going?" I asked, chasing after him until we both came to a stop at the clothesline. "What? The jacket? You want it? Take it! Just get the hell out of here."

Willard ran his filthy hand across the leather. "This was custom made, you know. I was a tailor before all of this happened," he said. "I made one exactly like it, for my oldest son."

"Great, it'll be like a souvenir of your time here. Take it," I said, knowing what his words implied.

Willard reached into his back pocket as I prepared to defend myself against an attack. Instead, he pulled out an old, weathered wallet, opening it to reveal a photograph. "You know these boys?" he asked. I reached out to take the photograph from his hand.

My heart sank as I looked at it. It was the two men from the pharmacy. Despite the lack of filth and injuries, I knew it was them. And standing between them was a much more kempt version of Willard.

"Why don't you tell me a little more about the men you killed, boy," he said angrily before reaching into his pocket a second time to pull out a butterfly knife.

"I don't know what you're talking about," I insisted.

"Bullshit!" Willard spat.

I took a step back to gain distance from him. "Take it easy. Nobody needs to get hurt here," I said gently.

"I got a good feeling it might help. An eye for an eye, boy," Willard replied, the crazed look back in his eyes.

We circled each other in sidesteps.

"I'm sorry. I really am sorry," I said sincerely.

"Sorry ain't gonna cut it. Not for that," Willard said.

The door behind Willard was eased open as Hazel crept out of the house with something in her hand. Beverly tried to pull her back inside, but Hazel wriggled from her grip.

"Stop! Please!" Mom screamed.

Willard waved his knife in the air, never looking away from me. "Shut your mouth, you stupid bitch!" he yelled over his shoulder. "If you know what's best for you, you'll all stay inside!"

As Hazel inched her way toward us, I could see what she was holding: a heavy cast-iron skillet. I knew what she was planning, but I had to occupy Willard just a while longer to keep him from turning around.

"How many?" I asked Willard.

"What? How many have I killed?" he replied. "Too many to count anymore. After the first few, you quit keeping tally."

"Why?" I asked.

"Can't barter anymore, not in this world. You see something you want, something you can use, you take it. Any way possible."

"That's what got your sons killed," I said.

Willard's face scrunched tightly in anger. "If you would've done what they said, this wouldn't be happening right now."

"They made it perfectly clear, they planned on killing us and taking what they wanted," I said.

"That's the way things work in this world, kid," Willard sneered. "But now I get my turn with you, and you're gonna pay for murdering my boys!"

"I had no choice, old man! My father is gone because of your trigger-happy kid," I replied.

Hazel was closing in on us, creeping closer and closer, now just a few feet from Willard, using both hands to grip the handle of the skillet like it was a baseball bat. Mom and Beverly watched anxiously from the porch, knowing that intervening could cause an even bigger problem. Violet was still asleep in Mom's arms, oblivious to everything around her.

"When I'm done with you," Willard said, "I'm going to kill every last one of those women, too.”

“You’d kill a baby? An innocent child?” I asked.

“Wouldn’t be the first time,” Willard said with a menacing look.

Suddenly, Hazel swung the skillet across her body, smacking Willard on the back of the head. He dropped, and his body hit the ground with a heavy thud. “Oh, Lord! Oh, my goodness, I killed him!” Hazel panicked, throwing the pan to the ground and covering her mouth in shock.

I looked down at Willard, who—though unconscious—was still breathing normally. “Calm down, Hazel! You didn’t kill him,” I assured her.

“Are you sure?” Hazel asked, not quite taking me at my word.

“He isn’t dead, but we have to figure out what to do with him before he wakes up.”

Hazel breathed deeply to calm herself down and nodded. “You got any ideas?” she asked.

I focused on a toolshed in the distance. “Anything in there?” I asked, pointing to the shed.

“Not that I know of,” Hazel replied.

“Well, that’s where he goes for now. It’ll give us some time to decide what to do.”

“Clint! Hazel!” Mom hollered as she hurried to us from the porch. “Are you okay?”

“We are. *He* might not be, though,” I said, glaring down at Willard.

“What were you thinking, bringing that man here in the first place? Why would you bring home a stranger?”

I smiled at her gently. “Once upon a time, we were strangers.”

Mom was taken aback, realizing the reason I had helped Willard in the first place was out of the hope that he was worth helping. “What’s next?” she asked. “Do you have a plan for him?”

I shook my head. "Not right now, but I know what we're going to do until we have one."

CHAPTER 12

Idon't know if I can hold this guy up for much longer," Hazel grunted through her teeth.

"We're almost there," I said, pausing mid-sentence to take a breath.

Hazel was holding Willard's legs up between her arms and rib cage, supporting his lower thighs with her hands. I was on the opposite side, walking backward, doing the same with his upper half.

"Okay, gently now," I said to Hazel as we approached the door of the toolshed. I laid Willard's top half down slowly. Hazel followed my example but forewent any degree of gentleness, carelessly dropping his lower half on the ground.

"Phew! That was tiring!" she grunted, bending over and breathing heavily, her hands resting on her knees.

I opened the door of the toolshed and was greeted by a thick network of cobwebs. Inside, the shed itself was no more than a cramped, empty space, with nothing but a small amount of junk on a single shelf and an even smaller amount of sunlight peeking in through the wooden boards.

I dragged Willard into the shed by his arms and pulled him over to a vertical support post in the back of the shed. "You got any rope in here?" I asked.

Hazel felt around in the dark for a moment and walked over to hand me a piece of rope about six feet in length. "Is this enough?" she asked.

"Yeah, it should work," I replied. I fed the rope through a small opening between the post and the wall. I propped Willard upright, with his back leaning against the post and his hands behind him as I tied the remaining rope around his wrists.

"Think that'll hold him?" Hazel asked from the doorway.

"For as long as we need it to, it should. We need him gone as soon as possible." I closed the shed door behind us, and we headed back to the house.

Once inside, we all assembled ourselves at the breakfast table, trying to work through a plan.

"What if we just leave him in there? Out of sight, out of mind," Mom suggested.

"Oh, Amelia, that's a little cruel, don't you think?" Beverly tutted. "Maybe he just needs some understanding and kindness."

"He came in here and ate all of our biscuits and tried to murder Clint in the backyard. I don't think he gets any second chances," Hazel argued.

"Yeah, all due respect, Beverly, I don't think that's such a good way to go about this," I said. "It was a big enough mistake, me bringing him here in the first place." I looked over at Mom, holding a sleeping Violet, her tiny snores sounding like a cat's purr. "There's too much at risk now, especially with the baby. I can't let anything happen to any of you. I'm sorry."

Beverly reached across the table to lay her hand on mine. "You have a big heart, Clint. That's nothing to apologize for. You didn't know he would be dangerous."

"Thanks, Beverly. But it still doesn't help figure out what we're going to do with him," I said, pausing for a moment before going on. "What if we tie him to a tree in the woods?"

Everyone at the table looked at me, dumbfounded.

"What's the difference in him being in the shed versus the woods?" Mom asked.

"We lead him outside, put a blindfold on him so he doesn't know where we are, and we tie him to a tree somewhere far away from here. Not so tight that he can't eventually get loose, but enough to buy us time to get back home."

We all sat quietly in thought, considering the idea.

"Sounds like as good a plan as any," Hazel said at last.

Beverly and Mom both nodded. "You be careful, okay? Do you need me to go with you?" Mom asked.

"No, no. Dad wouldn't have wanted to put you in danger like that. Heck, he'd probably be disappointed that I let it get this far," I said.

"No, he'd be proud of you for being brave," Mom said, giving me a warm smile.

"There's something else we should think about," I said nervously.

"What is it, dear?" Beverly asked.

"Through all that garbage Willard was spouting, he was right about at least one thing," I said. "Beverly, do we really know if Art and Gabe are coming back?"

Hazel looked at me with sadness in her eyes, but I could tell she understood the reality of what I was saying.

Beverly reached a trembling hand to pick up her teacup and took a small, unsteady sip. "That's something I've tried not to think about," she said as her voice cracked slightly.

"We're starting to run low on food. It's getting warmer outside, and the snow is practically gone. If we try, I know we can make it to Cincinnati."

Mom gave me an anxious look, then looked down at Violet's tiny form. "I think . . . I think he's right," she said as Beverly got up from her chair and walked to the kitchen window, its curtains pulled back to allow the sunlight in.

"It's a scary thought," Beverly said. "I've been in this house for thirty-four years."

I stood from the table and walked up beside Beverly. "I know you've been here a long time. But you just said it—'this house.' That's all it is now. A *house*. A home is a place where you can be safe, a place where you don't have to worry. What happens if someone else like Willard comes out of those woods? What if next time we aren't so lucky? Or worse, what if that person comes out with a swastika stitched on their sleeve?"

Beverly turned to face me. "When do we leave?" she asked gravely.

"In the morning, if that's okay," I said, turning to look at Hazel and Mom.

Everyone agreed, nodding silently.

"Okay, I think we need to get everything packed. We have a long journey ahead of us. Pack light; if we don't need it, don't take it. I figure if we only stop to eat and sleep, we can get there in five days on foot. If we keep our heads down and keep pushing forward, we'll be fine," I said.

Mom took Violet upstairs, and Beverly followed behind, the three of them going to get packed and ready.

Hazel stood from the table and approached me. "So, this is it, huh?"

"Yeah, this is it," I replied.

"I'm gonna miss this place," she said.

"Me, too, but we need to be somewhere safe. Today was a perfect example of what the world is really like now," I replied.

"I don't like the way the world is now," Hazel said.

"I know you don't; I feel the same way. But I need you to trust me. I need all of you to trust that this is the best thing we can do at this point."

Hazel took my hands gently, locking her fingers in between mine. She stood on the tips of her toes to get enough height to give me a peck on the cheek. "Of course I trust you," she said.

I smiled at her. "Think it's time we go out there and take care of our friend."

CHAPTER 13

I hope he's awake," Hazel said as we headed toward the shed, armed with her grandfather's rifle.

"Really? You hope that jerk is awake?" I asked.

"That guy's heavier than he looks. But of course, since you're a big, strong man and all, you probably didn't notice," Hazel joked.

"And don't you forget it!" I laughed.

"This thing loaded?" Hazel asked as she examined the gun.

"I don't know, but it doesn't need to be. He can't do much to us with his hands tied behind his back. Wait here in the doorway and keep an eye on him," I said to Hazel as I opened the door to the shed.

When the door was open, I could see Willard raise his head. "Oh, it's *you*. What the hell do you want, huh? Come back to finish me off?"

I walked over to him and crouched down to his eye level. "I already told you," I said. "I'm not going to kill you. Not everyone resorts to violence, you know."

Willard fixed a beady glare on me. "Still believe in that crazy Cincinnati pipe dream, huh?" he asked.

"Yeah, dreaming is all we got left. Maybe you'll learn to dream one of these days," I said, knowing that it was landing on deaf ears.

Willard scoffed. "I'd rather die a real man than live on stupid dreams," he replied.

"That's your call. But *we're* going to go get our lives back," I said, looking to the doorway to make sure Hazel was still keeping watch.

"Where'd you learn this load of shit?" he asked.

"The Bible. And it's not a load of shit."

Willard laughed. "You know why Adam and Eve betrayed God in the Garden of Eden?" Willard asked. "It's because forbidden fruits taste better. You see, every day—hell, every *second*—that passes, ignorant people like you dive deeper and deeper down into this lake of fire we live in now, and one of these days, you'll drown. You all will. And people like me, who took that forbidden fruit off that forbidden tree? We'll still be breathing. Your morals, your values will be your downfall. And you're going to wish you'd taken care of me when you had the chance. Because I'll be back. And I *will* make you suffer."

I looked down at the ground, having so much to say. Instead, I bit my tongue. "Are you finished?" I asked.

"I'll never be finished—not until you are. Not until *you* feel loss like I have," Willard sneered.

"If only you knew," I said.

"Just you wait, you'll see. Your God and your heaven have been replaced by a Führer and a Reich. You disgust me, you all do. This isn't your American dream, but, like it or not, this is the American way now. And there's no place for weaklings like you."

I stood. "Keep the sights on him," I instructed Hazel, nodding at the gun she held. I untied Willard, and he stood.

"This ain't over, boy," he said.

"Yes, it is. Move."

"Oh, look at you! You know how to use that thing?" he asked Hazel while I tied his hands together behind his back.

"I don't think you want to find out, jackass," she replied, clutching the rifle tightly.

"It don't matter, not really. You'll be handling a lot of guns soon enough, anyway. Them German boys need to get their barrels polished somehow," Willard replied, rasping out a laugh.

I growled in anger as I tightened the rope enough to leave a mark around his wrists.

"What's the matter? I make you mad?" Willard taunted.

"Walk!" I demanded, shoving Willard forward with my open hand.

"You'll be sorry, I promise you," Willard growled. He walked ahead of us into the woods, several hundred feet away from the house.

"Stop!" I demanded. He ignored me as he kept trekking forward. "I said stop!"

Willard turned to me slowly. "What?" he asked angrily.

I pulled out an old handkerchief from my back pocket.

"What? You gonna gag me? Blindfold me?" he asked.

"The second one, though they both sound pretty nice right now," I replied.

"Can't believe it. A couple of kids, pushing me around like a goddamn dog," Willard muttered.

I walked over to Willard to blindfold him, with Hazel at the ready on the sidelines. "I'm gonna put this on you, and we're gonna keep walking," I said as I wrapped the handkerchief around his head and tied the knot.

What happened next was something I should've seen coming. Willard thrust his shoulder into my midsection and sprinted off in the other direction, through the woods.

Hazel raised the gun to take aim, then lowered it again when he was out of sight. "Think he'll come back?" she asked.

I clutched my midsection, inhaling deeply to refill my lungs with air. When I'd recovered enough to speak, I responded. "I don't think so. We gave him a chance. If he comes back, we'll have to shoot," I said.

"Are you sure we'd have to do that?" she asked.

"If it means keeping you or any of the others safe, then yes."

When we arrived back at the house, Hazel and I both went up to our rooms. I figured I didn't need to weigh myself down with too much clothing, especially because they'd only slow our progress. I skimmed through the closet to find a set of thick flannels, which would be more than sufficient for the weather.

I stuffed the old, now-moldy duffel with canned food from the pantry and left enough room in the bag for water. I went outside to the well, raising and lowering a wooden bucket manually by rope to fill empty containers with water that had melted from the iced-over reservoir, noticing that something about the water didn't taste right to me—too earthy. But water was water, and it was something we had to have. I hoped they'd have a better substitute in Cincinnati.

When I was done, I went inside and upstairs to Beverly's room and knocked on the frame of the open door. "Do you need any help?" I asked.

"No, no, I think I have it under control, young man," Beverly replied, pausing for a moment. "Come here," she said, gently patting the bed next to where she sat. "There's something I want to give you." Her voice was quiet as she touched the wedding ring on her left ring finger and then slid it off. Before I could comprehend what she was doing, she presented it to me on her open palm. "I want you to have this."

"But Beverly—why?" I asked.

"I see the way you look at her, Clint, and I see the way she looks at you," she said with a smile. "If that isn't love, I don't know what is."

I laughed. "A little early to ask for her hand, isn't it? We're just kids, after all."

"*Just kids?*" Beverley shook her head. "The way I've watched you both grow in the last month alone proves you're not just kids. The way you talk to each other, I can tell you're both happy. Besides, time isn't guaranteed. You know that as well as I do. The day Art and Gabe left, I expected to see them again; I even set them a spot on the table, just like always. Time is a luxury more than anything."

I looked down at the ring I now held in my hand. "Think she'll say yes?"

"I *know* she will," Beverly replied. "Time, you may or may not have it to spare. So let the ones you love know what's really on your mind."

"Thanks, Beverly," I said, wrapping her in a hug.

"You don't have to call me Beverly, by the way. Call me Mamaw," she insisted with a warm smile.

"Okay, Mamaw."

"Do you know who Emily Dickinson is?" she asked.

"Yeah, she's a writer, isn't she?"

Beverly nodded with a surprised grin. "Why, yes. Well, a poet to be more specific. I've been thinking of some of her words for the last few hours. All the hope and how an idea is pushing us forward." Beverly paused with a look of focus and concentration. "I believe it goes something like this: 'Hope is the thing with feathers / That perches in the soul / And sings the tune without the words / And never stops, at all.'"

"What's it mean?" I asked.

"It means whatever you want it to mean. To me, it means that, no matter how dark things seem, how cold the world is, how hurt we may feel, hope will always see us through," she said.

I grinned. "I think I like that meaning," I said. "I think I'm going to see if the others need my help."

Beverly nodded.

I rose from the bed and walked to the doorway.

"Clint," Beverly said as I was leaving.

I turned around. "Yes?"

"I love you," she said with a smile.

"I love you, too, Mamaw," I said back.

I headed down the hallway, into the room that Mom and Violet shared.

"Shh! I just put this fussy little butterball to sleep," Mom said in a whisper.

I walked over to them. "Is there anything you need help with?" I asked quietly.

"No, I'm all done," she said.

"What about diapers?" I asked.

"If by 'diapers' you mean cut-up pieces of bedding, then yes, already taken care of."

"Good. Are you scared?" I asked.

"Of course I am," she replied. "I'd be lying if I said I wasn't."

"I hear you. I'm scared, too. I guess we got a little too comfortable and cozy here. Wasn't until today that we had a real wake-up call," I said.

Mom smiled at me, her face full of pride. "You've changed so much."

"How so?" I asked.

"You aren't the same boy that slept until noon and hated going to school. You're not even really a boy anymore. You're a man, and you remind me so much of your father. Always keep the values he taught you, Clint. He would be so proud," she said.

I could feel my eyes welling up. "I sure hope so. He wanted me to take care of you two," I said, wiping away a stray tear from my face.

"And you're doing a great job," Mom said. "There isn't anyone else I'd trust more than you. I'm just sorry you had to grow up like this. Didn't really have time to ease into it, huh?"

"I guess not, but that's behind us now. We're going to go back out into the world and fight for the good things," I said, hoping I sounded strong.

"And when we get there," Mom said, "Violet's going to need a little friend. Maybe once things settle down, you and Hazel can help out with that."

I laughed. "Funny you should say that," I said, pulling the ring Beverly had given me from my pocket. "Beverly's thinking along those lines, too."

Mom gasped. "What a coincidence," she said wryly.

"You two have been talking about this when we aren't around, huh?" I asked.

Mom smiled. "You got me."

Violet's brow began to twitch as her bottom lip puckered, and she let out an ear-piercing cry.

"I guess she's hungry again!" Mom exclaimed.

"Okay," I said, turning to leave. "I'll see you later."

I walked to the end of the hallway, making one final stop at Hazel's room. "Knock, knock," I said, peeking in.

"Hey, there, wise guy," Hazel said with a smile. "So, what should I wear tomorrow?" she asked, standing in front of her closet.

"Anything you want. I'm sure you'll be a knockout in whatever you choose."

"Thanks. But, you know, first impressions are everything. When you don't make a good first impression, next thing you know, you're getting hit in the head with a frying pan and being left in the woods, tied to a tree," she said, winking at me.

"Oh, of course!" I replied with a laugh.

Hazel turned to face me, serious now. "I love you."

"I love you, too," I said.

"You really think we'll make it to Promised Land?" Hazel asked.

"Promised Land?"

"Yeah. That's what I'm calling it—well, that's how I imagine it, at least. A place where everyone can move on, where everyone can be happy." Hazel placed her hand on my cheek. "Where we can be happy—together." She straightened to give me a kiss, then walked over to her bed and sat down with a sigh. "You really think we'll make it?" she asked as I took a seat next to her.

"I know we will," I said, wrapping my arms around her. "Have . . . have you ever thought of having kids?" I asked nervously.

Hazel looked caught off guard by the question. "Well, one day, maybe . . . Why?" she asked with an intrigued smile.

"Nothing," I said, laughing under my breath. "Your mamaw and my mom have been talking about us, is all."

"Oh, *really*? What have they been saying?" Hazel perked up with interest.

"They've been talking about us having kids someday, about how much we care about each other. That kind of stuff. I guess they're spying on us," I said with a grin.

"Spying, huh? I don't think you need to be a great detective to see that we spend almost all of our time together."

I looked into her eyes. "You're the best friend I've ever had."

"And you're mine," she replied, taking my hand.

"I'd like to be something more permanent, once we get to where we need to be," I said.

Hazel cocked her head to one side. "What do you mean?" she asked, though she'd obviously formed a good idea of what I was going to say. She just wanted to hear the words.

I reached into my back pocket to fish out the wedding ring and slipped it over the ring finger of her left hand, then took both of her hands into my own. I took a deep breath as I watched tears well up in Hazel's eyes. "Will you marry me?" I asked.

Hazel didn't speak. Instead, she pulled me toward her and curled into my arms.

"That a yes?" I asked.

She nodded enthusiastically, wiping tears from her eyes.

We spent the rest of our time together that day and night in our usual spot—the front porch. We sat on the steps with our hands locked, once again wishing upon the stars. Hazel asked if I thought Cincinnati had meatloaf and apple pie; I assured her it was there. She asked my opinion on which of us our children would resemble more, when we had them; I told her I hoped it would be her. She asked if I wanted to get married indoors or out; I told her it didn't matter—whatever she wanted. We talked and talked. We were happy; we were excited. The anticipation was like fuel on a hungry fire that needed hope for the future.

I hadn't even noticed that Dad's star wasn't out in the sky that night.

He must not have been able to watch what was going to happen.

He must have known.

Hazel spotted someone standing at the edge of the woods. I told her it had to be Willard, but something wasn't right. Something was off.

When I squinted to see into the darkness, I could make out something behind him. Several somethings.

It was when Hazel asked what that was prowling behind him in the moonlight that I realized what they were. Those somethings were *someones*.

In a voice so horrified it barely resembled my own, I said one word: "Nazis."

CHAPTER 14

G et inside. Get everyone together and go! Run!" I urged.

"I can't leave you!" she protested.

"I'm not asking you—I'm telling you! *Go!*" I said, more forcefully this time.

Willard turned to face the figures in the woods. "Catch 'em out back!" he shouted as three armed German soldiers sprinted from the woods.

I picked up a rifle that was leaning against the porch and aimed at one of them. Before I could shoot, I heard a crack of gunfire rip through the sky. My right leg was grazed by a bullet, and I fell to the floor of the porch, tumbling down the wooden steps. I yelled out in pain as I watched three more Germans emerge from the woods behind Willard.

"Please! Don't hurt them!" I pleaded with Willard as I lay on the ground.

He inched his way toward me. "You should've went too far left. Should've listened to me. And most of all, you shouldn't have killed my boys," he replied.

I heard Violet crying from the backyard, along with mixed screams of horror. Tears welled up in my eyes—tears of anger, sadness, and fear that overtook me as I heard Violet's infant cries slowly fade out.

I turned around and began crawling back up those steps, looking back to see trails of my own blood behind me, its crimson shade visible in the moonlight. "I have to find them. I have to keep them safe," I muttered, gritting my teeth in pain.

"Where do you think you're going, boy?" Willard shouted, laughing in a sinister way.

I heard his footsteps as they closed in on me, and felt his disgusting hand grab the back of my shirt as he pulled a pistol from his waistband, the elastic snapping back against his bony hips.

Willard pointed the barrel to the back of my head. "An eye for an eye, boy," he said.

I closed my eyes and heard the sickening, mechanical click of the hammer being pulled back. "I tried . . . I tried," I mumbled, awaiting my end.

In the next moment, I was back at that drive-in again, bending over to pick up that weathered, old baseball from the shrubbery. I turned around to see Dad, and I pulled the mitt off my hand and sprinted as fast as I could toward him. He met me with open arms. "Dad! Dad! I've missed you so much!" I said through my tears.

"I've missed you, too, son," he said, hugging me tightly.

"I'm so sorry I couldn't protect them. I'm so sorry I let you down," I said.

Dad pulled back and looked me in the eyes. "You didn't. I'm proud of you; I've always been proud of you," he said with a smile.

"It's so good to hear you say that," I replied.

Dad turned to face the lines of cars eagerly awaiting the moving picture. And in the middle, I saw our old family sedan, the same one Dad would always sit in, tapping the steering wheel whenever he got impatient. In front of the car stood Hazel, Beverly, and Mom, with Violet in her arms. Dad lit one of his trusty Marlboros and took a drag. I could smell the burning tobacco as it wafted past my nose. They were approaching us.

"Hurry it up, will ya!" Dad playfully shouted to them. "You married a good one, Clint."

"Married?" I asked, looking down to see a wedding band on my own finger.

"I was thinking we could go over to your place this year for Thanksgiving. That sound good?" Dad asked.

"It sounds great! It's perfect!" I replied with a giddy laugh.

Beverly and Hazel were standing in front of me now.

I smiled, then grew serious. "Are . . . are we dead? Is this heaven?" I asked.

"This is whatever you want it to be, young man," Beverly replied.

"I didn't mean for this to happen. I didn't want any of this," I insisted.

"It's okay," she said, gently rubbing a hand over my back. "Besides! They have apple pie and meatloaf here," she said with a laugh.

Mom walked over to me. "Look, Clint. Little Violet's cutting her first tooth!" she exclaimed. I took a closer look at my baby sister. Peeking just above the surface of her bottom gums was the tiniest pearly-white tooth I'd ever seen.

"At this rate, she'll be eating real food in no time!" Dad added. "Maybe we can go to Vicky's again. I haven't had a burger that good since Lord knows when!"

Mom scoffed. "I made you a burger last week!"

"Oh, lighten up. I'm just pulling your leg," Dad responded.

Mom grinned. He got under her skin—he always had—but she loved it.

"Hey! Bev!" I heard a loud male voice shout from a distance and turned to see Art in all of his husky glory, carrying back various snacks from the concession stand. "Cost me almost two dollars for all of this. You all owe me!" he said as he handed out various boxes of candy to everyone. He gave me a box of Good & Plenty. I didn't think I'd ever liked those, but it was fine. All things must taste better in heaven—I was sure of it.

"Now, don't tell me you lost Gabe again!" Beverly scolded.

"Oh, no, dear. Look! He's right over there, playing catch with a little girl he met." Art pointed a few feet off into the distance.

And there was Gabe, being a little boy like all little boys deserved to be, having the merriest time of his little life. That little girl, though—I wasn't sure who it could be, but she seemed familiar. After staring at her a little longer, I knew. It was the little girl I had seen when we'd been running from the bombs, the one frantically beating on her father's chest.

We watched the same film as we had the first time around. This time, though, we were able to finish it. As much as I hadn't cared for the film the first time, it had become my new favorite. I didn't even notice Marsha Hunt on the screen anymore. Sure, she was there on the screen, but with Hazel at my side, what did Marsha Hunt matter?

Mom and Dad were sitting in the front seat again, and Mom's head was on Dad's shoulder. Violet was fast asleep in Dad's arms. I was so happy he'd gotten to meet his daughter, the one that was a spitting image of him. I could tell he loved her immensely, and I think he loved Hazel like one of his own, too. I'd known from the start that he'd have approved of her.

Beverly and Art were sitting next to each other in the pickup truck beside us. I guessed it was getting a little late; Beverly had fallen asleep on Art's shoulder, and he began to yawn. Watching them nod off was sweet; it was as if they were there just to be around everyone else. They were happy to be there, though; I could sense it. And that was all that mattered.

Gabe was still running around with that little girl, collecting fireflies and trapping them in their empty candy boxes. They were too young to realize they'd just fly out whenever they wanted to take a peek at their collections, but they were laughing so loudly and intensely that I was afraid they'd suffocate on their own cackles. I had to have a chuckle at it, too. It was all perfect; everything was better in heaven.

And then, in an instant, the world froze around me.

I shook Hazel, but she sat immovably frozen. "Hazel! Hazel, talk to me!" I shouted. Mom and Dad were still. "Mom! Dad! What's going on?" I screamed. They sat there, motionless, their eyes still wide open.

Everything had gone silent. I panicked as I tried to scream; I couldn't even hear myself. The silence was impenetrable. My throat started to feel hoarse as I yelled out, trying to get someone's attention. I tried to reach the door handle of the car to let myself out, but I couldn't move, no matter how hard I focused or how hard I strained. It was as if I were bound to something, keeping me in place.

I started to hear something—sobbing. Not the baby's cries I had grown accustomed to in recent days, but they were still familiar somehow. The sobs were coming from Hazel and Beverly.

I could hear them intensify as an unpleasantly familiar voice said, "Knock, knock. Anyone home?" The words were followed by a stinging smack to the side of my face.

I came back to earth. It was all in my head; I must have been knocked out, and my mind had gone somewhere else. We were at the kitchen table, surrounded by armed German soldiers. Their pristine gray uniforms, perfectly shined boots, and sewn-on swastikas overshadowed us with their menacing presence.

I looked at the faces around me. Hazel and Beverly sat silently in front of me, staring directly in my eyes. The horrified expressions painted on their bruised and scratched faces told me everything I needed to know. It took me a moment to realize that Mom and Violet weren't there.

"Where?" I asked Hazel pathetically.

Hazel shook her head. "I don't know," she whimpered.

I looked down at the chair I was sitting in, the same chair I'd sat in every day to eat my meals. My arms and legs were bound with several layers of thick tape.

I looked up to see Willard glowering down at me. "Let them go, please," I begged.

Willard laughed. "Didn't I tell you that I was going to make you suffer?" he sneered.

"Make *me* suffer. Make me suffer all you want. Don't bring them into this," I implored him.

"You know, I tried to warn you. See these fine young men?" He indicated the German soldiers in the room. "I've been working with these guys for a few weeks now."

"You what?" I asked. "You betrayed your own people?"

Willard pulled his pistol from his waistband. "Never were my people. This country was corrupt! This country needed cleansing!" he insisted. "For all we know, this place would've let the fags get married and the coons in our schools. You really want to live in that backward bullshit?" Willard asked.

"You're scum," I replied in disgust.

"I'm not scum. It's my job, finding people like you all and leading my friends here to 'em."

"This was your plan all along, wasn't it?" I asked, livid.

"You bet your ass, boy. You just made it more personal for me," Willard said. He loaded a single bullet into the revolver. "Like I said: an eye for an eye. Only two of you will leave this room alive, but trust me, that ain't such a good thing. Let's just say you'll wish you were dead." He paced around the room for what seemed to be hours, though I'm sure it was only a matter of minutes. "Despite that shot-up leg of yours, boy, I think you'd do just fine working for us."

"Whatever you want. Just please, please let them go," I pleaded.

Willard ignored me, grabbing a lock of Hazel's hair in his hand. "And her, she'll do very well for herself where she's going." He looked at me one more time. "We'll find that mom of yours and that baby. Don't you worry." He shifted his attention to Beverly. "Too old to bear kids or work. What a useless waste."

Beverly looked at Hazel, knowing that Willard had made his decision. "I love you, sweetheart."

Hazel wept uncontrollably, begging Willard to spare Beverly's life.

Beverly looked at me. "Remember, Clint. *Hope*. Always keep hope. Goodbye," she said as Willard pressed the end of the barrel to the back of her head.

"Goodbye, Mamaw . . . I'm so sorry."

Beverly gave me one last smile as Willard pulled the trigger.

Hazel screamed as the side of her face was covered in her grandmother's blood.

"You son of a bitch! I'm going to kill you!" I shrieked at Willard, so loudly that even a dead man would have been startled, so angrily that I could feel my blood boil from within me.

Willard rolled his eyes, dismissing my threats as hollow. Hazel was senseless with horrified screams and cries. "Oh, shut them up already!" Willard demanded.

I watched as a German soldier knocked Hazel out from behind, using the stock of his rifle. Before I could react—if I even could have reacted—I felt the same force slam down on the back of my own head.

I woke up, unsure of how much time had passed. My arms and legs were bound behind my back, and it was dark wherever I was, but I could've sworn I was moving. Those bastards had kidnapped me. "Hazel!" I screamed.

A deep voice finally responded. "She ain't in here, pal."

"Who said that?" I asked.

The voice replied, "My name is Emmett Carver. And you?"

"Clint Brodsky . . . What's going on? Do you know?" I asked, my voice shrill.

"Yeah." Emmett paused momentarily. "We're going to camp."

I didn't know what that meant. I didn't know what to expect, but one thing was for certain.

Hold on, Hazel, wherever you are, I thought. *I'm coming for you. I promise. And, Mom, hold that little girl close. No matter what, don't quit running.*

CHAPTER 15

Camp? What do you mean, 'camp'?" I asked in the darkness.

"What I mean is that those Nazi bastards are gonna work our fingers to the bone, and as soon as we can't work no more, we're killed," Emmett said.

"Work? Why do they need us to work for them?" I asked.

"Well, that's an easy one," Emmett replied. "These animals want to win the war as much as the Americans do. They want to do that, they'll need help. And what kind of labor is cheaper than forced labor?"

"And if we refuse?" I asked.

"Beats me, pal. But for Hazel's sake—whoever she is—I don't think I'd test it if I was you."

"Where'd they take her?"

"Hell, I don't know. Can't be good, though," Emmett replied.

The vehicle we were locked inside of came to jarring halt as the brakes were slammed, likely on purpose. Emmett and I slid across the floor of the truck as our bodies hit the walls.

"You're gonna wanna fight 'em," Emmett said. "*Don't.*"

"Don't? What do you suggest we do?" I asked.

"I wanna get outta this spot as bad as you do. Ain't gonna happen if you get yourself killed, ya hear?" Emmett replied.

I could hear soldiers talking to each other in German.

"Showtime, pal. Keep your head down, and do whatever they say—for everyone's sake," Emmett said.

I could hear the handle of the back door rattle as it opened, letting in a ray of sunlight that made my eyes burn. A German soldier stepped up onto the running board of the truck as he climbed inside. I could get a good view of Emmett now, as we were face-to-face on the floor. He was a black man, probably in his early forties, with hair that was lightly peppered with gray and a face covered in stubble. "Remember what I said, pal," he mumbled as a German soldier unbound his legs with a knife and pushed him roughly out of the vehicle.

The German was coming toward me now; one of his hands had a tight grip on one of my feet as his other hand cut them apart. He did the same to me as he'd done to Emmett, grabbing me by the back of the shirt with both arms and shoving me out of the truck.

I was on the ground outside, but not for long, before I was pulled to my feet by another thickly accented Nazi and told to walk. My leg was pulsing in pain, but I knew better than to show signs of weakness. I was behind Emmett, and we walked toward a large building—an old, abandoned church with a white concrete steeple standing several tens of feet above the rest of the structure. The place was swarming with Nazis; I counted seven of them total: two walking around near us, two on the rooftop with rifles, and three in guard towers.

A chain-link fence with barbed wire crudely wrapped around the top was all that separated the church from the outdoor living area. Carelessly built shacks constructed from what seemed to be sheet metal and plywood scattered around the yard served as the living quarters. Some of the prisoners leaned against the fence, watching the new arrivals. Some looked emaciated, their skin stretched like tight leather over their skeletons. Some looked as if they hadn't been there as long and still had some body weight to them. But all of them looked as if they were dead inside, and all of them wore matching clothes: white pants and a long-sleeved shirt with blue vertical lines. I stopped to take in what I was looking at, but was soon shoved back into motion by a German soldier telling me to keep moving.

We were in front of the church, and a German soldier stepped ahead of Emmett to open the door for us. I looked down at my leg, feeling a strange warmth spreading over it. My pant leg was soaked in my blood. I prayed they wouldn't notice.

We were inside the church in the meeting hall, just before the nave. Our wrists were unbound, and we were told to stand against the wall on the farthest right side of the room next to two other newly captured men. Both of them stood there in terror, in nothing but their underwear. One of them was about my age, and the other around Emmett's. They both had black hair and a similar facial shape; I assumed they were father and son.

The two Germans from before stood on the other end of the room. "Take the clothes off," one of the Nazis demanded in broken English. We obeyed and stood next to the other two men.

"What's going on?" the younger man asked as I stood next to him.

"Don't," Emmett said out of the side of his mouth, indicating that it would be best for us to stay quiet.

I reluctantly ignored the young man's question.

It seemed to be hours that we stood against that wall, looking around at the dull white walls of the church lobby. A couple of wooden benches, a second metal door with stairs visible through a small window slit, withering potted plants, and pictures of Christ and religious icons scattered about provided an ironic setting. The two Germans on the other end stood there, completely silent with loaded rifles in hand, the entire time.

A heavy metal door leading to the nave opened as a third German walked out, carrying a bag in his hand. His boots shone in the light; his uniform was perfectly ironed and pressed. He appeared to be an officer rather than one of the grunts I had seen up until that point. For a split second as the door closed behind him I glimpsed pews lined up evenly in front of the pulpit with stained-glass windows and art behind it.

"Hello," the German officer said, his voice echoing off the walls of the lobby.

Emmett, the other prisoners, and I remained silent as the officer awaited a response.

"I said *hello*!" he screamed in impatience.

"Hello," we replied dutifully, afraid of what would happen if we didn't.

The officer approached the four of us and reached into his pocket to pull out a stopwatch. He dumped the contents of his bag onto the ground. Uniforms, obviously used heavily, with brown bloodstains on them. "Here. You will do what you're told. If you fail, you pay," he said as he started his watch. "Sixty seconds. Get dressed."

All four of us dove to the floor to grab whatever clothing we could. I was in possession of two pairs of pants, and Emmett two shirts. We swapped one for one with each other as the father and son were already getting dressed. I slipped into my pants and then my shirt as quickly as I could as the officer announced, "Fifteen seconds remaining." I got ready and stood against the wall next to Emmett, who had already completed the task.

"Time is up!" the officer informed us, looking to see who had successfully complied. He gave both Emmett and me a look of satisfaction before going over to the older man, who stood shirtless to my far right. "Where is your shirt?" he asked.

"There were only three. I couldn't get one in time."

The officer growled in anger, "I told you what happens."

"Please, give me another chance!" he pleaded. "I just need a shirt!"

The officer smiled wickedly. "I see," he said before unholstering a pistol on his side and shooting the younger boy in the head, his blood splattering on the wall behind him. "Take his! Sixty seconds!" the officer demanded.

"Jesus Christ," Emmett mumbled. "Don't let it get to you. Tune it out."

The older man was in a panic, trying to put his son's head back together in a desperate fit of shock and sorrow.

"Twenty!" the officer said moments later.

The man didn't care; he was still holding the warm corpse of his son close to him.

"Ten," the officer said.

Still nothing. The screams and yells coming from the man kept coming. And then they stopped as a bullet pierced his skull. Father and son lay there motionless, intertwined with each other in death.

The officer walked over to Emmett and me. "Congratulations!" he said with sadistic glee. We remained silent. "Happy! Celebrate! Clap!" the officer instructed. Emmett and I looked to each other and obeyed. "That's enough!" the officer barked suddenly. "This way, come."

We followed the German officer through a back door of the church and into the yard. The space itself was a wide-open plot of shin-high browning grass, about the same size of a high school football field. No doubt, the fences surrounding it were placed there deliberately to keep people inside. I looked back toward the building; on top stood two German soldiers keeping watch over the prisoners like wardens. Prisoners dragged their feet as they walked around helplessly. Most of them looked like they could drop dead at any second from malnourishment, while those who may have looked physically stronger didn't look as if they were in any better condition mentally.

I looked over at Emmett and noticed the number on a patch sewn onto the left side of his shirt. He was number 184, and I was 166.

Off to the left, I could make out a large ditch dug into the ground, several feet in length and depth. A thick cloud of flies and gnats swarmed over it. I didn't have to look closely to know it was a mass grave.

"How's that leg, boy?" I heard a voice from behind me say. It was Willard; I couldn't forget that voice, despite how hard I wanted to. I took a moment to collect my composure, then turned around to face him.

"What? Cat got your tongue, boy?" Willard asked.

"What did you do with her?" I said, my voice evenly measured but still threatening.

"It ain't what *I* did with her that matters now. It's what *someone else* is doing to her."

The Nazi officer noticed us talking. "Friend of yours?" he sneered.

My face was beet red with rage. Emmett must have noticed; he positioned himself beside me to give me a quiet word of advice. "I ain't trying to die today, and neither should you. That girl of yours ain't gonna make it if she ain't got no help. *Calm down.*"

Willard laughed at Emmett's advice, giving me the once over and smirking. "It's over—you lost," he said to me.

The officer instructed Willard to show us our living space and left to return to the church.

"This way, pissants," Willard said as we trailed behind him. "Here." He stopped in front of a poorly built shack and looked at Emmett. "What skills do you have, Negro?"

"I was in the Navy during the first war," Emmett said.

"Good. I'll tell the boss you can keep inventory," Willard replied before looking at me. "And you, I don't give a shit what a useless worm like you can do."

"Oh, but you care what I've done," I retorted.

Willard's cockiness dissolved into fury. "That smart mouth isn't going to help you. When the day comes and we put you down like the dog you are, I'll be the one behind the trigger. Just like that old whore back at the house. You'll be digging those ditches over there until your hands are nothing more than raw meat over bone, and then you'll be buried in the same hole you helped dig, boy."

I stared at him, trying not to look threatened.

"Breaking you down is going to be fun, I can tell. Now get inside, and get what rest you can. You'll need it for the morning," Willard rasped.

Emmett and I walked up the shoddy steps leading to the shack. What we saw inside was dismal.

Had there not been a poorly cut hole in the door used as a half-assed window, there wouldn't have been any light at all, and the smell was like nothing I had ever experienced. Four other men lay across the floor, their bodies covered in blisters that told of being brutalized and overworked. I wasn't sure if they were even alive. *Maybe that's what the smell is: death*, I thought. The floors were filthy, and a large pile of feces and other bodily fluids infested with maggots and flies occupied the far-most corner.

The facial expressions of the men in the room—I had never seen anything like it. All of them looked as if they would welcome death as a mercy, each of them clearly starved and so weak that every breath was a struggle.

Emmett took a seat against the wall, as far away as he could be from the other men inside the cramped shack. "I'm not gonna die here," he said as I sat on the floor next to him.

"What do we do?" I asked, hoping he had some kind of plan.

He looked around the room at the four men who still hadn't moved an inch since we'd walked inside. "I don't know, but we have to do something before we end up like them," he said.

"How did you get here?" I asked Emmett.

"We were trying to make it to Cincinnati. A caravan I was a part of from Indianapolis traveled here on foot. We got intercepted by the Nazis about halfway through. We fought the best we could. Some of us got away, and some of us were killed. I wasn't lucky enough to have either one happen," Emmett said. "What about you?"

"We were hiding just outside of Cleveland. Me and my parents. Dad didn't make it. Mom and I went out, found an old farmhouse, and stayed with the old woman and the girl there—Hazel. You've heard me say her name. We were getting ready to leave when Willard caught up to us."

"It all comes back to that prick, don't it?" Emmett asked. He turned his head to look at the malnourished beings sharing the room with us. "We can't end up like them. I hate to say it, but our roommates over there ain't gonna last another week."

"What do we do? We can't just try our luck with killing those guards out there. It's suicide!" I said more loudly than I'd intended.

I heard a sharp rap on the front door. "Pipe down in there!" a voice said in perfect English. A voice I had heard before, many, many times. A voice that was once comforting to me. I was confused as to why I was hearing it then.

I stood and looked through the makeshift window. "Riley!" I exclaimed in shock.

The uniformed soldier who was walking away stopped to turn around slowly, and I found myself looking into the eyes of my best friend.

Riley made sure nobody was looking and then jogged back to the shack. "Brodsky! What the hell are you doing here?" he whispered.

"I'm on vacation, you dumbass! What's it look like?" I retorted.

"I thought you were a goner!" Riley said.

"Not yet, but I will be if I stay here. I need your help. I need it now more than ever!" I begged.

Riley stepped back from the window. "I'm sorry," he said regretfully. "I can't . . ."

"You *can't*? What the hell do you mean, you *can't*?" I demanded.

"I mean . . . I'm not much better off than you. They have my mom, Clint. They said if I work and follow instruction, they won't kill her. You understand, I'm only trying to do right," Riley said heavily, obviously feeling immense guilt from what he was doing.

"Do *right*?" I spat.

"Do you think I *want* to do this?" Riley shouted, glancing around in worry that his outburst had been noticed.

"This ain't like old times, man. I'm sorry. Things change. We can't just be kids from Mayfield anymore. I hope one day you'll understand," Riley said more quietly before walking off.

"You backstabbing asshole! How could you let this happen?" I screamed from the window as Riley kept walking away from me, ignoring my words. "Goddammit!" I shouted, going back to reclaim my seat on the floor near Emmett.

"You seem to know a lot of folks in here," he remarked.

I shook my head. "I used to know him. He used to be my best friend. But that guy parading around with a swastika on his shoulder? I don't know him."

Emmett chuckled. "Sometimes we can't be who we really are. Only what we have to be to see another day."

Emmett's words resonated. They echoed, in a way, what Willard had said, but he was too much of a lost cause for me to truly understand what it meant. I only wished I had realized it sooner.

If I wanted to get out of that place, that hellhole, I'd eventually have to do it.

I'd have to go too far left.

CHAPTER 16

"Rise and shine!" Willard's scratchy voice said from the doorway of our shack.

The sun had just begun to rise, and the misty morning air had yet to settle.

A German soldier grabbed Emmett by the arm, and the look he gave me warned me to keep my anger in check while he was gone. After he'd been pulled outside, Emmett was escorted and followed by armed soldiers who would take him to his assigned duties.

Willard pointed at me. "Get up!" he commanded.

I reluctantly followed him to a large ditch several feet away from the shack.

"Hope it was worth it, boy. Welcome to the first of your last days on this earth!" he crowed.

"Let her go, Willard. This doesn't involve her," I said without preamble.

"Jesus Christ, you sure know how to beat a dead horse, don't you?" he asked, turning to give me a condescending look before laughing in my face. "Didn't get much sleep last night, huh?" he asked. "You look like hell—not that your scrawny ass looked too great to begin with." Willard turned around and resumed the walk to wherever we were going.

I stood in front of it before long. Dozens of naked, decaying bodies filled a large hole to the ridge. Some looked like recent additions, while others had varying degrees of rot. I could see decomposed flesh cracked and separated from skulls and bone, bluish-gray-pigmented skin, and bacteria-ridden stomachs that were bloated while still attached to their skeletal structures. Maggots crawled through a playground of empty eye sockets, gaping mouths, and skulls riddled with bullet holes. The number of flies was incalculable, and it sent a chill down my spine to know that I might have been wearing the clothes of one of the bodies inside that hole—someone else who had once been number 166.

Willard handed me a shovel and gestured to a large pile of fill dirt. "Cover it up. Better be done by nightfall."

"Or what? You'll kill me? That a threat or promise?" I asked.

Willard opened his eyes wide in mock shock. "Trying to be a tough guy, huh? Trying to make me think I don't scare you?"

"What's left to be scared of?" I asked.

"You can stop with the charade, boy. I can see it, them legs of yours, shaking like a drunk in front of a judge. Your fear stinks from a mile away," Willard scoffed.

"You know the funniest part about all this?" I asked. "The Germans don't give a damn about you. You parade around like you're some big shot, but all you are is a demented, bigoted joke. And as soon as you outlive your purpose, you'll be in that hole, too."

Willard smiled crookedly and walked off the way he'd come. "I'll be back to check on that hole, boy," he said over his shoulder.

I'm not sure how long it took me to cover that grave. Wasn't too long, though, before I started to feel the first layer of skin rub off of my fingers and palms from the friction of the wooden shovel handle. Muscle fatigue had set into my shoulders, and with each scoop of dirt, lifting the shovel got increasingly more difficult. And the smell was indescribable. I threw up seven times while digging, though I had nothing more than stomach acid to vomit by then. It burned my nostrils and throat, leaving a sour taste in my mouth, and my shirt collar and sleeve were eventually soaked in it as I wiped my lips to rid them of the residue. Adding to my misery, my leg was still sore and made itself the most troublesome when I had to rise after repetitive bending over my task. I could feel the warmth of blood trickling out of me as my wound ripped open more and more with the extension of my legs.

A dark shadow was cast over me in the setting sun as I was finishing up the job. "I need to talk to you," Riley said quietly.

I turned around wearily, sweat and dirt soaking my clothes and skin. "Why don't you learn German so you can talk to your friends?" I asked.

"You don't understand," Riley insisted, taking the shovel from my hand and placing it on the ground.

"Who says they're keeping their word? You always used your dick to do all your thinking, but I know you have a brain up there somewhere!" I said. "Do you really trust goddamned Nazis with your mother's life?"

"No, but what other choice do I have?" Riley countered.

I sighed. "You always—"

"Stop!" Riley interrupted. "After all that's happened, you're still going to believe that goody-two-shoes bullshit?" he asked. "Get a grip, Clint! Realize that we don't have an option! There's only one way to do things, and that way often causes us to become something we never imagined."

"Your father made the right choice. Not you," I said.

"*My father?*" Riley snapped, the bitterness clear in his voice. "*My father* left us because he didn't want anything to do with his family."

"What are you talking about?" I asked in confusion.

"The man was drunk from the minute he woke up to the time he went to sleep. And if he couldn't drink, he'd put his hands on us!" Riley said. "Here's a little secret, Clint: I hate sports! I only played them because it was easier to explain the bruises. But he's a hero because he put on a uniform, right? No, he left us because he hated us and hated his responsibility. And here I am on the other side of the fence just to protect the same woman he walked out on!" Riley calmed himself down, realizing he might be drawing attention. "*American hero.* A man who goes into battle to fight and defend, right? But what about the American *husband*? The American *father*? Isn't that just as important?"

"I'm sorry, Riley," I said. "But I've known you since we were in the first grade. This isn't you."

"I know it isn't. I've had to do some horrible things, Clint. But I have to protect her—*he* never did," Riley replied.

"I know how that feels. All too well."

"Come with me," Riley said, following me back to my shack to give the appearance that nothing was out of the ordinary. "How are your folks doing? You know, despite everything."

"Mom is running. I don't know where she is. And Dad's dead," I replied matter-of-factly.

"Oh, shit, I'm so sorry."

"It's fine. The baby was born—a little girl. She's with Mom."

"No kidding? Congrats on that," Riley said.

"Thanks. Can I ask you something?" I asked.

"Go ahead. Make it quick, though; can't be seen talking together for too long," Riley said.

"What do you know about Willard?" I asked.

"He's a real piece of shit, the type even the Nazis think is messed up. But he's devious, and as long as he can get more bodies in here, they put up with him," Riley said.

"All of these people suffering. He brought them here?" I asked.

"No, but he sure found a lot of them. They started out just killing them the first few days; then we put this shithole together. After a while, the amount of people wore thin, and then they found Willard. It was actually his idea to manipulate those poor people, sick bastard. He gets to know where they're either living or hiding, and then leads the Krauts to them," Riley said. "And you know what else? Those bodies with the bullet holes in their heads? He did some of that. Almost like he gets his rocks off on putting his own down. The more he did it, the more he realized how powerful it felt."

"And what about the other camp? The one the children and women are sent to?" I asked.

Riley took a second to respond, as if he didn't want to talk about what went on there. "You don't want to know."

"Riley . . . *tell* me," I insisted.

"I'm not sure who has it worse over there, the children or the women. But I do know it's a hotter level of hell than even this place. The kids, the ones old enough, do labor a lot like the people here do. Only difference is they're expecting the same output from a ten-year-old as they are from a twenty-year-old. And the consequences for failure are the same. The younger kids, they get experimented on—testing new drugs, mainly—for no other reason than to see if it won't cause a reaction. They seem real interested in modifying physical strength or pain thresholds. Most of their little bodies can't take it for long, and they die. The ones unfortunate enough to live suffer until they die, too. The sick, they're just starved to death—the easiest and least complicated outcome in a place like that. And the women—the ones they like, the ones that catch their eye—they're used as service girls against their will. Knowing my mom's in there, it's not something I like to think about," Riley admitted.

"I have someone in that camp. I met a girl; her name is Hazel."

"I'm so sorry, Clint," Riley said, sounding genuine.

"She's the most beautiful girl in the world, and I have to help her," I replied.

"If she's as pretty as you say, then . . ."

"I know, Riley," I snapped.

"I wasn't trying to be an asshole about it. I was just saying," Riley replied.

"I know that, too. Let's not talk about it."

Riley looked up to the rooftop watchpoint, at the armed guards atop it, as we approached my shack. "We'll talk more later," he said, looking slightly worried. "But we can't let anybody know we go way back."

I nodded and stepped inside as Riley walked away, carrying on with his normal duties.

Emmett was already waiting for me; I nearly tripped over his extended legs in the darkness. "Watch your step, pal," he said.

"Was it bad?" I asked.

"Wasn't fun, but—no offense—I wouldn't trade it for your job," he replied.

I squinted to see if anyone else was in the shack with us. I could only count the silhouettes of two other people inside.

"Two of 'em passed today. This little shack suddenly feels a lot bigger. Gotta think of something quick. Hey . . . by any chance, you get fed today?" Emmett asked.

"No," I said. "You?"

"They gave me half a cup of tomato soup—pretty much just red water," Emmett replied.

"We're going to end up like them, aren't we?" I asked.

"No. Ain't gonna happen," Emmett said. "I've seen too much shit to go out like this."

"You got a family?" I asked.

"No; not by blood, at least. My mom died in childbirth with me. Grew up an only kid with my dad. Saw him get shot to death a while back."

"I lost my dad, too," I said. "I know how that feels. These Nazis took everything, huh?"

Emmett chuckled. "Wasn't Nazis, pal. Not in my case. Dad's car broke down in a part of town he didn't know. Went up to a house to ask for help, and they shot him dead cold 'cause they felt threatened. If you ask me, it's 'cause they didn't like our kind," Emmett confessed.

"I'm sorry. I'm sorry you had to go through that," I said.

"It's all right. Motherfuckers never loved a nigger anyway, huh? I was sixteen years old when I watched my dad get shot down from the back seat of that car. Lived on my own for two years before I joined the military as a way out, eating out of garbage cans, sleeping on benches . . . You get the picture. Lived most of my later years in Indianapolis, usually kept to myself. Didn't trust anyone after what I saw happen to my old man. Couldn't afford much of a place to stay, though. Nobody wants to hire a black man if they don't got to, so I usually found myself doing odd jobs to get some cash. Mowing lawns, painting fences. That kind of shit. My neighbor, his name is Murphy. A white boy like you. It was actually his idea to get that caravan started. And he always saw me for a man instead of a subhuman. Best friend a guy like me could've asked for. Closest thing to family I had.

"And you, what's your story?" Emmett asked.

"A lot better than yours. Lived a cozy life with both of my parents. Dad was a steelworker; Mom stayed home. The American dream, pretty much. Now it's a nightmare. Only three things I live for now, three women who mean everything to me: my mom, my baby sister, and Hazel," I said.

"That's good," Emmett replied.

"How is that good?" I asked curiously.

"'Cause you still got something worth fightin' for. All these others in here with us? They gave up long ago. We ain't gonna die here; this ain't the last chapter for either of us," Emmett said.

"What keeps *you* going?" I asked.

"What keeps me chuggin' along is the fact I refuse to let some fascist fuck kill me. I ain't goin' out like that. Not in this lifetime. And think about it: What are the odds that me and you meet up here on the same day, and your best friend is an insider? All this? These are the ties that bind us together. There's a way outta here. We just gotta find out what it is before it's too late," Emmett said.

I nodded. "I'll follow you, but on one condition," I said.

"What's that?" Emmett asked with a yawn.

I lay down on my side with the intent of getting what rest I could. I stared out the window at the stars above, noticing Dad's star had returned, before facing Emmett. "When we get out of here, if it comes down to it, don't kill Willard." I paused for a moment, taking one more glance at that star. It served as a reminder of the man I'd known and how he would have wanted me to do whatever it took to escape that nightmare. I lay my head on the floor again and said, "I want to be the one who does it," before nodding off.

When the front door of our shack banged open hours later, we were commanded to wake up for work. They took Emmett first again, and then Willard made yet another unwelcomed visit to escort me. The entire time I followed, my mind savored the idea of murdering him right where he stood. The only thing that held me back was that I knew I'd have sealed my own fate in seconds.

"You did such a good job filling that hole in yesterday, I put in a good word for you to do it again today," Willard said.

We were standing about thirty feet to the right of the first freshly covered grave, and I looked down to see half a dozen bodies, naked and carelessly thrown on top of one another in a tangled mass. The body on top was one of the men who had been in my shack two nights before; his eyes were still open. He looked much the same in death as he had while he'd been "alive." I began to feel choked up as I came to the realization that I was about to bury someone I'd shared quarters with.

"What's the matter, boy? See a friend?" Willard said with a sneer.

I closed my eyes, fighting against the wave of anger that washed over me.

"Aw, ain't that nice!" Willard laughed.

I opened my eyes to see him reach down to grab the man's right hand and mimic a wave with it. "Hey there, it's me! Your friend!" he said in a childish voice, flailing the arm through the air. "Enjoy your time here in camp. I know I did! I was a fat slob when I first showed up, but look at me now! I got my girlish figure back!"

I looked away and huffed under my breath as my blood began to boil.

Willard let go of the corpse's arm and asked, "Why do you keep looking away? Don't wanna look at him? Something bothering you?"

"If you want me to dig your hole, leave me be and let me do it," I replied.

"I'm just makin' this as enjoyable as I can, boy," Willard said as he unholstered the same pistol he'd used to murder Beverly and aimed it at the dead man's head. "And you obviously don't want to look at him," Willard said with a disgusting grin.

"What's the point of this, you sick son of a bitch?" I asked.

"I'm just trying to be a good host, is all," Willard said before he pulled the trigger. "Wow! That was way messier than that old bitch at the house, huh?"

I bit back my response.

Willard thrust a shovel into my chest. "*Dig.* And if I don't like the hole, you'll be the first one buried in it." Then he walked away.

"I can't wait for the day to come, Willard," I said, and he stopped in his tracks.

Willard turned to face me. "Did you say something?" he challenged.

"I'm not going to let you get away with this. Beverly, Hazel, and wherever my mom and sister are," I replied. "You'll pay."

"And how you gonna manage *that*?" Willard asked, clearly amused.

"I'm going to do what I should've done the minute I laid eyes on you," I said. "I'm going to put a bullet through your skull."

Willard laughed. "You really think you got a chance, boy? Pathetic," he replied. "You and all the other empty shells wearing them stripes are done. Quicker you realize that, the better. We are the vultures, and you and all the other weaklings here are nothing more than the roadkill we feast on. Now, get to digging—or I may have to pay the other camp a little visit."

Willard left, and I walked toward the pile of bodies, breaking ground with the shovel a few feet away. It was nearly impossible to force the spade into the ground with my foot, so spent were my muscles from the day before. A sharp pain traveled through my body as I used all that was left in me to pull through. My arms, shoulders, and legs felt as if they had just gone ten rounds with a boxer. The deeper I dug the hole, the dizzier I became. Lack of food, water, and sleep were winning the fight against my own sense of determination.

By the end of the day, I could barely see. Not because of a lack of sunlight, but because I was starting to see black spots floating in and out of my line of sight from fatigue, dehydration, and hunger. The last thing I wanted was to pass out in a grave.

"Hey, Clint," I heard Riley's voice say.

I turned to see him standing at the edge of the hole, just above my head.

Riley squatted down just enough to hand me a small brown paper bag. "Take this. It's all I can do right now. Bury the evidence when you're done."

I opened the bag to find half a canteen of water and some type of cherry-jam-filled pastry. If I had to compare it to anything, it'd be a doughnut, but there was something different about it that I couldn't quite put my finger on.

"Don't eat it too fast or you'll just throw it up," Riley said. "Been there, done that."

I took Riley's advice and very slowly ate the first meal I'd had since I arrived in camp, using the water I had to help wash it down.

"You look like shit, you know," Riley said.

I looked down to see the white of my clothes had gone almost entirely brown from dirt. "How deep does this thing need to be?" I asked.

"Looks like you're at about six deep and ten wide right now. That should be good enough for a while."

I nodded and made a small hole at the bottom of the grave to bury my trash. I stretched a hand up to Riley, gesturing for him to help me out of the hole.

"I can't be seen helping you. Not even out of a hole. I'm sorry," Riley said.

I sighed, placed the palms of my hands on the dirt around the hole, and pulled myself up with the last ounce of energy I had, grunting my way to the surface. I lay flat on my stomach as I pushed myself up to my feet, wincing from the tenderness of my torn muscles. I got on my knees and pushed the bodies into the hole one by one, trying not to pay attention to the sounds the bodies made as they fell to the bottom.

"I gotta go now. Follow my lead from here on out," Riley said.

"Being a little vague, aren't you?" I asked, wiping the beaded sweat from my brow.

"Trust me. Just trust me," Riley said. "And, by the way, sorry."

I looked at him with confusion. "Sorry for what?"

Riley made a fist and punched me in the stomach, knocking the air out of my lungs.

I fell to the ground, "*What the hell?* What the hell was that for?" I panted as I stood up again, desperately trying to catch my breath.

"Can't let 'em know something's going on. Have to make this convincing," he replied.

Two German soldiers were walking toward another shack, catching Riley's notice. "I said you're done here!" he screamed at me. "Now go back to your hut and rot like the pig you are!" The Germans behind him nudged one another and laughed in amusement, then continued on their way.

Riley lowered his voice. "Go back and get some rest. You'll need it all for morning. Just remember, *trust me.*"

I gave a confused nod and limped back to the shack. *What in the world could Riley be planning?* I wondered as I watched two soldiers dispose of the bodies of the other two men from my shack, both of them walking backward with their hands wrapped around pencil-thin wrists, dragging the emaciated bodies on the ground. I sighed and climbed the wobbly, makeshift steps.

Emmett was already inside, in what had become his usual spot. "You see what happened just now?" he asked.

"Yeah. Guess it's just me and you in here now," I replied.

"Till they get someone else to come suffer with us," Emmett said. "You ask your buddy for anything to eat?"

"Didn't have to," I replied. "He gave me something while I was digging."

"Any leftovers?" Emmett asked, sounding hopeful.

"No, but it wasn't much to begin with."

Emmett scoffed, then said, "Well, I guess you needed it more than me, anyway. I ain't the one digging holes."

"What is it that you do, exactly?" I asked, trying to scrape together an escape plan from whatever information I could.

"You heard that asshole; I'm a little inventory bitch," Emmett said with a sarcastic chuckle. "I ration their shit out for them and write down what they have left. It'd be a cake job if it weren't for the fact I'm being starved to death and held in a camp against my will by a group of sick bastards who're lookin' for a reason to whack me. Christ's sakes, they already hate me because I'm colored. What else is new, though, huh?"

"You don't sound like the same guy I talked to last night," I said, surprised by the shift in his outlook.

"Hell, you keep goin' and goin' and goin' some more—almost to a point where you ask yourself why keep goin'? I can't find an answer, but I do know I ain't giving up, so don't think for a second I am. I told you once already, this ain't our final chapter. Not even close."

I nodded. "Riley has a plan, I think."

"Yeah? And what's that?" Emmett asked.

I shook my head and shrugged my shoulders. "I don't have a clue, but he told me to trust him."

"*Trust* him?" Emmett asked. "Look, kid, I know he's your buddy and all, but he's a Nazi now. You really wanna trust him with your life?"

"I would've trusted him with my life before this all happened. He gave me food and water today, and he didn't have to. He's still in there, somewhere under that uniform; he wants to help. I just don't know if he'll risk it," I said.

Emmett lay on his back and stretched across the wooden floor. "I guess we ain't got much of a choice anyway, huh?"

"No, not unless you think they'll let us out if we ask nicely."

Emmett laughed to himself as I lay down on my side a few feet away from him. "Riley said I'd need my rest for tomorrow," I said.

"There's a reason he said that," Emmett replied. "Go ahead, keep me updated what happens tomorrow."

I closed my eyes in nervous anticipation of the morning and went to sleep.

CHAPTER 17

"Why won't you tell me? A hint? Anything?" I said quietly to Riley as I followed close behind him toward the church.

"I would, but knowing you, you'd turn your campy little ass back and dig that hole until you die," Riley said.

"Then why even lead me over here?" I asked.

"Because once you're in those doors, your pride can't get in the way. You ain't got a choice once we're in there. Richter won't allow it," he said.

"Who the hell is Richter?" I asked.

"He's the ring leader here, a general for the SS. The guy you met inside the church when you got here. From what I hear, he used to be an artillery man in his youth, and I guess playing warden here is some kind of promotion."

"So, your plan involves me having a nice chat over tea with this prick?" I asked with hostility.

"And there you go, that stupid pride. I swear, you got it from your father," Riley replied.

"Watch your words," I warned.

"I'll put this gun on the ground and kick your little ass, Clint. I've always been able to kick your ass. Take it easy; I'm trying to help. And this is the only way I know how."

"What exactly is the plan?" I asked as we closed in on the church.

"Everything they want to hear, everything you don't want to say—say it, do it," Riley replied shortly.

"And if I don't?" I asked.

"You die. And I don't think Hazel or your mom would want that."

"I'm still not following you; what is it exactly that I'm doing besides playing nice?" I asked.

Riley shook his head slowly and stopped in his tracks for a brief moment. "Things you'll lose a lot of sleep over," he said.

I looked up to see that the guards watching over the camp were still patrolling the church rooftop, as well as the guards in each of the three towers and the few scattered around the campground itself, making sure all was in order. Realization hit me like a ton of bricks. "I hope you don't mean . . ."

"Yeah, you're going to play Nazi for a while."

We opened the side door into the church and walked into the same lobby Emmett and I had entered through when we'd arrived at the compound. Blood still faintly splattered the wall from when Richter had executed those two poor souls a couple of days ago. We approached the metal door leading to the nave; yet another armed soldier stood guard at the door on the right side.

Riley walked up to the soldier and spoke a single word in German—I wasn't sure what it meant, but I wasn't really interested in picking up the language. The soldier clearly understood, though, for he opened the door to the nave, and we walked in. Twelve wooden pews with blankets and pillows in the seats lined each side of the room beneath the vaulted ceilings; wooden crosses were engraved on the outer side of their frames. It was a large place of worship, complete with a sizeable platform at the farthest wall back. The pale walls were bathed in multicolored light that shone through panels of decorative stained glass, and I could read an oversized display of the Ten Commandments hand-painted on the wall to the right, just in front of the platform.

On the platform was a pulpit, towering high above everything else. Thick maroon curtains were pulled closed behind it. Without a doubt, though, the feature that stood out most was the large sculpture of Christ mounted just in front of the curtains. He hung on his cross, wearing his crown of thorns and pierced by nails through his hands and feet. The attention to detail was incredible. Thin, red streaks of paint flowed in a path from his arms to his shoulders to symbolize blood. His white loincloth had splotches of smeared brown paint to resemble dirt, and his entire torso had several paper-thin blackish-red marks to resemble the lacerations he'd received.

"What now?" I asked Riley as we approached the platform, walking up the steps as the sounds of our feet echoed through the vacant nave.

"Richter will be here in a moment," Riley said. "Have a seat in front of the desk, and remember, don't let your principles get in the way. And, especially, don't let him sense your fear."

"What makes you think I'm afraid?" I asked as I pulled a wooden chair from the writing desk that had been set up on the platform, its legs scraping noisily across the unpolished floor.

"I don't *think* you are. I *know* you are," Riley replied with a slight shake in his own voice.

I took a seat in front of the desk, scanning all that was scattered across it. An unevenly melted white candlestick sat inside a holder, the wilted wick looking spent and hopeless somehow. A dull metal cigarette lighter with a Nazi eagle insignia lay next to it on the desk, along with an ashtray laden with cigarette butts and a small mound of ashes sitting atop a stack of green folders that were overstuffed with documents and papers.

"I'm sorry," Riley whispered as we waited for Richter to make his appearance.

"I know. I guess you're right. Sometimes you don't have a choice," I replied. I turned my head toward the statue of a crucified Christ. I had so much to say to him, so much to ask. Yet, instead of speaking them aloud, I spoke them in my heart. Even there, in that hellhole that had once been a real house of God, I was sure he could hear them.

Forgive me, Father, I prayed. N*ot just for what I've done—and I know I've done enough—but for what I'm about to do. These monsters that patrol this hell—I guess they're your children, too. But what about your other kids? What about me? Hazel? Mom, Dad, Art, Gabe, Beverly, Emmett, and Riley? Do we not count? I know you have the power to end this, reverse this, and yet you don't.* I paused for a moment to rethink my next words. *Father, I'm angry. I'm confused, and you know why. And I know it might be wrong, but I'm either going to kill these monsters or die trying. I have no choice.*

I heard the door open, and I turned my head to see a figure approaching. My heart rate sped up, and sweat began to bead on my forehead. I looked to see Riley saluting Richter, who acknowledged him with a wave of his hand.

"Wipe that look off your face!" Riley instructed in a harsh but faint whisper, seeing the look of disgust and fear twisting my face.

Richter was at the bottom of the steps when I turned to face him again. I tried my best to grasp the gravity of the situation in front of me as I focused on appearing confident. I would need that if I were going to convince him that I could be turned. Richter's feet dragged sluggishly up the steps, almost as if he didn't even want to be there.

Richter pulled out his chair from behind the desk, reaching for a cigarette and his lighter as he sat. He squinted as he let out a drowsy yawn, then clamped his lips around his cigarette and lit it. We all stared at each other in silence for way too long; the discomfort of the encounter was intense.

"Name?" Richter finally asked me in a thick German drawl, yawning again and rubbing his temple.

"Clint Brodsky . . . *sir*," I replied, reluctant to address him formally.

Richter raised an eyebrow and crossed his arms as he sat back in his chair, its front legs almost rising off the floor. He looked away from me and over to Riley. "Brodsky . . . Is he a *Jude*?" he asked.

"No, sir," Riley replied.

Richter fixed me with an evil grin. "Very good. Last thing we need is a Jewish pig among us," he said, his sinister smile morphing into a hateful grimace. "So, this young man tells me you have experience."

I didn't know what the hell he meant by "experience," but I wished Riley had been clearer about what I was there for.

"That's correct . . . sir," I replied nervously, hoping to God he wouldn't question me further.

Richter nodded, sizing me up. He took a deep drag on his cigarette and exhaled the smoke carelessly; it wafted over my face. "Do you know the quickest and most effective way to control a nation?" he asked, finally breaking the silence.

"No, sir," I replied.

"Control its people! Break them down!" Richter shouted, slamming his fist on the desk for emphasis.

I nodded, a fake smile stretched across my face. "And having men like Willard to help find people?" I prompted.

"*Willard*," Richter said, shaking his head. "He's just an old man. An old man who has outlived his purpose. Getting less useful as the days go by. He sees himself as an honorary German." He laughed hollowly. "How wonderful that you have volunteered to be his replacement."

My eyes grew wide as I let Richter's words soak in. *Am I going to have to bring people here? Am I going to have to exterminate these poor souls like insects?* I wondered, sick with regret at having followed Riley into the church. But there was a silver lining. Richter had said that Willard had outlived his purpose. I had to know what that meant.

"So, then, what's going to happen to Willard?" I asked.

Richter looked almost annoyed. "He's just another mouth to feed. Before he showed up with you, he hadn't been of much use in nearly three weeks. Just a loose end. A waste. And Germans *hate* waste," he said.

"So he's going to be killed, then?" I asked.

"Naturally," Richter said, waving his hand in the air as if the decision to take a man's life was just casual small talk. "Do you object?" he asked, suddenly suspicious.

"No," I answered hastily. "Actually, I want to be the one who does it."

Richter leaned forward in his chair and looked me directly in the eyes, his lips stretched in a chill-inducing grin. "*Wunderbar*!" he boomed, looking over to Riley. "You get an extra ration today for a job well done!" he said. "And *you*!" Richter said, looking back to me. "Go with him. You both eat well today." Then he yawned again, rose, and left without another word.

Riley and I headed back to the lobby, and Riley led me through the last door, revealing a stairwell leading to an upper floor used for storage.

"That went better than I expected," I said, breaking the silence.

Riley sighed. "Did it?" he asked.

"I'm still alive, aren't I?" I asked.

Riley stopped walking up the steps and turned to face me. "Do you even know what you said in there?"

"What are you talking about? I said exactly what you told me to say," I replied defensively.

"Look," Riley said, "if you don't think I hate Willard, too, you're dead wrong. But the way you looked in there, the look on your face? That scares me."

"What look?" I asked.

"The same one Richter has when he kills. Clint. You smiled when you said it."

"I'm nothing like him! And besides, that was all an act. Just like you said to do," I said, unconvincing even to myself.

"Yeah, right," Riley replied. "You seem to forget that I've known you like a brother since we were knee-high. You can't trick me like you did Richter. This isn't you, Clint. You're better than they are."

"This is justice, Riley," I replied.

"So I can quit worrying about it now, huh?" Riley said sarcastically. "Justice my ass. This is revenge for you. Admit it, you're hungry for this."

"You can think what you want. But if this is the worst I have to do in order to bust outta here, then I don't see the big deal," I shot back.

Riley laughed mirthlessly. "So naïve. Thinking you're running the home stretch when, really, your lanky ass ain't even seen the first pitch." He scoffed at me and turned around to walk up the steps.

We both remained silent the rest of the way, the tension between us growing thicker as we neared our destination.

Riley opened the door at the top of the stairwell. The room was wide open and resembled a miniature warehouse more than it did the storage room of a church. Boxes upon boxes of food-and-drink rations, rifles, machine guns, and pistols were stockpiled in a corner, with a German soldier watching over them, his back toward the arsenal. At the opposite end of the room was Emmett, a clipboard in hand, counting out the ammunition individually.

"General Richter needs you to patrol outside. I'll take it from here," Riley said to the other soldier keeping watch, who walked hastily outside.

The door slammed shut behind the German as Emmett stood up to address us. "So? What's the deal here?" he asked.

"I wish I knew," I responded, turning to Riley.

"*You*—what *you* need to do is pull your head out of your ass for a minute and forget this obsession you have with killing Willard," Riley said to me.

"You don't understand," I said.

"I understand, Clint," Riley said. "I'm trying to get us out of here, all of us. But we need to be on the same page, so forget your vendetta. Put on the uniform and do as you're told!"

"What's he talking about?" Emmett asked.

"I'm going to be one of them . . . till we get out of here, at least," I said.

"Okay, so you play dress-up. Then what?" Emmett asked.

I shrugged, turning to Riley for some clarification.

Riley walked over to the weapons stash, unlocked the latches of a gray metal storage container, pulled out a German-issued combat knife, and handed it to me. "I got one just like it. We should be out of here before they notice it's gone. You'll be sleeping with me and the rest of the Germans downstairs. We'll wait for the right moment and strike." Riley turned to Emmett. "And you. I overheard Willard say something about your military experience."

Emmett nodded. "That's right. Why?"

"After we take care of things here, we're going to pay the other camp a visit and break my mom out of there," Riley said before looking at me. "Hazel, too." He looked back to Emmett, whose arms were crossed, an interested look on his face as he considered the plan Riley was proposing. "I'd be willing to bet you can handle yourself better than we can if you run into trouble. Your job is to haul ass to Cincinnati and alert the Americans about what's happening here."

"What about the guards on the roof and in the towers?" I asked.

"We've only got one manned at nighttime. The plan, as crazy as it sounds, is to get to the rooftop, take care of the guys up there, and then focus on the tower. We need to make as little noise as possible."

Emmett sighed. "Sounds like suicide."

"It just might be, but what else can we do?" I asked.

Riley shrugged. "Nothing. I stayed up and thought about every little detail before I went to sleep last night, and this seems to be the only way we even have a shot," he said. "Don't let them see you with that knife, Clint. I doubt they trust you enough yet."

Emmett and I agreed to Riley's plan, knowing it was the only chance we had. Time was wearing thin, and the last thing we needed was for Emmett to wither away from starvation to the point that he couldn't fight.

"Here, put this on," Riley said as he handed me a Nazi uniform.

I stuffed the gray shirt into matching pants, cringing at the sight of the swastika on my shoulder. I slipped on a pair of polished black boots and concealed my knife inside one of them, then walked over to a window that lit the dusty old storage room and gave me a vantage point of the camp. I could see Willard parading around like a hotshot, clearly puffed up with delusions of grandeur. But most disturbing to me was what I saw reflected back at me in the window glass, my morals and mental health barely hanging on by a brittle thread. I didn't like the way I looked. I hated it, actually. And that uniform . . . It wasn't some kind of honor to wear the same clothes as those monsters. It was a curse.

But I didn't fear it; I couldn't. So I embraced it, because the only thing I knew for sure was that I was going to fight. All three of us were, even if it meant not playing fair. Killers were quiet, like the night itself. And even though I'd promised Riley I would put my rage behind me, I still knew that Willard would die by my hand. We were going to make them all pay, and I wasn't going to live the rest of my life without Hazel, Mom, or Violet with me.

Riley looked at me one last time. "So, what do you think?"

I turned to face him and said, "That they're going to regret messing with the kids from Mayfield."

CHAPTER 18

G onna be the talk of the town, aren't I?" I asked Riley as the three of us left the church.

I saw blank stares locked onto me, beady eyes sunken into pale sockets whose gazes projected fear, disappointment, and disgust.

"That answer your question?" Emmett asked, noticing the reaction I was receiving.

"Yeah, unfortunately," I replied.

"Better get on back to your shack now!" Riley shouted at Emmett, taking up his role.

"Keep me updated," Emmett whispered to us before he walked away, looking duly obedient.

"So, what is it exactly that I should do?" I asked Riley as we made our rounds through the camp.

"Just play it up and act like you're one of them," Riley replied. "Richter's going to want to show you the other camp, too. He's mighty proud of it."

"You mean the one where—"

"Yeah," Riley interrupted. "The one where they are."

"Will I get a chance to see her? To talk to her?" I asked, overcome with excitement.

"If you don't seem overly interested, yes. But you need to act like you want to see her for other reasons," Riley said.

"What do you mean?" I asked, knowing deep down the answer to my question.

"You know what I mean," Riley said grimly, pausing before he went on. "Hey, Clint?"

"What is it?" I asked.

"If you see my mom in there, let me know how she's doing? All right?"

"Sure, I can do that," I agreed.

"Thanks. It'd mean the world to me," Riley said softly.

"What the hell is this?" I heard a familiar raspy voice shout from behind us. Riley and I turned to see Willard. He was fuming at the sight of me in my new uniform. Riley and I approached him cautiously.

"What does it look like, asshole?" I asked.

"How fucking *cute*. You come in here and think you're just going to make an idiot of me? After you killed my sons? After everything I've done to watch you suffer?"

"Your sons had it coming, Willard. And so do you. The end is closer than you realize," I said calmly.

Willard turned to face Riley. "What the hell is he talking about?" he sneered.

Riley shrugged, looking bored. "That General Richter decided to replace you."

"Bullshit!" Willard screamed. "You think you have what it takes to fill my shoes, boy? You really think you're going to make it in here?"

"I think I already have," I replied. "Look at you. A pathetic old man. Shit, they didn't even think enough of you to give you a uniform."

"Go to hell!" Willard shouted.

"How ironic," I replied. "That's what your son said . . . right before I sliced his throat open and watched him bleed out like the miserable mutt he was."

"This isn't over," Willard threatened through clenched teeth, his face turning a violent shade of red.

"For you, it is," I replied with a sly smile.

"Why don't you go on, old man? You've said enough," Riley said, intervening.

"No. If you're going to end me, don't just talk about it like a coward. Act!" Willard said, reaching for the revolver in his waistband.

"This is your last chance! Go! Don't make us ask again!" Riley shouted.

I saw Richter come through the church door, watching our altercation from a distance. His arms were crossed, and I could swear he was smiling. I locked eyes with him, and he gave me a nod to go ahead with the kill.

"Give me your knife," I said to Riley.

"This isn't you, Clint. Remember what I said," Riley said under his breath.

"He's watching. Even if I didn't want to kill this piece of shit—which I do—I can't show weakness. Remember?"

Riley reluctantly handed me his knife, his hand shaking at what was about to happen. He knew the demons I would have to fight all too well. Willard seemed to realize what I'd said about Richter watching, and he turned his head to look toward the doorway. In that split second, I had my chance.

I reared back and plunged the knife into Willard's side. I could feel his flesh being ripped apart from the blade's impact as I drove it in all the way to the hilt and twisted the blade before pulling it back out. Willard screamed in pain and shock, realizing that he had lost. The look of fear and pain that filled his evil eyes was something I had been longing for since the moment he'd come back to the farmhouse with the Nazis in tow.

Willard reached down to his waistband, fumbling for his pistol again in a last-ditch effort to take me out. But he was too slow. Before he could even react, I drove the knife into his side again, leaving the blade in as I reached down to grab his revolver.

I cocked the hammer back and shot him in the right kneecap, sending a pink mist and fragments of flesh and muscle into the air.

Willard fell to the ground and began dragging himself toward Richter. He seemed to think it was his only choice, but he was turning to the very man who had deemed him expendable. A trail of blood poured from his fresh bullet wound.

I glanced up as I came level with Willard, catching the look Richter gave me. He approved—thrilled to it, even—if the look on his face was anything to go by. I wish I could say I didn't share that thrill, but I did. Willard was as good as dead.

I dug my foot in Willard's back. "Didn't I tell you how this was going to end? A bullet through your head?"

Willard twisted his head to look up at me. "No mercy in there, huh?" he asked, his voice a strange mixture of hope and soullessness.

I laughed harshly. "Mercy for *you*? What's the matter? Don't wanna be a vulture anymore? You think I went too far left?" I spat.

"I forgive you for my boys . . . ," he said weakly.

"That's how it could've been, how it should've been, from the beginning," I replied. "It's good to know you forgive me. But after Beverly, Hazel, my mom? I can't say you've got forgiveness for any of that," I replied.

Willard shut his eyes tightly, knowing I had made my mind up.

Tears formed in the corners of his eyes.

"Rot in hell," I said before bending down to shove the barrel against the back of his head. "Remember when you had this gun pointed at the back of my head at the house? Guess you should've done it," I said before pulling the trigger.

I stood with bone-deep satisfaction, feeling the corners of my mouth stretched to what felt like their limits. When I turned to see Riley, the look on his face was a clear display of fear. Disgust. *Horror*.

"Who *are* you?" he mouthed.

My smile dissolved as I came to understand what I had just done. I looked down at what was left of Willard. He was nothing more than a mangled pile of meat. I stared at the pistol I held in my hand and dropped it to the ground as I realized how far I had fallen, what I'd just become. I fell to my knees, the bloody palms of my hands pressed against my forehead. I turned to face Riley. "I don't know," I moaned. "I don't know who I am."

I had killed this man like an animal, and it had been *my* choice. My own selfish desires had taken priority as I'd made the decision to execute him like a pig in a slaughterhouse. Had I lost my grasp on the person I'd thought I was—the person I'd been raised to be?

This wasn't like our escape plan, quick and silent.

I'd tortured him.

Part of me died then; part of my humanity was gone. It was at that very moment I understood what Richter had meant about breaking people down. He wasn't speaking about enslaving innocent people. He'd been referring to claiming souls, to bringing people into evil and stripping them of their morals. He'd known about my desire to kill Willard, and he had exploited it. That was what this was—a test to break me. And I had failed. I had failed myself, my parents. My Hazel. I was just as evil as them now. And it was all because I'd let my desire for revenge get in the way of who I really was.

A shadow came over me as I stared, unseeing, at the ground, and a gloved hand reached down to help me up. *Richter*. I took hold of his hand and rose to my feet.

"Excellent! I hope you do just as well later tonight!" he said. His eyes widened as he took a closer look at Willard.

"What do you mean, sir?" I asked, confused. He smiled at me without speaking, almost as if he were debating how much he wanted me to know. But I could see now that he'd wanted to see me in action, had wanted to give me the push to exact my revenge. His movements, facial expressions, the emptiness of his eyes . . . Richter was insane. But he was also a genius, and I knew that insanity and intelligence were a dangerous combination. Willard had been the scum of the earth, but he was still just a thug. Richter, on the other hand, was bred for evil.

"Sir?" I asked again.

He snickered. "A bloodthirsty young man like you! An ice-cold machine! You will join me in tonight's execution."

My heart sank as I looked at Riley. He turned away, unwilling to look me in the eyes. That was what he'd been talking about; that was what he'd known would make me lose sleep, what I couldn't live with.

"Who are we executing?" I asked with a shaky voice.

"The weak!" Richter replied like a giddy child. "The ones about to go anyway. I'm sure you'll enjoy it."

"I'm not sure I'm ready for such an honor," I replied, trying to talk my way out of it.

"Nonsense!" he shouted back. "Look around you."

I looked around the camp to see weakened men peeking out of shacks, others frozen in motion with their attention on me in obvious fear.

"See?" Richter boomed. "You've struck terror! And the best way to keep that is to prove that *you* are in charge, that *you* have control!"

I didn't know what else to say besides "Yes, sir."

"Let me show you what else can be yours!" Richter went on.

I followed him back inside the church, then out the front door. Three German personnel vehicles were parked out front, the same type I'd been thrown into the back of when I'd first arrived in camp. Richter opened the driver's door of the vehicle farthest from the church entrance, gesturing for me to sit beside him, and I complied.

Richter pointed to the glove box. "Keys!"

When I opened the compartment, a pistol tumbled out and fell to the floor at my feet. I picked it up from the floorboard, and Richter took notice.

"German weaponry! The finest, *ja*?" he said.

"It is, sir," I replied with a nod.

"It is yours now. No good soldier is complete without a weapon!" Richter said.

"Thank you, sir," I said as the thought of putting a bullet through his head skittered through my mind. All I would have to do was shoot that sick son of a bitch and go find Hazel and make my way to Cincinnati. But I wasn't sure where the other camp even was. I also hadn't a clue about how I'd get Hazel out of there. I couldn't exactly fight my way out—not alone, at least. And what if that weapon wasn't loaded? I couldn't give Richter the opportunity to end me now. Besides, I couldn't leave Riley and Emmett behind; they wouldn't be able to make it out without me. I gave Richter a fake grin as I replaced the gun back in the glove box compartment and handed him the keys to the truck.

"I'll get it later," I explained as he started the engine.

The drive lasted all of ten minutes, mainly limited to Richter's chatter about his accomplishments. But my attention was largely focused on the sights outside of the truck window, which were unlike anything I had ever seen before, once we were past the guarded gate.

That seemed to be a trend: just when I thought I had seen it all, I saw something new. Our surroundings—despite being devoid of all signs of human life—were in pristine condition, and it was nice to see a place evacuated rather than demolished for once. We were in a small town, and other than quaint old houses, there was hardly anything there. A pizza parlor attached to a single gas station, a firehouse, a few storefronts. I did finally recognize where I was, however, with the help of some billboards and signs—a small place known as Lucasville, about a hundred miles from Cincinnati. It was a considerable distance, but it could've been much worse. If Emmett hauled ass, then he might be able to make it with enough time to inform the Americans before Riley and I had to take matters into our own hands.

We made a stop at a supermarket called Scioto County Grocery just outside of town. The market, of course, was vacant—though that vacancy seemed not to be the result of recent events. It looked to have sat empty for years. Thick vines grew up the sides of the building's structure, and FOR LEASE signs and boarded-up windows left no doubt that it had long been abandoned. Perhaps the oversized store had been too much for such a small town to sustain.

There were no fences, no guards. It was as if this were an underground operation that desperately relied on being nondescript.

Richter pulled to a stop and hopped from the driver's seat, leaving me to scramble behind. It was quiet.

"Are we here, sir?" I asked.

He turned to face me. "*Ja*," he said. "What do you think?"

"It doesn't look like much of a camp," I said, confused as I looked around.

Richter let out a cackle, as if he had just been told a great joke. "Camp? Who told you this was a camp?" Richter asked.

"Riley did, sir," I replied.

Richter shook his head in silent amusement.

"Come this way!" he said at last, walking around to the back of the supermarket. There was a large bay door, no doubt used to allow trucks to flow freely in and out and drop off shipments. Next to it was a black metal door with peeling paint. Richter reached into his pocket to fish for a key to unlock the back door as we approached it.

"If this isn't a camp, then what is it, sir?" I asked nervously.

Richter turned to face me again, this time looking more serious. "For the weak, this place is a grave. For the youth, this place is a research facility. And for the women, in order to spread the German bloodline, this place is a brothel."

I stared daggers into Richter's back as he turned around again to focus his attention on the door. It opened, and we were in a large, spacious stockroom. Wooden pallets and various expired goods were neatly stacked and shelved around us, with a single German army truck parked inside the space, as well. Two German soldiers on the other end of the room slept with rifles at the ready atop makeshift mattresses consisting of stacked bags of dog food, with sleeping bags covering them.

Coming from behind the stockroom doors, I could hear cries, screams, and shouts that bled together in one looping, unintelligible noise. I couldn't define any of it, but I knew Hazel was in there.

I knew I wasn't going to like what I saw on the other side of those walls.

I knew that those walls were built for evil.

CHAPTER 19

I closed my eyes tightly and braced myself for whatever might lie ahead as Richter unlocked the door to the sales floor. Then I heard the heavy door squeak open as a wave of gut-wrenching noise washed over me.

When I opened my eyes, I saw about a dozen women sitting in a tightly packed circle at the center of the store, like sardines in a tin can. Their faces were caked in filth layered over bruises. My eyes scanned the mass of hopeless souls, looking for the one who mattered to me most, and on the far left side, I caught a glimpse of blonde hair.

Hazel! I wanted to scream out for her; I wanted her to notice me, but I was wearing the Nazi uniform now, and I wasn't sure if Richter knew of my connection to Hazel. Until I figured out a way to get through this, I'd have to act like I didn't know anyone or anything.

"This way," Richter said to me as he began to walk the perimeter. "Isn't it beautiful?" he asked, gesturing to our surroundings as we made our rounds.

I was caught in an emotional battle during the entire tour, keeping my facial expressions in check, forcing smiles and frowns and furrowed eyebrows. Richter watched me carefully all the while.

"It's astounding!" I said.

He nodded and looked around again, marveling at his own creation.

My back was toward a men's restroom door as I followed his gaze. The store was lit by only three fluorescent lights across the ceiling. The other four were either dead or flickered as if they were nearly spent. Apart from Richter, I counted six other armed German soldiers inside the market—one in each corner of the store and the two sleeping in storage. If Riley, Emmett, and I executed our plan with absolute perfection, then this should be a walk in the park—especially with the help Emmett was going to find for us.

I took in every detail I could—the features of the building, the layout, who was where and what they were doing. I needed the most vivid mental image I could form in case Emmett couldn't return with help in time. The layout was simple, with a wide-open, rectangular floor plan. Unfortunately, that meant there weren't many places for Riley and me to take cover, but it also meant that there were just as few places for the Nazis to hide. Apart from the three concrete pillars that provided structural support, it looked to be an open field of play.

Wall dividers and stained white bedsheets separated the rest of the space from the farthest corner of the room. To my eyes, it looked like a makeshift medical clinic. I could only assume that was where they experimented on the children.

"Come, I will show you the rest!" Richter said.

I opened my mouth to respond, but I was suddenly hit from behind by the force of the bathroom door being slung open. I regained my balance as I watched a girl of about my age rushing past to take a position with the other women seated in the middle of the room. She was clearly distraught, her tears making visible tracks in the filth caked on her skin as they streamed down her cheeks. She was soon followed into the room by a German soldier, who nodded to me in wordless greeting, his fingers working his pants zipper and belt back into place. It was obvious what he'd been doing in there to that poor girl.

Nazi bastard number seven, I thought silently.

Richter chuckled to himself. "Boys will be boys, eh?"

I grinned back, nodding in affirmation.

"So, where were we?" Richter asked.

"You were just showing me around some more," I replied with false interest.

"Ah, yes!" Richter replied. "Come. This way!"

"Actually, sir," I said, seeing Hazel now sitting in the middle of the room, her eyes focused directly on the ground and her legs tucked closely to her chest. I pointed to her as my words caught in my throat. "I'd like a turn with that one."

"Ah!" he said with a wink. "Good choice. She's very popular, if you know what I mean."

I could barely contain my anger, but I managed to force another smile.

"Go inside! She will come in just a moment," Richter instructed, nodding to the bathroom.

"Yes, sir," I replied, walking into the men's room in anticipation of the reunion I longed for. I stood against the wall farthest from the door. One urinal, one stall, and one sink lined one side of the room, while the other side was an open space. Despite all the horrible things that I knew had gone on in there, it was considerably cleaner than the rest of that shithole, though I doubted that the plumbing was functional.

Suddenly, the door creaked open and Hazel was shoved into the room. She hadn't looked at me yet—she was far too busy yelling at the guard who had thrown her in.

"I'm not going to do it anymore! You hear me? You'll regret this! I have people looking for me!" Hazel screamed at the top of her lungs, giving the door several punches and kicks to emphasize her words. Had it not been for her petite stature, she might have ripped the door off its hinges with her bare hands.

"He's already found you," I said quietly from behind her.

Recognizing my voice, she turned her head slowly to face me. She ran clumsily to me with open arms, nearly tripping on her own feet. "How did you find me?" she sobbed as she clung to me in a hug so tight that my arms were pinned to my sides. Her face was buried into my chest, and I could feel the warmth of her tears soaking through my clothes.

I leaned down and kissed her head gently, returning her embrace. "It's okay. You're going to be okay," I soothed.

"The things they're doing to us, Clint," Hazel said, her voice muffled by my chest. "I don't know if I can take it anymore."

"You won't have to. Before you know it, it'll all be over," I replied, trying to sound confident.

"I'm so scared . . . so, so scared," she said.

"I know, but I promise you'll make it out. I'm coming for you," I murmured.

"I've missed you so much—and I was so worried that you were gone," Hazel said as she lifted her head from my chest to look into my eyes.

"You should know that I would never give up—especially not on you," I replied.

Hazel smiled at me, and the sight of it made me tear up. It was the most beautiful thing I had ever seen, and it warmed me to my soul. In that instant, I felt safe, and even if it was for just a moment, it took the pain away.

"Why are you dressed like that?" Hazel asked suddenly, finally registering the uniform I was wearing.

"I'm doing whatever it takes to save you," I said, hoping she would understand.

"You're going to end up getting yourself killed, Clint! What are you thinking?" she asked incredulously. "Just go! Just go to safety and forget about me—doing this won't work!"

"*Forget about you?* How in the hell do you expect me to do that?" I asked.

"You can't save the world, Clint! It's over. It was over as soon as Willard killed Mamaw," Hazel said, sounding lost and resigned.

"You don't have to worry about him anymore. He's dead."

"Dead?" Hazel asked, her eyes wide. "Did you . . . ?"

I nodded.

The look on Hazel's face was one of both surprise and relief.

"I'm sorry," I said.

"Don't be. I understand," Hazel replied, sinking her head into my chest again.

"I'll be back in a couple of days, okay? Hang in there," I said.

"What did I just tell you?" she insisted. "Go on, you won't do me any favors by getting yourself killed."

I shook my head, dismissing her words. "It won't be Promised Land without you. Nothing would ever be worth it without you," I replied.

Hazel placed a hand gently on my face. "I'm saying this because I love you," she said.

"And I'm ignoring it because I love you back." I took a breath as I rested my hands upon Hazel's shoulders, looking into her beautiful brown eyes. "One day—one day *soon*—I'll be standing next to some preacher, seeing you in a long, white dress. My mom'll be there, and little Violet can be the flower girl. That's what I'm fighting for."

Hazel turned her head away, wiping tears from her eyes. "That sounds fantastic," she breathed.

"And one day," I continued, "we'll get a cozy house—big one, little one, who cares? It'll be *our* place, a place of our own. Waking up every morning to the birds chirping, rabbits hopping around in the woods. Little rugrats who, I can only hope, favor their mother. A little dog or cat running around . . . It'll be perfect. But it can only be perfect if I have *you*. Understand?"

Hazel nodded, sniffling. "But what if it doesn't work? Whatever it is you have planned? What if you die trying to make that happen?"

"I won't! I have to do this. I got us into this mess; I'm the reason Beverly isn't here and why I don't know where Mom and Violet are," I said regretfully. "I have to make that right."

"You don't need to blame yourself, Clint. You did what most couldn't do in your situation," Hazel insisted.

I nodded, trying to believe her words, and gave her a small smile. "By the way, one day we'll die, but not until we're old and gray, and you'll still be just as beautiful as ever. We've got a whole life ahead of us, and who knows what the future holds? I just need you to trust me." I stopped to run my fingers through Hazel's hair as I leaned in to give her another kiss. "You trust me, don't you?"

She nodded. "Of course I do—and I always will," she said. "But how will I know what to do when you come back? You can't do all this yourself."

"I have a plan, and I have someone to run to Cincinnati and let the army know where you are. I've got help, but when you see me again, stay out of the way and keep yourself safe until it's over. How many people are here, do you know?" I asked.

"Thirteen women and five children," Hazel said.

I looked around at the room. "This should do," I said, trying to estimate how many people the space could hold. "Tell everyone to hide in here, but under no circumstances do you risk yourself. Okay?"

Hazel nodded.

The sound of knocking on the door echoed through the bathroom. "Having fun in there?" I heard Richter ask.

I gave Hazel one last hug. "I love you," I said.

"I love you too, wise guy," she said back, giving me a smile laced with hope.

I let Hazel leave the restroom first, then followed through the door to see Richter giving me a wink. Hazel scurried back to the middle of the room. "Making the most of it, *ja*?" Richter said with a grin.

"Yes, sir," I replied.

Two Germans walked over to the center of the room, slinging their rifles behind their backs as they pulled the corpse of a dead woman from the middle of the huddle. They spoke in German, but I could hear notes of disappointment as one of the men threw her over his shoulder and began to walk outside, leaving the second man behind to reclaim his post.

"What a pity—she was a favorite among the men, too," Richter tut-tutted. "Such is life, *ja*?"

I looked into the lifeless face of the woman as she was being carried out of the building. Her facial structure, her raven-black hair, the small mole to the right of her upper lip—I knew her all too well. *Priscilla Jennings.*

I knew Riley would ask about her when I got back to camp.

But how was I going to break the news? The only thing I could do now was give him the truth. I just hoped Riley could think straight when I told him his mom was dead.

CHAPTER 20

Impressive, isn't it?" Richter asked on our drive back to the church.

"Yes, sir," I said simply, then falling into silence.

"That's it? No questions?" Richter asked, curious. "You must be tired from too much fun."

I smiled despite feeling sick to my stomach. "Why a grocery store?" I asked, playing along.

"Why not?" Richter asked back. "Do you know how many times those American pigs have likely passed by without noticing? Without wondering what is inside?"

I nodded.

"You can't spread the German line, you can't perfect the genes of the youth if you have an army of swine getting in the way," Richter explained. "Work in plain sight. It's genius."

"True," I replied, watching the landscape go by as we drove.

I was silent the rest of the way back, dreading what I would have to tell Riley when I saw him. Thankfully, Richter seemed satisfied to let me sit quietly. He drove on, whistling something I didn't recognize. I had hopes that soon enough that whistle would be silenced.

That brings me to where I am now, sitting in one of the pews in the very back of this church that I can't wait to leave. I toss my empty dinner plate to the side after a filling meal of sauerkraut and bratwurst. I've never cared for the stuff, but beggars can't be choosers.

I look over to Riley as he stands from the pew next to mine, walks toward me, and takes a seat. "Glad you're back, finally," he whispers. "So, did you see my mom in there?"

I take a deep breath before replying. "Yeah," I say, knowing I have no choice but to tell him.

"Well?" he presses, his voice barely a whisper.

I look at him, shaking my head. "I'm so sorry."

Riley leans back into the cushions of the pew. "My entire family . . . gone." Riley pauses. "You know what, though?"

"What?" I ask.

"I don't think I have it in me to be sad anymore. I mean, what she was going through . . . could it really have been any better than death? That anger you had, that rage you took out on Willard—I understand now," he says.

I nod. "You still have family left, Riley," I reply.

He faces me and raises an eyebrow in question.

"We've known each other for eleven years. A lot of memories, am I right?"

Riley snickers. "Yeah, too many to count. And looking back on it, I think you're the reason I was grounded all the time, all that wacky bullshit you had us do."

"*Me?* Whose idea was it to skip school when we were twelve and hang out at the drive-in burger place all day?"

Riley smiles. "Okay, so that one was me. Still can't believe my old man stopped by and caught us."

"Yeah. But at least he didn't make us ride our bikes back

home," I say.

"Hell, I don't think I could've if I'd wanted to—not with the ass-whooping he gave me right in front of everyone," he replies.

"And remember that time we put the fish we'd caught in the lake in Mr. Buchanan's desk?" I ask.

"Hey, that one was *your* idea, pal!" Riley says, his smile and eyes both wide.

"Sure, but I didn't expect you to actually do it!"

"That's your own fault, then, for underestimating me," Riley replies. "And let's not forget the time you—yes, you, goody-two-shoes Clint—wanted to build some janky-ass treehouse with all the boards your dad spent a good ten dollars on the day before. Whose ass got beat then?"

I laugh. "You got me," I say. "My point is, we aren't just friends anymore—we're brothers. We're family." I pause for a moment before looking at Riley again. "I love you, man."

Riley nods, one side of his mouth forming a smile. "Likewise, brother," he replies.

I look at the backs of the German heads sitting several rows in front of me. "Ready?" I ask Riley, my voice hushed now.

"Ready as I'll ever be," he says with a nod.

"This is for my dad, for Beverly . . ." I take another look at Riley. "For your mom . . . It all ends tonight, when they least expect it."

Riley directs his attention past the German troops ahead of us and focuses on the statue of Christ watching over the nave. "Think we should say a prayer or something? You know . . . just in case?" Riley asks.

I chuckle. "There is no 'just in case,' pal. The good guys always win, right? It isn't us who need to say a prayer right now."

"Damn right," Riley replies.

I take a look at Richter sitting at his desk up on the platform, his pen moving quickly over paperwork.

"Leave him for me," Riley mutters under his breath, sounding determined as he follows my gaze.

I nod. "You got it, man." I can almost hear my own bones shaking from the nervousness of what's about to happen, and I can see that Riley is feeling it, too.

Richter rises from his desk, and all activity in the room comes to a halt, blanketing everyone in silence thick with anticipation. He doesn't have to say a word, for everyone knows what is going to happen. Everyone inside follows Richter from the church and into the yard, some looking overcome with excitement, while others look bored.

Riley leans in to whisper in my ear, a whisper so quiet that it's almost inaudible. "Whatever he makes you do, whatever you see, whatever you feel—don't let it break you."

I nod as we both rise from our pew and join the line of soldiers streaming out of the church. Once we're outside, all the guards— Riley and I included—stand with our backs against the wall as we face the shacks, and prisoners scatter about. Richter looks back at me with a wink and a sly grin, then walks over to hand me the pistol he gave me earlier in the day. Making his way back to the front of this long snake of assembled soldiers, Richter pulls his own gun from his holster and fires a shot into the air.

The attention of all the prisoners is captured; they stare at us in horror, knowing what will probably happen next. Richter points to three prisoners, each of whom look weakened past their breaking point. Two are older men, the third much younger—though their ages are hard to gauge, all of them being so frail and brittle. The youngest of the three men has a ghostly white cast to his skin that indicates some type of severe illness. Richter turns and cocks his head at the first few soldiers in line, sending them to do a roundup.

The pleas, the cries, the looks of hopelessness—that shit's getting to me. I glance over at Riley; I can see it bothers him, too. I guess there are some things you never get used to, even if you have to.

"Don't . . . break," Riley mutters quietly from the corner of his mouth.

The first two prisoners give up easily without much of a fight; they know there isn't any hope in resisting or trying to delay the inevitable. The third is trying to squirm and fight back through his bloody coughs. He's weak, though, and a couple of swift punches to the stomach are all that's needed for him to submit.

The three men kneel, with their backs facing us, while the soldiers who rounded them up cover their eyes with handkerchiefs. The yard is loud with the sound of sobbing as the three men await their deaths, and I watch Richter point his pistol at the back of the head of the first man and pull the trigger. The second man lets out a horrible scream of terror and begs to be spared, but he is next. One by one, the three men are shot, and as their bodies fall to the ground, blood pours from their open skulls. Their cries cease, and there is nothing but sickening, deathly silence.

Richter turns his attention to me. "Now it is your turn," he says with an evil smile before glancing at the soldiers who had rounded up the first three prisoners. "Get the Negro!" Richter demands.

"Oh, shit! What now?" Riley whispers frantically to me.

"What happened to not breaking?" I whisper back, nervous.

I watch as the two men run inside Emmett's shack.

"Get the fuck off of me!" I hear Emmett scream as he's dragged out, resisting as much as he can. Emmett breaks one arm free and punches the guard on his left, catching him square in the face. He stumbles to the ground, blood trickling from his nose as he gapes at Emmett in surprise and confusion. The one on his right seems to have it worse, though. Emmett breaks free from his grasp and throws him to the ground, getting on top of him, punching his face relentlessly until it looks like raw hamburger meat.

The soldiers in line all raise their weapons, but Richter waves them off. "No!" Richter says. "We could use some entertainment."

We all continue to watch as Emmett wraps his legs around the soldier from behind, locking him in a chokehold. Screaming in rage, Emmett places his hand on the side of the German's face as the soldier desperately tries to break free, and with one swift yank, Emmett breaks the other man's neck. I can hear the snap from where I stand.

The second soldier reclaims his composure and fires a shot into Emmett's leg using his rifle, and Emmett howls in pain as he fruitlessly attempts to stand. Riley and I look at each other, not saying a word, but both of our faces communicate our lack of knowing what to do. The German slams the butt of his rifle into Emmett's head three times, splitting his forehead open and covering his face with blood. Emmett finally succumbs, and another soldier joins to help drag him to a spot next to the other victims, making him kneel directly in front of me.

"Go on," Richter says to me. "Finish him!"

I pause for a moment, desperately looking for any way out of this. The man in front of me is one of the only two people in this place I can trust, and now it's I who has to end him.

"I said kill him!" Richter screams, his face reddened with impatience.

Taking a deep breath, I walk reluctantly up to Emmett and position my pistol at the back of his head. My hand is shaking uncontrollably, and I know I will never forgive myself for what I am going to do.

"Yes . . . yes . . . ," Richter encourages.

"Go ahead, pal," I hear Emmett say. "I know this ain't you."

I cock the hammer on my pistol.

"Do it!" Richter says.

I glance over at him, and I know what I have to do. Our original plan is shot; we had one chance, and it's now or never. I have to take a stand, a final stand. I move my hand as fast as I can, aim the gun directly at Richter's chest, and pull the trigger.

The gun clicks, but nothing happens.

It's empty.

It was all a test.

Richter lets out a maniacal laugh. "What did I tell all of you?" he shouts, facing the Germans lined up on the wall. Richter raises his pistol again and fires a shot into Emmett's head. He hits the ground in a lifeless thud.

"No!" I scream.

Richter aims his pistol at my torso and fires a bullet into me.

I fall on my back, my vision blurring. I look at my stomach and see blood—so much blood. *My* blood. It pours out of me in a never-ending stream.

"Remember when I said that walls are paper thin?" Richter asks me, his voice and face both shrouded in fury. "These walls, bathroom walls—*all walls*. You must think me stupid!"

Out of the corner of my eye, I can see that Riley's holding back from crying. Richter approaches me and places his gun to my head. The burning pain in my stomach is unbearable, and I know that I'm dying. This one last shot will be almost a mercy.

"No! Don't!" Riley screams suddenly.

Richter looks coldly at him and moves his gun again, firing a shot into his chest. Riley groans in pain as he falls to the ground next to me, a streak of his blood leaving a trail down the wall.

"Riley . . . I'm so . . . so sorry," I mumble through agonizing pain.

Richter grabs me by my hair, drawing me closer to his face as he leans over me. "Repeat after me," he says between gritted teeth. "*Heil Hitler.*"

"Don't!" Riley shouts in pain. "Don't you say it!"

Richter aims his gun at Riley again, keeping hold of my head. "Say it, or he dies. You don't want to lose two friends at once, do you?" he asks with a grin.

"He . . . he . . . ," I force myself to say.

Richter laughs at me again. "Come on, be a good boy and say it."

"He . . . he . . . ," I say.

"It's okay. Our fearless leader doesn't need the praise of a mutt like you, anyway." Richter lets go of my head, sending it falling back to the ground. He unloads another shot into Riley's chest, and the open wounds glisten in the light as he stares at me with a haunting look of shock and confusion, as if he can't believe this is happening to him.

"Ri . . . Riley . . . ," I pant.

"She will die," Richter leans down again to whisper in my ear. "Seven days. I will be back to visit for our weekly supply run. That will be her last day on earth."

"Pl-please . . . ," I beg, knowing it will do no good.

"You're pathetic," Richter sneers. "Your pleading does nothing but prove your weakness." Richter stands and shouts at all of the other prisoners watching. "Let this be an example to never go against German might! Let this show all of you what resistance does!"

I look to my right to see Emmett's lifeless body, the shell of the man who was going to be our way out. I turn to face Riley, wearing that same look of horror on his face, as he coughs up and gags on his own blood. And I look down to my own wound, bleeding endlessly. So much blood.

"Get rid of the bodies!" Richter shouts before walking back inside the church.

I feel two sets of hands grab me, and then I'm carried away. One man has me by my feet; the other, by my arms. My head dangles as I see Riley next to me, being carried to the same fate. Our faces speak our goodbyes.

My vision is going out now, and I see where they're taking me. That hole. They toss me in, and I land on the decomposed body of someone else who probably thought he had a chance. I'm looking up the dirt walls of the grave now, and in the distance, through all of the blur, I can see a vulture perched on the watchtower. He looks hungry. I see Riley's body thrown into the grave, as well. His body lands on mine with a thud, and he's looking at me now.

"Another one of my stupid ideas," he says with a smile, coughing on his blood.

"Stop," I beg him.

"In a hundred years, when they dig us up—they're gonna think we're Nazis," he says, his voice weaker now.

"Shut up. We're not dead yet," I beg of him.

"Couple of kids from Mayfield should've known better. It's the end, brother," Riley says.

Tears well up in my eyes, and I watch as Riley slowly closes his own. A third body is thrown on top of us—Emmett's.

"It's pretty bright, Clint," Riley says. "White, even . . . just like they always say it's going to be."

"Don't . . . don't you die," I mutter, trying to sound commanding.

"I can see her," Riley says. "Hey, Momma . . . hey, Momma! I'm home now . . . I'm home!" he says before his eyes shut completely.

I move my weak hand over to Riley and place it on his back, trying to shake him awake. "Wake up! Wake up . . . please," I beg, but he isn't breathing. They killed him, and I had to watch him die. *I'm so sorry, Riley. I shouldn't have ever gotten you involved.*

It's ironic, isn't it? Back when I was in that cellar, I kept telling myself I wouldn't die in a hole in the ground. Now, I think I just might.

My stomach doesn't hurt as much now. I can barely feel it, actually. I do feel cold, though—really, really cold.

I can see it, too, now. What Riley was talking about. It's fading in, and I can see people in the distance. Sitting at a huge table, waiting for me . . . Looks like there's a turkey with all the fixings sitting in the middle of the table. I inch my way closer, just to see if I know them, and I do. Mom and Dad are there, Hazel, Violet, Emmett, Riley, Beverly, Art, and even Gabe. It's just the way I said this would all end—just the way I pictured it, but somehow even better.

They turn their heads to face me, inviting me in with smiles. I'm gonna walk toward them and join the gathering at the table. I think I finally found my way. I think I finally made it to Promised Land.

I'm getting a little tired, though. I'm not dead yet, so I think I'll just close my eyes for a minute, take a little nap, and see how I feel when I wake up. Think I'll pray tonight before sleep. Should've taken the chance to pray when I was in the church . . .

It isn't very easy to talk right now, so I'll just think it in my head. That's still praying, right?

Now I lay me down to sleep,
I pray the Lord my soul to keep.
If I should die before I wake . . .
I pray the Lord, my soul to take.
Amen.

CHAPTER 21

The light has faded away, and now I'm shrouded in absolute blackness. I can hear screaming . . . gunfire . . . It sounds so real, so haunting. Am I dead? Is this hell? It has to be; I don't think heaven was built for people like me. I can hear footsteps approaching. There's a confusion of injured yelps and shouts and cheers of victory in the background. But what stands out the most to me is the words I'm hearing.

They're all unmistakably in English.

"He's alive! Quick! Pull him out and ask this asshole what we need to know!" a voice says from above. I force my eyes open and see nothing but the thick morning mist. Then I feel strong hands reach down and grab me by the shirt, dragging my body up the side of the hole.

As my vision focuses, I see bodies littered everywhere. Some German, some prisoners, and some that seem civilian. *What could possibly have happened? How long was I out?*

My eyes close again. I need to rest a little more. I don't know who these people are, but if they kill me, at least it'll be quicker than rotting in the ground. As my vision fades out and I lose consciousness again, I can see that they're dragging me just outside the camp and into one of the German transport vehicles. I try my best to understand what's happening, but it seems impossible.

Who are these people? What do they want from me? I wonder as I drift out again.

"He gonna make it?" a man asks in the same voice I heard before.

"I can't answer that. He's lost so much blood," a woman replies.

"We just need to ask this dirtbag a few questions. After that, let him die, for all I care."

"Rise and shine, shit bird," that voice says again, this time to me.

Again, I force my eyes open to see a man standing before me. He looks to be in his late twenties, and he stands tall with a full, muscular frame, and rough patches of stubble along his chiseled jawline.

Judging by my surroundings, I seem to be in a clinic. I see a woman about my mother's age leaving the small exam room, shutting the door behind her. Balled up in a pile near the door is the bloodied soldier's uniform I'd been wearing, and I look down at my now-topless torso. A patch of gauze and medical tape conceal my wound, and the smell of rubbing alcohol and disinfectant lingers in the air.

I look back to the stone-cold stare I'm receiving from the stranger. "Where am I?" I ask.

"You speak English, then, huh? Sounds like you're American. Makes you even worse scum," he sneers, crouching to meet me at eye level. "Where are they?"

"Who? I don't know what you're talking about," I say, genuinely confused.

"Bullshit!" the stranger booms.

"It isn't," I groan.

"Your boss! He fled with his tail between his legs as soon as we invaded the camp. *Where is he?*"

"I want him dead as bad as you do, believe me," I reply, taking in a deep breath to ease the sharp pain in my chest. "I'm not one of them . . . trust me."

"So you were just wearing the uniform, then?" the stranger retorts, grinding and pressing the tip of his thumb into my wound.

I let out a short series of groans and yelps before the stranger releases the pressure from my wound. "I can't answer your questions, so if you're going to kill me . . . please, just do it," I say, panting through the pain. "If I was truly one of them, explain the bullet hole. You think a prisoner did that to me? You think they would allow that to happen?" I ask, feeling overcome with exhaustion.

The stranger stands upright, obviously finding some sense in what I just said. "Go on, then. Keep talking," he demands.

"I was with my people, my family. Long story short, we got captured," I say.

"Where are they now?" the stranger asks.

"My girl—my fiancée—is in the other camp. Rest of them got away. Least, I hope they did," I reply.

"What other camp?" the stranger asks, a dubious look on his face as he bends down again to look me in the eyes.

"An old grocery store in Lucasville. Hell, you might've passed it when you found my camp."

The stranger chuckles condescendingly. "A *grocery* store? You expect me to believe that shit?"

"Think about it," I counter. "Perfect place to hide, where no one would look. Check it for yourself," I say, hoping he believes me.

"Who are you? What's your name?" the stranger asks.

"Clint. What about you?" I respond.

"You don't need to know me," he replies. "Now tell me about your boss."

"He isn't any boss of mine, but his name is Richter," I say. "He's a psycho. Thinks he can control everyone with violence and make the country like another Germany."

"Was it him? Richter? Did he kill the black man?" the stranger asks with an uneasy tone.

"Emmett? Yeah. Richter did it," I answer, wondering why he's so interested.

"You know him by name?" the stranger asks, surprised.

I nod. "He and the other guy in the German uniform inside the hole with me were the only people I could trust. Emmett and I arrived on the same day. We had a plan; things went sour. Why? Did you know him, too?" I ask.

"He was in our group leaving Indianapolis. We hit a fork in the road, and Emmett got captured. He was like a brother to me," the stranger says. "This Richter guy—he has to pay."

"That other guy in the hole, he was my best friend since we were little kids. I want Richter dead as bad as you do. You aren't the only one who's had your brother taken away by him." I pause for a moment and take a long look at the stranger before saying, "You're Murphy. Emmett mentioned you. Said you were the best friend a man like him could've had."

"Yeah . . . that's me," Murphy affirms, finally realizing he can believe me. "So where do you think Richter is?" he asks.

"The only place I can even guess is the other camp I mentioned. Take me with you when you go. I'll help you in any way you need. But I need your help in return."

"With what?" Murphy asks.

"My girl. Her name is Hazel. I need to save her. I promised her she'd make it out."

"I'll consider it," Murphy says noncommittally.

"There isn't any *time* for considering it!" I snap, a surge of sharp pain shooting up my chest. "I know from what Emmett said that you aren't a bad guy, just like I'm not. You just need answers, need a way out of this. We all do, but I've told you everything I can."

Murphy stands up, obviously considering my request. "If you can help us find the place, I'll try my best to get them out. We'll leave in the morning. Get some rest. You'll need it," he says as he turns his back to me, walking out the door. He turns to face me as he stands in the doorway. "If you're lying about any of this, I'm going to put you down. Keep that in mind before you try anything stupid."

In that moment, I find peace in knowing that maybe it all wasn't in vain. Maybe I'll be able to pull through. Though I have to admit, I feel pretty crummy sending someone else to do what I should've been able to do. In the end, though, it doesn't matter—as long as she's safe. As long as we can make it out of this. Murphy seems like a good man. A hard-ass, but a good man. I think our common enemy will prove to be what brings us together in the end. Richter must die. I just hope they get to the camp before it's too late.

I take Murphy's advice, try to get some rest. I close my eyes and slip into the all too familiar darkness again. I've fallen asleep thousands of times before, but my new awareness of the darkness that slumber brings creates a sense of unease in me.

This darkness seems more intense than the deepest black and brings a level of loneliness and helplessness I've never experienced before. All I can visualize, if my eyes close for any more than a simple blink, are things I can never have. Things that fate itself has forbidden me from having—pleasures of the mind, soul, and flesh that have never been meant for me and will haunt me all the way to an inevitably early grave.

Though I see nothing in the darkness, I can hear children laughing, playing, singing. I can hear the words spoken by lovers. I can hear the sounds of nature all around. I can hear everything that has ever been worth hearing. Everything that sounds like *life*.

But why is it so dark?

I feel a sea of guilt drowning me. I don't know why I'm overcome with this guilt all of a sudden, but I have a feeling I'm about to.

The sky is suddenly alight with the glow of a round sphere. It's the moon—too perfect to be the real moon, though. So proportionate, so bright, without even the smallest visible blemish. There's a sound off in the distance, a strange buzzing just loud enough to be heard. I look down at my feet to see them bare, planted firmly on a cobblestone path that is overgrown by weeds. I begin to walk forward, and as I close in on what the light guides me to, I see a small gravestone ahead. I inch toward it, walking closer until I see what it says.

Clint Brodsky

May 2, 1926–May 3, 1943

The day the bombs fell.

I feel chills rush up from my toes to my temples as I realize that I should have died by now. It was my destiny to die.

That buzzing is louder now, loud enough for me to realize that it's voices—voices of the ones I once knew and those I still know.

"I'm ashamed of you! *Murderer!*" I hear Dad hiss.

"You never came back! You let me die!" Hazel shrieks.

"We would have been safe if it weren't for your stupidity!" Mom screams.

"This is all your fault—you had to blow our only chance!" Riley shouts.

"Please! Please stop, I'm sorry!" I plead. "I didn't mean for any of this to happen!" I'm so desperate to make the voices stop, but they keep repeating themselves, over and over. With each word of blame, they get louder and increasingly condemning.

"I take you in as part of our family, and you doom us all," Beverly groans.

"I should've known better than to trust some kid with his head up his ass!" Emmett howls.

"Please, God, make it stop! I'm sorry! It's all my fault, and I'm sorry!" I scream, so loudly I swear I can taste the metallic flavor of my own blood as my vocal chords seem to rip apart in my effort to be heard.

"They heard me," I whisper now as the voices cease to a haunting silence. I look around and see nothing but blackness apart from my own headstone, illuminated by the artificial moonlight. I look again at my burial plot. It's different now; I no longer have a death date inscribed on that stone.

"How does it feel, little reaper?" I hear two deep voices say in unison from behind me. I turn to see the faces I hate the most staring back at me. Richter and Willard, side by side, grotesque grins stretching across their demented faces.

"Haven't I suffered enough?" I demand of them.

"*Suffered? You're* the one who's suffered? What about *them*?" Willard asks with his finger stretched out to point at something behind me.

I turn to face my headstone again. It has company now.

Seven other markers have joined mine to form a perfect line, each inscribed just as mine is. I look down the line and read the birth and death dates of everyone. Mom, Dad, Hazel, Beverly, Violet, Riley, and Emmett. Carved at the bottom of each are words that rip at my soul.

Betrayed in the End

"I'm not a traitor! It isn't my fault!" I scream at Willard and Richter as I turn back to face them.

"Isn't it?" Richter asks.

"Is that what you tell yourself? To sleep at night?" Willard interrupts with a maniacal chuckle. "You're just as evil as we are," he insists. "Was it not enough to kill my boys? You had to go off and kill your own, as well?"

"I'm nothing like you!" I scream at them.

Richter inches closer to me, nearly bumping against my chest. His eyes look down into mine. "Why are you here? Why did you not give up when I threw you into that hole?" he asks.

I stand silent. I have no answer.

"How many have to leave this earth for you to understand that there is no place for you?" he demands.

"You're a liar!" I shout.

Richter leans forward and whispers into my ear, "Your existence is the worst thing that could have ever happened to them."

I press my hands to my eyes, a stream of tears flowing between my fingers. "Leave! Get out of my head!" I demand.

"We'll never leave," Willard says. "We're going to haunt you until you take your last breath. So. How's it feel, little reaper?"

Their laugher grows in intensity and volume, like the devil himself is cackling at my torment. I press my hands harder to my eyes as my knees weaken, my arms and legs go numb.

And then, suddenly, the laughing stops. I drop my hands from my face to look ahead. Nothingness. A pitch-black, empty void. I look down at my hands and see that there's blood everywhere, soaking me from my wrists to my fingertips. I turn to face my tombstone again. And in place of the grave markers are the lifeless bodies of those I love, carelessly tossed atop one another.

"How does it feel, little reaper?" an unfamiliar voice whispers softly into my ear. "How does it feel?" it repeats, over and over and over again.

"Their blood is on your hands," another voice chimes in.

The ground rattles, shakes, and eventually separates as my grave gapes open, moved by a supernatural, otherworldly force.

"It's time," I mumble.

"Yes . . . it's time," the serpent-like voices repeat in my ears.

But I don't want to go in that hole.

"You can't run forever, Clint," the voices whisper.

A force, a power greater than my own will to stay above ground, drags my feet closer to that hole. I try to fight back, but to no avail. I've accepted death's warm embrace; I've accepted that my very existence is not only futile but has an everlasting, negative impact on the ones I tried to keep safe.

My feet are at the edge of my plot, and I feel the weightlessness of my descent. It feels a lot deeper than six feet; it's as if I'm going to be falling forever. And just like that, I stop and look up from the bottom of that hole. Six dark silhouettes stand above me, surrounding my grave, and I hear the high-pitched crying of a seventh off in the distance. Not a single one of the visible six are mourning, and I watch as they drive shovels into the dirt.

They're going to bury me, like I buried them.

The first load of dirt cascades over me as some of the tainted soil finds its way into my eyes and mouth.

"We hate you!" they chant, their individual voices ringing loud and clear.

"We hate you!"

"We hate you!"

"We hate you!"

Over and over again. More dirt falls onto me, and before I know it, it's up to my ankles. Shovelful after shovelful, they won't stop—not until they completely bury me in the earth.

Thunder rips through the night sky, and torrents of rain fall from the heavens, drowning me in thick mud that threatens to swallow me. A flash of lightning illuminates the scene, but for only a split second. They're decomposing, all of them, nothing more than reanimated corpses. Their skin and muscle hang loosely from their bones; maggots and larvae crawl over them like living flesh. Their rotting, blackened teeth are fastened loosely in diseased gums.

"We hate you!"

"We hate you!"

"We hate you!"

They continue to chant, growing louder and louder with each word.

"They're not real! They're not real," I whimper, trying to convince myself. "Please! Leave me! I'm sorry! I'm so sorry! Please! Don't!"

The chanting goes on, never letting up, never showing any mercy.

The mud is up to my neck now, filling the hole with increasing speed.

"Stop! Please!" I scream.

I scream . . .

And scream . . .

And scream until my ears ring, and then I scream some more.

I close my eyes, breathe in until my lungs are full, and let out one more plea.

Suddenly, I wake from my tortured sleep, springing upright in my cot and screaming. Cold sweat drenches my skin as it trickles its way down my chest and back. I'm panting as if I've been running, and crying uncontrollably.

"Make it stop! Please, make it all stop!" I whimper.

"Shh . . . it's okay," a kind voice says as a gentle hand rubs my forearm.

"No . . . it can't possibly be," I murmur in disbelief, turning to face the voice that soothes me. "Mom? Is it you?" I can barely make out her features in the darkness.

As my eyes adjust, I see that it really is her. Violet is asleep in her arms. "It's me, baby . . . it's me," she says as she rubs her gentle hand across the side of my face, a sheen of tears in her eyes.

I swing my legs over the side of the bed, completely ignoring the sharp, aching pain that fills my body, and wrap my arms around her in a tight embrace. "Please don't hate me . . . please don't hate me . . . I'm so sorry," I sob.

Mom places her hand on my back and begins to pat me gently. "It's okay, Clint. I love you. We all do. It's just a bad dream."

"I just try and try," I cry into her shoulder, "but I don't know what to do! I don't know how to protect everyone, no matter how hard I try. You think you're doing the right thing, and you end up losing someone. You decide to do the wrong thing, and you lose a piece of yourself! I can't take it anymore. I can't take it!"

"Would any of them want to see you like this?" Mom asks. "Do you truly believe any of them blame you for what happened? Clint, this isn't your fault. You never asked for this."

"Even if they don't, I blame myself. There's so much I should have done, but I didn't know how . . . ," I say hopelessly.

"We'll make it through this, Clint. Hazel needs you. Violet needs you . . . I need you. And no matter what, we aren't giving up on one another."

"I'm just so happy you and Violet are safe," I say.

"Think of it this way: if you hadn't warned us, we may not have been. You saved us, Clint," she replies.

"I love you, Mom."

"I love you, too, sweetheart."

As I fall back asleep, I remind myself that I made a promise, and if nothing else, I intend to keep it. We have to make it through this.

CHAPTER 22

Rise and shine!" Murphy says.

I open my eyes and yawn to see him extend a hand toward me. I grab it, and he helps pull me up into a seated position. "I'm going to give you the benefit of the doubt and trust you. You knew Emmett, so I'm going to let that vouch for you. But I'll still be watching you."

"No apology, then, huh?" I ask drowsily.

"Don't push your luck," he responds. "How are you holding up? Think you can walk?"

"I don't know. If I can, won't be for too long," I reply.

Murphy nods. "All right. We'll have a chair rolled in here to take you out to the truck."

"What's your plan?" I ask.

"Found a set of keys in the vehicle we took. Only one is a key for a vehicle. We're hoping it was Richter's personal set and that the others fit the doors of this place you've been talking about."

I nod. "Okay. And then what?"

"I guess we'll just hope that we get lucky enough to get in through the back without being seen and have a chance to see what we're dealing with. Then, the plan is to fire away."

I shake my head. "There are too many innocent people in there. It's going to get some of them killed."

"Then what do you suggest we do, kid? Ask them nicely to let everyone go? It's the only option we got, with the walls being boarded up. Can't see a thing through that."

I sigh. "Be careful. Please be careful."

Murphy nods. "We will. But best thing for you to do is lay low and let us handle it. I got a few guys coming along who know how to handle themselves. A couple of cops, a couple of angry old Marine vets. I feel good about our chances."

"So what do you want me to do?" I ask.

"You'll be riding along in the front seat. You'll be our eyes and help us spot the place," Murphy says.

"Okay . . . sure," I reply nervously. I'm torn between emotions, anxious to finally free Hazel and end this nightmare, and fearful that things will go south. With my track record, I'm not all that optimistic that things will run smoothly.

The doorknob turns, and the door slowly swings open. Four men wearing tattered, unwashed clothing walk into my room, all of them differing in age and physique. The two in front have many years on the two at the rear; they give the impression of being experienced and trained in all things war. The first is a larger man who has a hardened look in his eyes. The second wears the same expression. These must be the Marine vets Murphy mentioned, haunted by the memories of combat and tormented by the fact that it's happening again on their turf. Most importantly, however, they look downright pissed and ready for a fight. These old dogs are looking for a reason to take back what's theirs.

The two men in the back—presumably the former cops—are

much younger. Both seem to be in their late twenties, maybe early thirties. Both seem much less rough around the edges, as well, but what they may lack in experience, they make up for by being considerably younger and in better shape. Their faces are cocky and smug, their hair perfectly slicked back despite looking as though they just pulled themselves out of a manhole.

"Nice to meet you," I say to the quartet.

No response from any of them, not the slightest acknowledgement.

Murphy laughs. "Don't worry about them, kid. Just help us find the place, all right?" he says before turning his attention to the four men. "It's okay. He's on the same side we are. Don't be too hard on him."

They nod, and the youngest of them leaves the room.

"Look, kid," Murphy says, turning back to me. "I realize the shit you've been through. I think maybe it's time you get a break."

"It's *been* time," I reply with a slightly bitter laugh.

I open my mouth to ask about my mom but decide against it. I'll see her again soon, and she's safe. The last thing I need is her finding out that I'm going to be in harm's way again. I'll tell her about this someday—maybe tomorrow, even. But right now, I need to rescue Hazel.

"When're we doing this?" I ask as the young man walks back in pushing a wheelchair.

"Looks like now. You ready?" Murphy asks.

"Born ready," I reply.

"Remember, I've got my eyes on you. Don't try anything, and don't try to be a badass. I find out you're crooked, you're done. You mess this up, I've got no promises for what will happen to you. Got it?"

I nod. The wheelchair is rolled right up to my bedside, and I start to climb into it.

"Need any help?" Murphy asks.

"No. I got it," I reply.

Murphy stands behind me and wheels me out the door, following the other four men out of my room. I'm rolled out into a hallway and then into a nondescript lobby with multiple chairs and a dusty, old reception desk. As I'm pushed to the front door, I spot the "borrowed" transport truck sitting in the parking lot through the glass door.

"This is it," Murphy says. "If we pull this off, by nightfall we'll all be free again. Are everyone's weapons ready in the back of the truck like we agreed?"

Two men nod; two say yes.

"If anything happens to us—" the oldest begins.

Murphy interrupts. "Stop. This isn't anything you've never seen before. Gonna take a lot more than this to take you or any of us out."

The oldest man grins. "You always know what to say, Doc," he says.

I turn and look up at Murphy. "'Doc'?" I ask curiously.

"I'm a psychologist. *Was* a psychologist," Murphy says, gesturing toward the oldest man. "Jack here is a patient of mine. A damn good one, too."

"Well, I have a damn good doctor," Jack replies.

"Clint," Murphy says, looking at me, "I'd like to get to know you better, once we make it out. Think it'd do you some good. What do you think?"

"Sounds great . . . Doc."

"I'm glad to hear you say that," Murphy replies. "Everyone else in hiding?" he asks the group of men before me.

"Yeah," one of the younger men says. "I told them to come find the place we'll be at in a couple of hours. We should be done by then,

I figure. I guess they're off somewhere else, keeping themselves occupied right now."

Murphy wheels me out the door and into the parking lot, and as
we approach the truck, the four other men hop in the back. Murphy
opens the passenger door and helps me into the cabin of the truck.
The pain from the wound in my stomach makes me groan. "Are you
good?" he asks.

"Fine," I grunt. "I'll live."

I buckle myself in and lean back, struggling to find a position
that provides some degree of comfort. The driver's door opens, and
Murphy hops in and inserts the keys in the ignition.

"Hey," he says to me, pausing.

"What is it?" I ask.

"Sorry about yesterday. Couldn't take any chances, you know?"

I nod. "I know. Trust me, I understand."

Murphy faces forward. "All right then," he says, turning the key
to start the engine. "Get ready, and stay low. It's showtime."

As we drive down these vacant, dusty roads, I watch out for the
route Richter took during our drive to the store. We pass the church
after four or five minutes, the sight of it flooding me with haunting
memories. Bodies are littered across the plot of land; blood paints the
sides of the shacks and patches of grass.

"What happened to the rest of them?" I ask.

"The guards? We gave them a choice. Something that doesn't
come around too often, it seems. Either come willingly or go down
fighting. Most of them chose door number one. The prisoners—what
was left of them—got transported for medical care." He pauses as we
come to a stop sign. "Right or left?"

I think for a moment before saying, "Right." As we turn right, the
memory of the long, straight road into Lucasville forces itself back

into my mind. "It's about ten minutes or so from here. Just keep going," I say, looking out the window.

"Are you sure?" Murphy asks.

"Yes. What's the matter? Don't you trust me?" I ask back.

Murphy grabs a pistol, this time an American model, from a holster on his belt and hands it to me. I see that the chamber is loaded. "That answer your question?" he asks.

I chuckle to myself. "Thanks," I say.

"Just because you have it doesn't mean you need to use it. That's just to defend yourself on the off chance you need to help us."

"Gee, that's reassuring. Thanks."

"Welcome to Lucasville," a rustic wooden sign in the distance says. Murphy notices it and praises me for my navigation.

"It's at the end of town," I say. "Big grocery store, looks out of place. Yellow paint. Can't miss it."

"You did well, kid. Thanks," Murphy says.

"I'm the one who should be thanking you," I say. "You could've just gone on, but you decided to stick around and save them."

"Don't thank me. Don't need it. If I leave them behind, their blood is on my hands. We look out for one another. It's what *real* Americans do."

Our surroundings come into focus, a tumbleweed town of barren roads and vacant buildings that echo with abandonment.

"You didn't lead us to a ghost town, did you?" Murphy jokes.

"That's why they picked this location, remember? Last place you'd expect."

"Crafty bastards," Murphy mutters under his breath.

I can see the peeling, cracked yellow letters of the grocery's storefront in the distance. "That's it," I say.

"Damn . . . you weren't kidding. That's the last place I'd expect,"

Murphy replies.

He brakes about forty feet away from the back of the store, pulling over to the side of the road. "Engine's loud; best to take this on foot if we want to catch them off guard," Murphy says.

I nod and sink lower into the passenger seat, pistol in hand, preparing myself for any conflict.

My eyes are barely peeking over the dash as Murphy asks, "What in the hell are you doing?" with a raised brow.

"Trying not to get my head blown off, if that's okay with you," I reply.

"You'll be fine. It'll work out. Don't worry," Murphy replies, sounding sure of himself.

I give a short bark of laughter. "Yeah. Nice try, but you're a shrink. You're supposed to say stuff like that."

"Good point. Now that'll be ten dollars," Murphy says dryly.

"Left my wallet at home. Ask me later," I reply.

Murphy grins. "Just sit tight. It'll be over before you know it," he assures me. He opens the truck door carefully, closing it quietly before sneaking around to the back.

It isn't long before I look out the side mirror to see Murphy and the four men armed to the teeth with various types of rifles and submachine guns in their hands and pistols and knives strapped around their waists. Murphy is holding a small black German SMG. I remember hearing some kids at school talk about them from time to time—an MP 40, if I recall correctly. No doubt he picked it up at the church, which makes me think he may not be as experienced in combat as the others—or the guys he's going after, for that matter. But one thing I do know is that he's smarter. I don't need to know this guy's life story to know he's intelligent—just the way he carries himself, the way he can tap into your psyche simply by speaking a sentence. He is a doctor, after all, so I suppose it comes with the job.

All five of them walk silently past the truck and sneak to the back of the building, hugging the walls of the store as closely as they can. The back door isn't visible from where we're parked, but maybe that's for the better. I don't know if I want to see this bloodbath unfold.

I close my eyes as my heart beats itself nearly out of my chest. *Breathe in . . . breathe out* plays over and over in my head as I try to keep my composure as much as I possibly can. I feel so helpless; this is my battle to fight, after all. Why can't I hop out of this truck and help them? I've cheated death so many times now that I feel almost invincible. I take a deep breath, and just like that, I know exactly why I should keep my ass in this truck. A painful reminder shoots from my chest through every inch of my body.

Oh, yeah. That's right: I can barely stand right now, I think.

My heart rate isn't as fast now; I think I've calmed myself down enough to see what's happening. And to my relief, it seems that step one is a success—they've found the right key and have managed to make quick work of the men inside the storage area. The group drag the bodies of two Germans out the back of the store and lay them along the side of the wall, out of sight. From my seat in the truck, I can see that their throats have been slit open, and their entire bodies are drenched in a tide of crimson.

Murphy glances back at me, lifts up his arm, and signals me a thumbs-up from where he stands. I return the gesture.

I'm giving myself a pep talk now. Telling myself that this is it, that before I know it, I'll be with all three of my girls again. I've come so far. I've witnessed some awful shit; I've done some awful shit. But all of those things led me to where I am now, so close to victory I can taste it. To hell with this war; I don't care about that anymore. I just want them back! I want to teach Violet how to ride a bike and make a snow angel. I want to do something young and stupid and be chastened by my mom, to be able to cry on her shoulder when things get rough. I want to start a life with Hazel, to have her be the last thing I see before drifting off at night and the first thing I see when I wake in the morning. I want us to hold each other close.

I want to live. I want *all* of us to live. We've earned it.

Come on, guys! I urge the five fearless men I know inside. *I believe in you, you gritty sons of bitches! We've all lost something in this fight—now show those animals in there how that feels!*

I wait to hear gunshots, to have them ring through this silent sky like a symphony. I want them all killed so that we can move on.

From where I sit, I can hear the faint sounds of shouting. Then the screaming gets louder and louder, so loud that I think it could drown out the sound of gunshots.

And then the first shot echoes through the air. I hear Murphy shout, "Get down!" so clearly that it's like he's sitting right next to me. A barrage of gunfire drowns out every other sound, and I can see birds flying away in a frantic attempt to escape.

I sit with my fingers crossed, hoping it's not too late, hoping that Hazel doesn't have to pay for my mistake. Though the fight seems as if it's gone on for hours, I'm sure it's probably only been a matter of minutes. The sounds of gunshots and shouting are lessening; it feels like it's almost over.

Suddenly the world falls silent again. Sweat trickles down my face as I nervously watch the front door slowly creak open. A line of women and children walk slowly out of the store, and I study them all, one by one, watching and waiting for the one who matters most to me. I pull the handle to the truck door and grit my teeth in pain as my feet meet the pavement. I'm limping over to get a closer look, and then I see her.

My Hazel.

CHAPTER 23

I can't believe this is really happening. We did it! After all we've been through, we've finally woken from this nightmare.

Hazel is just a few dozen steps away, and she breaks into a run. Fighting through the pain, I pick up my own pace and make my way toward her as quickly as my beaten body can. She's so close to me now, and we open our arms to one another, intertwining our bodies like vines on a chain-link fence.

"We did it! We did it!" Hazel cries into my chest.

"We sure did!" I say back through tears of happiness, ignoring the pain. "Told you I'd come back for you."

Hazel pulls back and looks up into my eyes. "What now?" she asks.

"Now? Now we do everything we planned on doing. Go somewhere safe and new, get married, buy a house, and have kids. Our fight is over—now it's time for us to be happy," I say.

She looks up at me with her beautiful brown eyes and that stunning smile and hugs me even tighter, burying her face into my chest again.

I look over to the doorway to see Murphy and the others come out of the building. The two older men are helping one of the younger guys walk; it looks as though he took a pretty nasty shot to the leg.

Murphy approaches Hazel and me, where we stand, still locked in each other's arms. "What happened to staying in the truck, huh?" he asks with a wink.

"Couldn't help myself," I say, grabbing for the pistol tucked in my waistband and handing it to him.

He looks down and acknowledges the weapon. "Keep it, kid. Let it be a souvenir."

"No thanks. I won't be needing it anymore, anyway," I reply, shaking my head.

"Suit yourself," Murphy says, taking the gun and putting it in his holster.

"You find that asshole?" I ask.

Murphy nods. "Sure did."

"I hope you made him pay," I say, gritting my teeth.

"Didn't have to. We found him in the corner of the room, foaming at the mouth. He offed himself before we had the chance to do it," Murphy says.

"Coward," I reply, wishing he'd met justice in the way he'd deserved.

I hear the sounds of vehicles pulling into the lot and turn to see trucks arriving to pick up the survivors. Mom climbs out of the back of one of them with Violet and waves me over.

I look at Murphy. "Remember what we said we'd do when we get out of here."

"Haven't forgotten. I'd love the chance to help you," he replies.

"Good," I reply. "Now, let's all get the hell out of here."

Murphy goes back to the truck and jumps behind the wheel, and

Hazel and I walk hand in hand toward Mom and Violet. We all climb into the back of the truck, with me in the middle, between my mom and Hazel, so relieved that we're finally all together again.

"We made it, Mom," I say as I rub my fingers along Violet's cheek.

"I'm so proud of you, Clint," Mom says. "Do you want to hold your baby sister?"

"More than anything!" I say enthusiastically. I look at her sweet little face and hold on to her tiny baby hand, whispering softly to tell her how much I love her. I offer a promise to her that she'll never have to worry, that I'll always keep her safe. She gives me a little yawn in reply.

"Would you like to hold her?" I ask Hazel quietly.

Hazel looks at me doubtfully.

"Oh, come on!" I insist. "You know you want to!"

"Clint," Hazel says. "Hold who?"

"Violet! Who do you think?" I reply in confusion. I look down at my arms. My empty arms. "Mom!" I scream as I swing around to look at her. There's no one there. "She was right here, Hazel! They both were!" I stammer.

Hazel sits upright, holding the side of my face as she stares into my eyes. "It's okay, Clint. Once we get settled in, we're going to get you some help. You're going to be okay," she assures me.

"It seemed so real," I whisper.

"You need time. I'll be there for you the whole way, don't worry," Hazel says, holding my hand tightly.

I find myself wondering where they are. I hope they're safe; all I can do is hope.

As the truck engine cranks to life, the back fills with escapees.

"We're on our way!" Hazel says with a smile.

"Yeah, I guess we really are. Hey, Hazel . . ."

"What is it?"

"You ever blame yourself for anything? Ever wonder if you could've changed the way things ended?" I ask.

"All the time, and I know what you're getting at," Hazel says. "It's normal to think that way. But no matter how hard you think about it, it isn't going to change the fact that you're pinning the blame on the wrong person."

"I'd like to believe you, but chances are, if it weren't for me, you'd already be safe," I reply.

"Is that so? Do you really feel that way?" Hazel asks. "If it weren't for you and your mom coming, Mamaw and I would still be waiting helplessly back at the house. And look around you at all these people."

My eyes scan the inside of the vehicle to see several women and children seated, all waiting to start over in a better place.

"What about them?" I ask.

"You helped give these people a chance. You helped all of them live to see another day. If there's something to blame yourself for, let it be that."

"You always know what to say, don't you?" I ask as she curls up next to me.

"Yeah, I do, wise guy."

The truck begins to move, and the first day of the rest of my life begins. Time passes as I hold Hazel in silence.

The whole truck is quiet. We need time to recover and collect ourselves; all of us do. It's like the initial shock of waking up from a nightmare.

I look down to see Hazel fast asleep with her head buried in my lap. A few of the other women inside the truck are asleep, as well. It isn't until a couple of hours later that the truck jolts to a stop and jars everyone awake.

Hazel sits up and looks around in confusion. "What's going on? Did we make it?" she asks.

The truck still isn't moving, and I can hear the driver's door hinges open and then slam shut.

The back door opens, and Murphy is standing there to let us know that we finally made it. "You guys," he says, clearly holding back tears. "You have to see this."

Murphy and Hazel help me out of the back of the truck, and as soon as my feet touch the ground, I can smell it. The warm air of a busy city that I missed so much, complete with the scents of restaurants cooking food and freshly mowed grass. I can hear it—angry motorists shouting at one another, the honking of horns, the conversations between adults, and the playful squeals of little children. I can see it—tall buildings surrounding me in every direction, ferry boats gliding across the river, a playground filled with kids, men and women making their commutes to and from work.

It's all here—a whole new world, so similar to the one I miss so much. The world I promised us. The *life* I promised us. Hazel and I begin to walk deeper into the city together.

"You're not going to stick around?" Murphy asks as Hazel and I walk away from the truck. Hazel is still helping me walk a bit. "We'll be in touch!" I shout over my shoulder to Murphy.

"But where are you going?"

I look into Hazel's eyes and smile. "Promised Land," I say.

EPILOGUE

It's been a month now. Things are going great. I thank the universe every day for the second chance it has given me. I've been talking to Murphy once or twice a week—free of charge.

The Axis powers surrendered last week. I guess we were able to use those bombs to our advantage, after all. We won, and now the main focus in our country lies in rebuilding it. Mine is on rebuilding myself. I was able to find a job. Nothing flashy, but it's a job. I work at a grocery store stocking shelves, just your standard nine-to-five. Pay isn't anything special, but if we live modestly, Hazel and I should be fine until I find something better. The job can sometimes be stressful, but mainly because of things totally unrelated to the work. I still see Mom sometimes, but I try my best to ignore it and remind myself that it's all an illusion.

I spent most of my first two paychecks on our future. We had been sleeping at one of the convention centers in the city, most of which got converted to a shelter for people trying to get back on their feet. There comes a time where you have to move on, though. My first check went toward a down payment on a little one-bedroom apartment I found in the city. It's a cozy place, and, best of all, it's our place. My second paycheck was used to help buy another wedding ring for Hazel, to replace the one that was taken away while she was at the camp. You can't ever replace some things, but I tried my best, and she loves it.

All in all, I've been having the time of my life focusing on living more than surviving, if that makes any sense. And in minutes, it's going to be official.

I'm standing across from the most beautiful girl in the whole world, in her beautiful white gown. We're inside a small wedding chapel. The pews are empty except for Murphy in the front row. I wish everyone could've been here to see this.

"Do you, Clint Brodsky, take Hazel Maxwell to be your lawfully wedded wife? To have and to hold, from this day forward, for better or worse, for richer or poorer, in sickness and in health, till death do you part?" the pastor asks.

"I do," I reply, gazing into Hazel's eyes.

"And do you, Hazel Maxwell, take—"

"Yes. I do," Hazel interrupts.

"I now pronounce you husband and wife. You may kiss the bride," the preacher says, obviously holding back a chuckle.

I bend down to kiss her, and doing so, I see a bright light out of the corner of my eye.

I look down the aisle, and I see Mom again, holding my baby sister. The heart-shaped locket around her neck must have caught the sunlight from the open doors behind her.

Hazel looks to see what has my attention.

"It's all right," I murmur.

Hazel smiles at me. "Yes, it is. Yes, it is . . . because I see her, too," she says.

My lips curl into a smile as welcome tears run down my face.

ABOUT THE AUTHOR

Brandon Dean resides in Sevierville, Tennessee, with his wife, Haley, and two sons, Layne and Nolan. Promised Land is Brandon's debut novel and his first published work. Brandon has been writing since he was twelve years old, and everything he knows is self-taught. When Brandon isn't writing, he enjoys spending time with his family or watching baseball.

www.ingramcontent.com/pod-product-compliance
Lightning Source LLC
Chambersburg PA
CBHW050341190726
48284CB00007BB/2100